MEG'S
Melody

KAYLEE BALDWIN

MEG'S
Melody

KAYLEE BALDWIN

BONNEVILLE BOOKS
SPRINGVILLE, UTAH

The views expressed within this work are the sole responsibility of the author and do not necessarily reflect the position of Cedar Fort, Inc., or any other entity.

This is a work of fiction. The characters, names, incidents, places, and dialogue are products of the author's imagination, and are not to be construed as real.

ISBN 13: 978-1-59955-477-8

Published by Bonneville Books, an imprint of Cedar Fort, Inc., 2373 W. 700 S., Springville, UT 84663
Distributed by Cedar Fort, Inc., www.cedarfort.com

LIBRARY OF CONGRESS CATALOGING-IN-PUBLICATION DATA

Baldwin, Kaylee, 1983-
  Meg's Melody / Kaylee Baldwin.
    p. cm.
  Summary: A woman discovers she is pregnant shortly after her husband
leaves her. She finds comfort in her music and in the friendship of a tender-hearted
gynecologist.
  ISBN 978-1-59955-477-8
  1. Pregnancy--Fiction. 2. Divorce--Fiction. I. Title.
  PS3602.A59536M44 2010
  813'.6--dc22

                        2010032796

Cover design by Danie Romrell
Cover design © 2010 by Lyle Mortimer
Edited and typeset by Heidi Doxey

Printed in the United States of America

10 9 8 7 6 5 4 3 2 1

Printed on acid-free paper

To Jeremy, who always listens.
I love you.

Acknowledgments

Thank you to DeAnn Huff, Rachel Rager, Sarah Albrecht, Peggy Urry, Anna del C. Dye, Bonnie Harris, and Kari Pike for reading this manuscript and giving me some much needed feedback. Also, thank you to all of the ANWA sisters who answered my endless questions. This book would still be filed away, unfinished, without your support.

Thank you to the staff and editors at Cedar Fort, especially Jennifer and Heidi. Thank you for giving me a chance.

Thank you to Jaimee, Lyndsie, Carol, Mary, Marie, Kali, Grandma Green, Grandma Ruth, and all of my other friends and family members that read it. You read it in Africa, woke up at three a.m. to finish it, read it all day instead of doing things around the house, loved Johnny too much (you know who you are), read it in one sitting, and told everyone about it. All of you gave me confidence to keep on writing.

Thank you, Mom. You have read every version, every deleted scene, every plot tangent that I've presented. You've read this book as many times as I have and then listened to me talk about it even more—including our very creative title discussions. You and Dad always encouraged me to write and to follow my dream. Thanks for helping me do that and being the best parents I could ask for.

Thank you to my wonderful husband, Jeremy. You have been so supportive throughout this whole process, encouraging me, brainstorming with me, reading a "chick book" for the first time ever for me, and loving me. I'm so glad I introduced myself to you.

Prologue

eg Sanders stopped humming when she saw the piece of notebook paper on the table.

"Not again," she muttered as she threw her heavy backpack on one of the dining chairs. She avoided the note and instead went into the kitchen to find something to eat. The last thing she was in the mood for was more of Austin's platitudes and excuses. Because if Austin wrote a note, it was only to notify Meg of something he didn't have the time or guts to tell her in person: He was leaving again.

Austin worked for an accounting firm that had offices in Tucson and Phoenix. On the "fast track" for a promotion, he was required to take a lot of last-minute weekend trips to their main office in Phoenix. Inevitably, he received notice of his impending trips sometime in the middle of the day on Friday, giving him just enough time to drive home, pack a bag, jot an impersonal note to his wife, and lock the door behind him.

Meg grabbed the last apple from a basket next to the stove and took an unsatisfying bite from it.

"Looks like another dinner alone," she said to her reflection on the stainless steel fridge before pulling open the door. Nothing but questionable leftovers, condiments, and yellowish milk. A glance in the freezer yielded two burritos that had succumbed to freezer-burn many months ago. The empty cupboards were no better. Her frustration grew as she slammed the last cupboard door shut.

Tiny granules of her mushy apple coated the inside of her mouth. She forced herself to swallow each bite, all the while thinking about the great dinner Austin would most likely be eating, compliments of his firm.

Meg attempted to push away her hurt feelings that—once again—she hadn't been invited to go with him. More than once, Austin had told her that his trips consisted of him working hard and late, leaving him little time to entertain her. Meg tried to explain that she enjoyed just being with him, but he waved away her words as though they amounted to nothing more than the residue of exhaust fumes. Apparently the fast track only had room for one.

Meg unwrapped the burritos and brushed away as many of the ice flakes encrusting the tortillas as she could. She plopped them into the microwave and headed toward the table to face the inevitable.

I'm sorry, was all the note said.

"I'll bet you are." Meg dropped the note and headed for the master bedroom.

She pulled on a pair of comfortable basketball shorts and an extra-large Arizona State T-shirt that engulfed her long, lean frame. She decided to call Austin and make sure he'd made it to Phoenix before settling down with her burritos. Later she could vent by pounding out Prokofiev on her piano.

When she opened the closet doors to grab a pair of ratty slippers that she only wore in her husband's absence, the desolation of dozens of bare hangers assaulted her.

She backed out of the closet and ran to the dresser. His drawers boasted a space as empty as the kitchen cupboards—barren with the exception of lint and one unpaired sock stuffed in the corner.

Meg left the drawer open in her haste to get back to the kitchen. Hands shaking, she unzipped the front pocket of her backpack and rifled through all the junk she stored in it. Not finding her cell phone, she turned the backpack upside down and shook it violently over the table. Old gum wrappers, sheet music, a baton, hair ties, mints, and other small candies scattered before her cell phone fell on top of the mess.

She flipped it open and tried to call Austin, her unsteady hands making it difficult to press the buttons.

She finally pressed the ringing phone to her ear.

"This is Austin. Leave a message—"

She ended the call and dialed again. This time the call went straight to voice mail.

Then she remembered the note. This must be a misunderstanding. Austin wouldn't leave her. Sure, they had their problems, but they'd only been married eight months. They needed time to adjust to life together. Things weren't bad enough for him to actually leave.

Then where are all his clothes? A persistent voice niggled in the back of her mind.

She pushed the thought aside when she found the note. She read it again and turned it over, hoping for more of an explanation. Nothing. Just those two little words.

Meg put the crumpled paper back on the table and redialed Austin's number.

She sat on the hard kitchen chair for almost an hour while she dialed and let the phone ring until his voice mail picked up. Then she rested her head against her arm and kept the phone pressed to her ear. It almost didn't register when the ringing stopped.

Meg sat upright when she realized someone was on the other end.

"Austin?"

He cleared his throat. "Hey."

"What's going on?"

He paused. "I'm sorry, Meg."

"Sorry for what?"

He didn't say anything.

"Sorry for what?" she repeated through gritted teeth.

"Meg . . ."

"Where are you?"

"Phoenix."

"When are you coming home?"

"I didn't want it to be like this," he finally said.

"You're not answering my questions."

"I just can't do it anymore," he said as though he didn't hear her. "It's not like it used to be. We're not good for each other."

"Is there someone else?" she forced herself to ask. The thick silence gave Meg the answer. "Come home," she pleaded, pushing aside feelings of betrayal. "We'll talk about this."

"I've already talked to a lawyer, Meg. It's done."

"*It*? What's *it*?" Meg's voice rose. "What did you do?"

"I'm sorry."

"Stop saying that!"

"You'll probably get the papers next week sometime."

"Austin, please—" She heard the click and knew he'd ended the call. She stared at her phone, trying to process what had happened. It fell from her limp fingers and clattered onto the table. Meg buried her face in her hands and released the broken sobs from her chest.

PART ONE

The Surprise

Chapter One

"Are you sure you want to do this?" Cathy Wilkes asked her son as she helped him carry the last couple of boxes from his car into the house.

"I'm sure, Mom," Matt grunted from behind the cardboard. He tightened his grip on the box of books as he began his ascent up the stairs. His mom followed close behind him.

"I don't understand why you have to go so far away."

Matt sighed, the muscles in his arm twitching with the desire to let go of the box and run his fingers through his hair. Instead, he had to relieve his frustration by grinding his teeth. It felt like they'd gone over this again and again. Every time his mom asked why he was leaving, he questioned his decision to uproot his daughter from their lush home in the Pacific Northwest to move to the arid desert of the Southwest.

"There are medical practices for sale in Washington," she continued, persistent as ever. It was this persistence that had gotten him through the past year and had helped his dad become some semblance of the man he used to be. But his mom also had the ability to drive him crazy with her endless reasoning. "I'll watch Lilia for you while you work. There's no need to go all the way to Arizona."

Matt got on his knees and pushed his box into the corner next to the other boxes they'd already hauled up to his childhood bedroom. He stayed on the floor just a second longer than necessary, gathering his patience against his mother's well-intended words. Then he stood and brushed the dust from the knees of his jeans before looking her in the eye.

He swallowed once, then twice, but his voice still scratched with sorrow when he spoke. "Mom, please. I can't be here anymore."

"Daddy, are you coming? I'm hungry!" Lilia yelled from the bottom of the stairs.

"I'll be down in a minute," Matt called back to his four-year-old daughter, grateful for a reason to hurry the good-byes. He glanced back at his mom, her sympathetic gaze piercing him to the core. It was the only way anyone seemed to look at him anymore.

His mom let out a sigh long enough to stretch from Washington to Arizona. "Well, make sure you don't teach Lilia your bad habits, then," she admonished. "And you'd better stop and get that girl some food on the way. And find somewhere to sleep tonight. Don't try to do the whole drive in one shot."

Matt nodded, grateful that his mom had stopped pushing. He only had so much fight left in him. A small bit of doubt twisted his heart as he took a final look at the items not going with him to Arizona, but he shook it off and followed his mom down the stairs.

"Grandma!" Lilia exclaimed as his mom leaned down to give her a hug. "We're going on an adventure!"

"I know," she said, sounding resigned.

Matt caught her eye and pleaded silently with her to understand. He needed to leave. He took his mom's cool hand in his and tried not to feel how frail and small she seemed. Over the past year, she'd lost weight that she didn't have to spare.

"Thank you, Mom. For everything. I never could have made it through this year without you." He swallowed the lump in his throat and pulled his mother into a hug.

"You're going to be fine." She held him tightly for a minute and then pulled away.

"And you," she said, crouching in front of Lilia. "You better make sure you write and email me pictures. Don't let your dad forget."

"I won't." Lilia threw her arms around her grandma's neck. "I love you, Grandma."

His mom didn't say anything for almost a minute. "I love you too," she finally choked out, clutching Lilia to her chest.

Matt turned to his father and once again had to reconcile the man who had raised him with the one who now sat confined in a wheelchair. He tried not to think of the wheelchair as a painful reminder of everything they had lost.

"Drive carefully, son," his dad said gruffly.

Matt leaned over the arm of the wheelchair to give him a hug. "I will."

Lilia crawled into her grandpa's lap and kissed him on the cheek. She rested her head against his chest, and her sniffles broke the silence.

Matt's dad nudged Lilia's head off his chest with his shoulder. "Hey, I've got something for you." He ruffled her hair and handed her a present he had stowed next to the wheel of his chair.

"Open this when you get to your new home."

"Can't I open it now?"

"Nope. It'll give you something to look forward to."

Matt picked Lilia up and again pushed down the surge of emotion that threatened to overtake him at the sight of his parents. His mom stood next to his dad with her hand on his shoulder.

He waved one last time before getting into the car. As he settled into the driver's seat, he caught his reflection in the rearview mirror. It must have been jostled at some point when they were loading the car. He reached up to adjust it, but not before he saw his haunted image reflected back at him. The paleness of his skin and the hollows in his cheeks attested to how overworked and undernourished he'd become in the past year.

He hardly recognized himself anymore. His daughter needed more of him than shadows and the shell of a father, but painful reminders of everything they had lost chased and tortured him. Maybe if they left, he could find himself again.

"Sing the elephant song, Daddy," Lilia begged from the backseat.

Matt glanced in his rearview mirror one last time, and he

began to sing Lilia's favorite nursery song, her high-pitched voice joining in. He turned a corner, keeping his eyes forward, and was surprised to feel anticipation squeeze past the sorrow in his chest.

A new life awaited them in Arizona.

Chapter Two

Meg stopped at her parent's house on the way home from work, unable to face spending the rest of the afternoon alone. Since Austin had left, the quiet in her house seemed thicker, more suffocating.

Maybe it was time to bring Cliff home. She'd had to give up her chocolate Lab when she got married because Austin had allergies. Her parents had taken him while she was at Arizona State, and they kept him after the wedding. She'd missed her dog.

The scent of fresh bread met Meg when her mom opened the door.

"How are you, sweetie?" Sandra wiped floury hands on an ever-present apron and ushered Meg inside. Meg followed her mom's steady footsteps, forming them into a song and pattern in her mind. From the time she was little, she heard music in everything and everyone. Her mom's melody was always solid and predictable.

"Meg?"

"I'm here to get Cliff."

"Good, he needs his walk still. He's out back with Kaitlyn."

They walked to the back door and Meg called out Cliff's name. He responded with a bark and bounded toward her. Meg scratched his neck and kneeled down to give him a hug.

"When do you think you'll be back with him?"

"I'm not bringing him back, Mom. I'm taking him home."

Her mom nodded. "And Austin . . ."

"The divorce is final." Meg swallowed and shrugged her shoulders, trying to pretend she didn't care. She stiffened when her mom put a hand on her back.

"Meg, you know I'm here if you need to talk—"

"I'm fine." She stepped away. "Kaitlyn!"

Her four-year-old niece popped her head out of the tree house. "Aunt Meg!"

Meg's mom sighed behind her as Meg ran to the tree house. She helped Kaitlyn down into her arms and gave her a hug. "Do you want me to push you on the swing?"

Kaitlyn squealed as she ran to the swing, her small legs tapping an excited, staccato beat against the ground. While Meg pushed, Kaitlyn leaned back until her long blonde hair brushed the ground and her foot swiped the leaves of the tree above her.

"Did you see that, Aunt Meg? I touched the tree! Higher!"

Meg pushed her for a few more minutes until she saw her older sister, Missy, waving from the doorway. She grabbed the chains on the swing and pulled it to a stop. "Look who's here, Kaitlyn."

When Kaitlyn saw her mom, she popped from the swing and rushed into the house. Meg followed at a slower pace, not sure how eager she was to see her sister. Missy always reminded Meg of all the areas where she fell short. It wasn't anything Missy did; it was just who she was.

Missy's petite body curved into clothes like they were made especially for her. Meg towered four inches over her sister and had almost no curves to speak of. Missy had silky blonde hair and creamy skin. Meg had unruly brown hair and a spattering of freckles across her nose.

As Meg gathered Cliff's toys and food, she watched Missy hug their mom, her sister's tinkling laugh drifting to where Meg stood. Missy and their mom had always been close. They even looked alike—so much so that people assumed they were sisters when they went out together. No one ever mistook Meg and her mom for sisters. Of course, Meg couldn't remember the last time she and her mom had gone anywhere together.

"Meg!" Missy squealed, pulling Meg into a suffocating hug. "I haven't seen you in forever. You're so thin! What have you been doing?"

"Getting a divorce."

Missy's spirited smile didn't dim a watt at Meg's flat tone. "Oh, right. Well, Mom, I need to get Kaitlyn home so I can start dinner before Tom gets off work."

"Wait." Mom put her hand on Missy's arm. "I wanted to ask you how your lesson's coming."

"Lesson?" Meg asked.

"I was just called to be a Relief Society instructor," Missy explained. "I'm teaching for the first time this Sunday."

"Oh." Meg shifted her feet. She should've known they were talking about church stuff.

"You should come and support her, Meg."

"Oh, yes. Please," Missy begged.

Church had been another thing she'd given up for Austin, but anxiety accompanied the idea of going back again.

"We'll see," Meg said, avoiding a firm commitment. She called for Cliff and opened the back door of her car for him. He settled in next to his toys and food. "If I missed anything, I'll get it later."

"All right, Meg. I'm glad you stopped by." Her mom thrust a small loaf of bread into her hands. Meg glanced at Missy and her mom while she backed out of the driveway. The two looked serious as they talked about something—probably her. A glimpse in the rearview mirror confirmed that they still stood there, looking like twins at that distance. Just another reminder that Missy and her mom were best friends, and there was no room for Meg to squeeze in.

✺

Matt halted abruptly, appalled at the mess that awaited him in his new house. Ripped carpet exposed stained cement floors. The entire house smelled faintly of cigarette smoke and urine. Droppings from some sort of rodent littered one corner of the front room. He gripped Lilia's hand tighter as they stepped further into the dark house.

Light fixtures had been torn out of the ceiling, and their left-over wires hung over his head. All the kitchen appliances were gone, and the smashed-in cupboard doors dangled from bent hinges.

"Daddy, this house is messy."

Matt pulled his cell phone out of his pocket and found the real estate agent's number.

"What happened to my house, Rob?" Matt barked when his agent answered.

"Why? Is there something wrong?"

"Did you know it was trashed when you sold it to me?" Matt gripped the bridge of his nose and tried to relieve the pressure mounting there.

Rob paused. "I thought you understood. I told you that the previous owner had a 'foreclosure party.'"

"Okay . . ."

Rob swore. "You know what that is, don't you?"

"Should I?"

"It's when the people who are getting foreclosed on trash the house before they move out. They take everything that's not bolted down and destroy what they can't take with them. The current condition of the house is the reason I got you such a great deal in that neighborhood."

"I don't have time to fix this up. I would've spent more money on something I could move into right away."

Matt tried to calm down when he noticed Lilia's bottom lip trembling. "What are my options?"

"At this point, you don't have many. We can turn around and sell the house, but that will end up costing you a lot of money."

"Is there anything else we could do?"

"You already signed the papers and put money down. Other than recommending a good cleaning crew, there's not a whole lot I can do for you."

Matt ended the call and looked around the kitchen in dismay.

"Can I open my present now?" Lilia asked.

"Sure. Let's go get it." He needed a breath of fresh air anyway.

They retrieved the wrapped box from the car and went back

into the house. After Lilia ripped the paper off and threw it onto the floor, Matt kicked it into the corner to cover the droppings.

"It's Grandma and Grandpa!" Lilia squealed. "And you, me, and Mom."

She held out a hinged frame with two pictures resting side-by-side. In her other hand she gripped a small, silver necklace with a half-heart pendant. It looked like one of those friendship necklaces he'd seen his sisters wear as children.

Lilia handed him the note to read after he fastened the chain around her neck.

"'I hope you had a fun trip,'" Matt read. "'Always remember that you carry half of our heart with you. Put this picture somewhere in your new home so that we will always be close by. We love you. Grandma and Grandpa.'"

"Are we home, Daddy?" Lilia looked up at him with her trusting green eyes. Matt glanced around the room. The price and time required to fix up a home concerned him. They would have to stay in a hotel until he could at least get an exterminator and someone in to clean it. He'd need to find somewhere to store all their boxes so they could return the moving truck. Yet his hands already itched to smooth out the walls and reconnect new appliances.

He watched his daughter clutch the picture of the family they left behind. She needed stability—something to anchor her to this new place. Plunging head first into the living nightmare of this house, he gently took the frame from Lilia and set it on the gouged counter.

"We're home."

Chapter Three

Meg sat in her parked car with both hands on the wheel, elbows locked, as if bracing her body from the cream stucco building. Twice she tried to pry her white-knuckled fingers from the steering wheel and open the door. Both times she chickened out.

A glimpse in the rearview mirror confirmed the sorry state of her appearance. Between sleepless nights and loss of appetite caused by the stress of divorce, Meg's body had suffered. Her sallow skin—improved only slightly by blush—showcased her puffy blue eyes and sunken cheeks. At least the soft, natural curl of her brown hair hid any evidence of thinning.

Meg pulled her eyes away from the mirror when people got into the car next to her. No one looked in her direction as the last door shut and they reversed out of the parking spot. Her tense spine relaxed once the car was gone. Until she looked at the church again.

Almost two years. She'd done something faithfully, willingly even, for twenty-three years. Then she stopped for less than two, and suddenly she felt like an intruder.

She just couldn't take one more minute of the quiet in her house. Memories of Austin hung around every corner, reminding her of everything they'd bought together, planned together, done together—except church. He'd never gone with her to church.

Meg released the steering wheel from her death-grip before

she could change her mind and exited the car as quickly as the safety pin in the slit of her skirt would allow. She derived some satisfaction from knowing that Austin would've hated that she made the already conservative skirt even more so, and then she halfheartedly berated herself for caring about what he'd think.

Meg studied the ground as she walked across the parking lot and into the chapel. She slipped into the back pew. Sneaking a glance out of the corner of her eye, Meg confirmed that the widows still congregated on this bench. She fidgeted with the hem of her shirt but looked up when someone nudged her shoulder. She started when she saw her mom—who always arrived at least twenty minutes early to claim their family's unofficial spot on the second row—standing next to her.

Meg blinked when she noticed her sister's family and her dad standing behind her mom.

"Can we sit with you?"

Meg nodded and scooted over so that her family could squeeze in next to her. She avoided looking at the widows, who now sat scrunched to one side of the pew.

"Mom," Missy whispered. "Are you telling her?"

"What?" Meg asked.

"Look to your right," her mom ordered. "Have you met the man wearing the dark suit? He's standing next to Brother Williams."

The man next to Brother Williams was tall, probably a little over six feet, and in his late twenties or early thirties. Even through his suit, Meg could tell that he had a nice build, although he was a little on the lean side. He had coffee-colored hair that brushed his shirt collar. She could only see his profile, but from this angle he seemed good-looking, in a clean-cut way.

He nodded at something Brother Williams said, and his head turned to look around the room. His eyes met Meg's, and the edges of his mouth started to turn up into a smile before a little girl threw her body at his legs. He staggered back, all of his attention refocused on the girl who wrapped her arms around his legs. Meg pulled her eyes away from the scene and turned back to her mom.

"No." Meg cleared her throat and fought to keep from looking over at him again.

Her mom gave her a strange look. "Are you sure?"

"Positive. Why?" Meg asked nervously. She had an ugly suspicion that she knew where this was heading. She wasn't ready to go there.

"No reason."

"Great." Meg turned to the hymn book in her lap and pretended to be fascinated with the raised image of the organ pipes on the hard green cover. She ran her finger over it, and her mind drifted to the songs printed inside. She'd missed singing hymns when she had stopped going to church.

"He moved here about a week ago, and Sister Perkins says that he's single."

"Who is?"

"You know who. The man I asked you to look at. You practically ogled him. Really, Meg, I thought you'd be a little more discreet. If people weren't talking before, they will be now."

"Mom," Meg warned. She glanced around the room to see if anyone was looking at her. Most people appeared involved in their own conversations and pre-sacrament meeting activities.

"You haven't said anything to him about me, have you?" She sank lower into the seat. Why had she thought coming to church was a good idea? It was so much safer at home. Cliff never gossiped about her or tried to set her up on dates.

"Of course not. I haven't even met him yet. I just thought you should know. People are already talking about the possibility of you two. Single man, single woman . . ."

"Divorced woman."

Her mom sighed. "I just thought you should know what's circulating."

"He just moved here, and this is my first week back at church. How can things be circulating already?"

She shrugged. "Honey, you know I'm not a gossip. I don't know how these things spread so quickly."

"I wish people wouldn't talk about me."

"I know it doesn't seem like it, but they care about you. We all want you to be happy," she finished as the bishop stood and the prelude music ended.

"Then let me get through this my way," Meg whispered over the first announcement. Her mom smiled in response and looked back at the bishop, unwilling to talk while someone stood at the pulpit. Meg could practically feel her own blood pressure rising.

While the congregation sang the opening hymn, Meg's eyes drifted toward the man her mom had pointed out to her. He sat in a side bench two rows up and to the right from where Meg sat with her family.

The little girl who had run to him and hugged his legs so tightly now cuddled into his side. She looked maybe three or four years old. Her blonde hair was combed out smoothly at the ends, but the top of it looked tangled and frizzy. The man had his arm around her and sang solemnly from the hymn book. They appeared content.

Meg absently cracked her knuckles, and her eyes drifted toward the bishop. He smiled at her, and she averted her gaze down to the hymnal. *No more looking up,* she told herself. *It gets you into trouble.*

Somehow she made it through sacrament meeting and slipped out to her car. She worried that someone would strong-arm the new man into meeting her. That was the last thing she needed. What she did need was a hot bath and something to calm her churning stomach. She felt like she might be coming down with the flu.

❀

"She has a degree in marriage from BYU. And come Thanksgiving, she makes the best pumpkin pie." Sister Forrester—or was it Foster?—smacked her lips. "Can't find a better girl than my Kendra."

Matt nodded and forced his smile to remain in place while wishing the Sunday School teacher would begin the lesson.

"Tall, beautiful, and a good cook. There's no better combination. Gets her looks from me, of course."

Of course.

"She's good with kids, too. You have a daughter, don't you?"

Matt nodded, not liking where this was going.

"She's just the kind of girl you need. I'll give you her number. She goes to the singles ward in Tucson."

"I'm sure your daughter is a wonderful girl, but I'm not interested in dating right now."

"Just take it. You never know." She thrust a paper into his hands.

"Leave him alone, Irene." A middle-aged woman in front of them turned around.

"What? I just don't want him to miss out on a fabulous opportunity."

"He says he's not interested. Kendra would be embarrassed if she knew what you were doing."

Matt shifted as the women's conversation continued.

"He's not going to be interested in Meg, if that's what you're thinking," Sister Forrester whispered.

"Excuse me?"

"Sandra, he needs a girl who could raise his daughter with strong values, not someone who married a nonmember and got a divorce just a few months later."

Sandra's eyes narrowed. "My daughter is a wonderful young woman. She needs love from us, not judgment."

Sandra's gaze slid past Matt before she turned around, and he flashed on why she was familiar. He'd seen her in sacrament meeting sitting next to the pretty young woman with the smile that didn't reach her eyes.

Sister Forrester didn't say anything else but slipped her daughter's number in Matt's scriptures during the lesson. The beginnings of a headache pulsed at Matt's temples, and he wished he could be at home, working on the repairs. The steady amount of work he needed to do to fix up the house kept him busy, and it kept his mind on things that he didn't want to think about—like this constant pain he felt rubbing at the raw edges of his heart. His mind flashed again on the girl he'd seen in sacrament meeting, and he suspected that she also knew this familiar ache.

❦

Meg scoured her fridge for something to make for dinner, but she was running low on supplies. She rejected another microwave dinner, and her stomach churned as she checked out the assorted sandwich meats in the crisper. She let the door shut and rested her woozy head against the cool stainless steel surface.

Her appetite had left the same day Austin did. Her pants hung off her body so much that she'd had to start wearing a belt again just to remain decent.

It didn't seem worth it to go to all the trouble of making a meal that only she would eat and appreciate. Meg decided to skip dinner again and dragged her body toward the dark living room. She wanted to lose herself in her music, close her eyes, let her fingers fly over the piano keys, and pretend that life was different. Pretend that Austin never left. Or that they'd never gotten married at all.

A dark, chaotic melody pounded from the belly of the piano until its rhythm matched the pulsing pain in Meg's head. But the depressing song only worsened her mood. Ending on a minor chord, Meg groaned and dug her fingers into her hair.

She considered praying, but it still felt so awkward to her. What would she say? *Hey, God. I know I stopped coming to church when I found someone I liked to be with and it was inconvenient to make time for you, too. But now he's ditched me, and I'm a mess. I need help, so here I am.*

Tears pooled in her eyes, and she swung her legs around the bench. Sitting here was accomplishing nothing.

Food. She needed to eat. Memories of the contents in the fridge did little to help her stomach and headache.

The nausea, headaches, and mood swings she experienced made her feel like she was on her period. Except, these symptoms had been constant since she'd read Austin's note.

Meg's heart dropped, and she jumped up from the bench. Bursts of black floated in front of her eyes as she stumbled into the kitchen where her calendar hung. Meg put her finger on the date, her haggard breathing evolving into something that bordered on hyperventilating.

She flipped the calendar back a month, and dread took a firm root in her clenched stomach. With all the stress of the divorce, she hadn't even noticed.

She was late.

Meg grabbed her keys from the fireplace mantle and rushed out the door in her pajamas and slippers. She decided to drive into Tucson, where she would have less risk of running into someone she knew. The drive to a drugstore in a seedy part of town went by too quickly, and Meg's heart raced as she stepped from the car into the well-lit parking lot.

The first time she walked past the family planning aisle, a man stood there, so she circled the store and tried to calm her nerves. On her second lap, the row was empty, so she eased in front of the colorful boxes, finally picking a two-package, supposedly error-proof test.

Once Meg got home, she locked her bathroom door even though no one else lived in her house. She attempted to convince herself that she was overreacting to her period being a month late, but her hands still shook while she pried open the box.

She paced the small confines of her bathroom as she waited the obligatory two minutes for the result. Yet, part of her sensed the truth. Not only did Austin take her self-esteem and plans for happiness, but he also took her get-out-of-this-marriage-free card.

The plus sign glared at Meg from the white plastic frame of the pregnancy test. The test fell from her hands and clattered into the bathtub as Meg's back slid against the wall until she reached the floor. She pulled her knees up to her chest and buried her head, the coldness of the tile seeping through her cotton pants.

She had no one to tell. No one was waiting, supporting, or celebrating with her. No one to laugh with. No one to cry with. With the hard wall pressing against her spine, she listened to the sound of water dripping rhythmically from the sink.

"I'm pregnant," she said into the quiet. She threw the test into the trash and flipped the lever for the shower.

Her clothes came off easily, and as she stood under the hot spray, she placed her hand on her flat abdomen. A baby.

She didn't feel pregnant. Not that she knew what it meant to feel pregnant. Missy had been sick for the entire first half of her pregnancy with Kaitlyn. Lately Meg had felt queasy some mornings, but she'd blamed it on stress and low blood sugar from skipping breakfast most of the time.

The shower water turned cold before she decided to get out. She stood in the bathroom, wrapped in a towel, growing chilled as the steam dissipated. Her legs buckled, and she sat on the toilet.

She was tired of thinking about Austin. She didn't want to worry about the divorce, what people thought of her, or even Austin's betrayal any longer. And now he was going to be a part of her life forever—for better or for worse.

Meg buried her face in the soft towel as her bare shoulders shook.

I'm sick of being me.

PART TWO

The First Trimester

Chapter Four

Dr. Cohen's secretary set up Meg's obstetrician appointment for four weeks away before informing Meg of some changes that had taken place at the office. Dr. Cohen was going into semi-retirement and had sold her medical practice to another doctor. She'd be on an extended vacation until after Christmas, and then she would only be working one day a week, which meant Meg would need to see the new doctor.

Meg confirmed that this was fine. Then she hung up and called into work to ask for her last sick day. After jotting down a note to pick up some prenatal vitamins, she used the second pregnancy test.

It also came out positive. Her stomach fluttered the second time she saw a plus sign.

Meg knew she needed to make another call. It couldn't be put off any longer. Austin had a right to know before anyone else, no matter how much she dreaded telling him. Her finger hovered over the *send* button for a second before she pushed it down.

The phone rang once before an automated voice came onto the line: "The number you dialed has been disconnected." The digitized female voice repeated the message three times before Meg pulled the phone away from her ear. Rejection slammed into her with the realization that he'd changed his phone number. She had no way to contact him except through her lawyer.

As Meg drove to her lawyer's office, the message from Austin's number looped around in her brain until only the word *discon-nected* repeated over and over again. Flashing blue and red lights and the bleep of a siren knocked the words from her mind.

She looked in the rearview mirror and saw the familiar cop car come up behind her as she pulled over. "Great. This is just what I need."

Meg stewed while she watched Tom's muscular, six-foot-three body unfold from the car and saunter her way, note pad in hand. He'd pulled her over more times in the past month and a half than in her entire life combined. The fact that Tom had married her sister led Meg to believe he should give her a break, but it only seemed to make things worse. Since his and Missy's wedding five years previous, he acted like he had a brother's right to tease her and did so relentlessly.

He'd only actually ticketed her once—just a few days ago—because she ran a stop sign while he was with his partner. He gave her a remorseful look the entire time. Before the divorce, he would have smirked.

"Speeding again, Meg?"

She didn't know what look she gave him, but it was deadly enough to stop him in his tracks.

"Hey," he said, putting the pad in his pocket and then resting his hand on the ledge of the open car window, "What's going on?"

A cramp seized her stomach before she could vent her frustrations on Tom.

"Are you okay?"

Suddenly Meg wasn't okay. She really hadn't been okay in about a month. Or longer, even. But at this very moment, she for sure was not okay.

Meg flung the car door open, knocking Tom off-balance in the process, and heaved the glass of water she'd had for breakfast. She straightened in her seat, swiping the back of her hand across her mouth.

"I'm taking you home."

"No," Meg croaked, her throat still burning from stomach acid. "I need to go to my lawyer's office."

"You need to go home. Or to your parents' house so your mom can take care of you."

"Tom, get out of the way, or I'll run you over."

Tom wouldn't budge from where he stood inside the open door. He put his hand on Meg's forehead, and she pushed it away.

"I do not have a fever," she snapped.

"And I'm not going to let you drive like this. Anything that you need to do at the lawyer's office can wait until tomorrow when you're feeling better."

"I need to talk to him now. Please move."

"What's going on?" Worry laced the frustration in Tom's voice.

"I'm pregnant," Meg blurted out almost against her will. She pushed her fists into her eyes to ward off the tears she felt building. Tom let out a huge gust of air as if he'd been holding his breath for a month. Maybe he had. It seemed like everyone held their breath whenever she came around.

"Are you sure?"

"Yes." She whispered so he couldn't hear the strain in her voice. Her eyes were still covered and she didn't see him move until she felt herself being hauled out of the car. Tom's thick arms wrapped her in a comforting hug.

"Oh, Meg," he said quietly. "What did Austin say?"

She buried her face in the warmth of his shoulder, even as she felt her tears seep into his shirt. "He changed his phone number, so I couldn't call him."

"Let's go," he said, steering Meg toward his patrol car. She let him lead her to the front seat without argument. Her head pounded with the combination of no food, throwing up, and crying.

She kept her eyes closed while Tom drove, wondering how she was going to tell her mom. *As if I'm not already a big enough failure. Here's just one more thing to add to my growing list of disappointments.*

Tom eased the car to a stop.

She opened her eyes. They weren't at her mom's house. Tom had taken her to her lawyer's office. "Thank you."

Tom followed her into the brick building, and Stan's secretary waved them back to his office. Stan, who was Meg's lawyer and her cousin, stood up when they entered, offering Tom a hearty handshake before taking in Meg's watery eyes.

She explained the situation to Stan, who agreed that they needed to somehow contact Austin. He called Austin's lawyer, who said that he'd get back to them within forty-eight hours with Austin's reply. Meg figured Austin would just call her when he heard the news, probably before the end of the day. She thanked Stan and left as his sympathetic stare followed her and Tom.

Tom and Meg rode in silence to her parents' house. He pulled into their driveway, and she saw the blinds slide up before the front door opened. Her mom jogged out of the house.

"What's wrong?"

"Nothing's wrong, Sandra," Tom said as his arm went around Meg's waist to help her into the house.

"I can walk by myself," Meg snapped.

He grunted in argument. Meg resisted the urge to yank away from him. Sometimes he took the big brother thing a little too seriously.

The smell of whatever her mom was cooking sucker punched Meg as she walked inside the house. She bent over, her empty stomach clenching as she gagged.

"Tom, pick her up and take her to her old bedroom," her mom ordered.

Tom lifted Meg with ease and carried her down the hall. Her head fell onto his chest for the second time that morning. Once again she realized what a lucky woman her sister was.

Tom set her on her old bed, and her mom bustled in behind him. She sat next to Meg and put a wet cloth on her forehead.

"Do you want some water, honey?"

"No, that's what I had this morning."

"All you've had today is water?" her mom asked, aghast. Meg felt like she just told her that she'd run over the neighbor's cat again.

"Tom, get a snack for Meg, please."

Tom retrieved some crackers and then excused himself to go back to work.

Meg was relieved to see him leave so she wouldn't have to worry about him accidentally spilling her secret. Once she forced a couple crackers down, her mom left the room. The combination of a little something in her stomach and a brief respite from her mom helped her to relax. She looked around at her unchanged room.

Three boy-band posters from junior high still decorated one of her walls. Dance pictures and old handouts from Young Women lessons were stuck to a cork board. She pulled out the journal she used to write in faithfully from the night table next to the bed. When she opened the first page, a picture fell out.

Johnny Peters.

She and Johnny had grown up in the same ward. He was a couple of years older than her and had always been friends with Missy, but Meg had usually tagged along with them because of her crush on Johnny. The last day of her junior year, Missy told her that Johnny had signed up for the army and would be leaving for boot camp within two months of graduation.

Missy had dared her to kiss Johnny. Somehow Meg convinced Missy to do it too, and they got a friend to snap a picture while they simultaneously kissed him on each cheek.

He told the girls he needed a copy of that picture to take with him to boot camp, but he ended up leaving early, only one week after graduating. From what her mom had told her, he now lived in Southern California.

Meg set the picture on the nightstand when her mom came into the room with a bowl in her hands.

"Do you want some soup?"

"I don't know if I can keep anything down."

"Have you called the doctor, yet?"

"No. I'm sure I'll be fine with a little rest." *Nine months of rest.*

"It's been so long for me that I just don't remember how everything went," her mom replied, wringing her hands. She actually looked stressed. Of course, Meg was growing accustomed to seeing that look directed at her over the past month.

"Mom, it hasn't been that long since you were sick."

Her mom's hands stilled. "I mean the pregnancy."

The spoon stopped halfway to Meg's mouth as her mom's words registered. "When did Tom tell you?"

"Tom knows?"

"He didn't tell you?"

She shook her head. "I've known you were pregnant for about two weeks."

"Two weeks!" Meg moved the soup bowl to the night table when she realized it had already sloshed all over the bed. "I just found out last night. How could you have known before me?"

"I didn't know for sure. I just suspected. I knew you skipped your period last month because you usually have cramps so bad that it's hard for you to even leave the house. But you came to Kaitlyn's birthday party without a problem. Then there was the light-headedness, the nausea, the emotions."

"Couldn't that have all been because of stress from the divorce?" Meg countered, her mind whirling. She felt thrown off-balance, almost as if her privacy had been violated. Meg had no idea her mother had been watching her that closely and monitoring her habits so religiously. It made her wonder what else she may have observed.

"Individually, yes. But collectively? I figured you were pregnant." The revelation settled into the cracks of their silence. Her mom jumped up and grabbed the soup. "You need to go get in the shower while I wash the sheets on this bed."

"Mom, who else knows?"

"Just me and Tom, I guess. I haven't even told your dad. I figured you would tell us when you felt like the time was right."

"Then why did you tell me that you knew?"

"I didn't want you to have to do everything alone." She glanced at Meg one more time before leaving the room.

Chapter Five

On the morning of Meg's first OB appointment, she left school early to drop by Stan's office at his request.

"What's going on?" Meg asked after he asked that she sit.

"I talked to Austin's lawyer." Stan leaned forward, resting his elbows on his desk. "Austin's been out of town for the past few weeks, and before that he was busy with the wedding, so he couldn't get back to you."

"The wedding?"

"Yes. He got married two weeks ago."

Meg wanted to throw up, and this time it had nothing to do with the pregnancy. Their divorce had been final barely a month, and he'd already remarried.

"What did he say about the pregnancy?" Meg forced the words out past the rising bile.

Stan hesitated. "He was angry. He said that he thought you were on birth control." Stan looked a little uncomfortable as he relayed Austin's message. "He also said that this doesn't change anything now because he's already remarried."

Hearing this a second time did not make it any easier for Meg. She couldn't look at Stan. *When did Austin become such a jerk?*

"Did he say anything about the baby? Is he going to call me so we can work out what's going to happen after the baby's born?" Meg's voice rose, and she fought her growing hysteria.

"Meg," Stan began. She wanted to cover her ears and run away. This was not going to be good. She'd known Stan all her life and had heard that tone before.

"No." Meg shook her head before he could speak. He continued to give her that sympathetic look.

"He wants you to get an abortion. He said that this kind of thing happens all the time and that he'll send you money for it."

"This kind of thing happens all the time! To who? The woman he cheated with?" Meg's chest tightened, and she tried to take a deep breath. She began pacing in front of the desk, her rapid breathing matching the frantic rhythm of her steps. Every step she took shook a little of the anxiety out of her system until she collapsed back into her chair. She ran her shaking fingers through her hair. "I don't know what I did to make him hate me so much."

They sat in silence, and Meg's statement crackled in the air until Stan cleared his throat. "As your lawyer, who also happens to be your cousin, I can tell Austin's lawyer exactly where to stick that abortion money. Once the baby's born, we'll discuss monetary support. The last thing you need right now is more stress."

Meg impulsively reached over the desk and gave Stan a hug. He started with surprise before patting her on the back. She pulled away with a glimmer of a smile. "I don't suppose you could actually shove that money yourself to make sure it gets put in the appropriate place?"

"Honey," he said with a grimace, "that's a place I hope I never have to see."

Meg couldn't quite laugh as she left his office. She still felt like there was a rock in her stomach. She stopped outside the doorway of Stan's office and released the pressure by throwing up in his bushes. Looking around to make sure no one saw, Meg hurried to the car, glancing behind her once to see if the acid had started wilting the flowers yet.

PALO VERDE OB/GYN
PATIENT INFORMATION FORM

MOTHER: ___Megan Sanders___
AGE: __25__
OCCUPATION: __High School Music Teacher__

FATHER: ___Austin Sanders___
AGE: _25_
OCCUPATION: ___~~Loser~~ Accountant___

☐ SINGLE   ☐ MARRIED   ☐ WIDOWED

Meg looked at her choices on the form at the doctor's office and resisted drawing an additional box and writing next to it *jilted*.

FAMILY MEDICAL HISTORY
MOTHER: ___Maternal Grandma: diabetes. Maternal Grandpa: high cholesterol, heart disease. Paternal Grandpa: lung cancer. Mom: arthritis___

FATHER: _____

Meg tapped the pen on the paper and realized she didn't know any of Austin's medical history. She didn't even know if his grandparents were alive or not. In the excitement of their romance, Austin had convinced her to elope, so she had never met any of his extended family. Family wasn't something Austin ever really talked about, anyway. She left it blank and took her papers to the receptionist at the front. She only had to wait a few minutes before the nurse called her back, weighed her, and led her to the bathroom.

"We need a urine sample. When you're done, head back into the exam room."

Meg held the offending cup as if it already had urine in it. When she was finished, she set her sample on the counter and the nurse led her to a room.

She settled into the chair and thought of questions for the doctor. Her nausea and resulting weight loss troubled her. She'd lost twelve pounds in just a couple of months. Her clothes hung off her very unattractively, according to her mom.

Meg looked up when a man walked into the exam room, his steps calm and confident. He was young, probably early thirties with thick brown hair that curled a little over his tan forehead. He looked familiar to Meg, but she couldn't place where she'd seen him before. She was waiting for him to act embarrassed for walking into the wrong room when she noticed his out-stretched hand.

"Hi, I'm Dr. Wilkes."

"What?" Meg asked.

He smiled at Meg, and warmth filled her entire body.

"I'm Dr. Wilkes," he said again, releasing her hand and walking over to the counter. "Your urine sample looked good."

Meg felt like she'd wandered into an alternate universe. Was she really talking to a man—a handsome man—about her urine? Blood rushed to her face when he looked at her expectantly.

"Great," she squeaked.

"It looks like from your dates here, you're about nine weeks along." He made a few notations in her chart before he looked back up at her. He had the most amazing green eyes.

"The only thing that really worries me is your weight. You put here that you've lost twelve pounds since you got pregnant." He waited for Meg's confirmation.

She nodded.

"Are you having a hard time keeping food and liquids down?"

His efficient tone snapped Meg out of her reverie. *This is my doctor, not some man I met on the street*, she reminded herself. She glanced down at his hands while she answered him. Nice hands to go with a nice ring. Married, of course.

Meg cleared her throat, horrified at herself. She couldn't believe she just did a ring check on her doctor. She'd just found out what a jerk her ex-husband was, for heaven's sake.

"The main problem isn't keeping the food down, it's getting things in," she answered, banishing all other thoughts from her mind. "I've only thrown up a handful of times, but the thought of eating . . ." She shuddered.

"Do you feel weak?"

"Yes," Meg admitted. "I teach music and drama, and I have a hard time conserving enough energy to make it through the day."

"Oh, where do you teach?" he asked with his pen posed above the chart.

"At Sahuarita High. I love my job," Meg started. "Well, I used to anyway, before I became miserable."

Dr. Wilkes laughed, and his eyes crinkled in the corners. Meg couldn't help but laugh with him, wondering at the fact that she could laugh at all on a day like this.

"I think you mean before you became pregnant."

"So far it's the same thing."

"I don't like that you've lost so much weight so quickly. I'm going to write you a prescription to help you with the nausea. It's not a miracle drug, but it should help you to be able to eat again."

"Okay," Meg agreed, willing to try anything.

"Do you have any more questions for me?"

"No," she said, shoving her bladder-related questions away. She could ask Missy instead. Or better yet, buy a book.

"All right," he said slowly, giving her a moment to change her mind. "I'll just enter your information into the computer, and then I'll come get you for an ultrasound to see how many babies you're carrying in there."

Meg wiped sweaty hands on her pants and tried to wrap her mind around seeing the baby—or babies. She hadn't considered the possibility of multiple births.

"I didn't realize I'd have an ultrasound so early."

The doctor shrugged, and his lips turned into a half-smile. "I just bought this equipment, and I'm trying to use it as much as possible to get used to it. Plus, I just like doing ultrasounds."

The doctor left the room, and Meg grew excited at the prospect of seeing the baby. She wished that she would have brought someone with her. She pushed aside a momentary pang of sadness that Austin wasn't there. He had made his feelings clear regarding her and the baby.

After a few minutes, the nurse came in and led her into another room. Dr. Wilkes was already there, bending over a keyboard that hooked up to a monitor.

"Go ahead and lay back."

He typed in a few more things, verifying the spelling of Meg's last name, before he pulled out a little paddle and squeezed a glob of gel onto it. She gasped when the cold gel squished onto her stomach.

"Sorry. I got really busy this morning, and I forgot to put the gel in the warmer."

Meg nodded, her gaze locked on the screen.

Dr. Wilkes pointed out areas of interest, like her bladder, on the screen. He moved around, making notations now and again with the keyboard, before he stopped. There in the middle of the screen sat a tiny oblong shape.

"That is your baby," he said as he focused on taking a measurement.

Meg's eyes locked on the screen. That was her baby. She forgot for a moment about Austin, her family, and even the good-looking doctor sitting about a foot away from her.

"There's only one baby, and you're eight weeks and five days along according to the measurements. That fits right in with your dates." He paused the screen and pushed a button. "I'm going to print you a few pictures to take home and show your family."

He took the paddle from her stomach and handed her a towel so she could wipe off the gel. Meg pulled her shirt down over her belly. Even though she'd just seen the evidence, it was still hard to believe she was actually carrying a baby. Her stomach still lay as flat as it had three months ago. Actually, it was a little sunken in now because she'd lost so much weight.

Dr. Wilkes handed her the ultrasound pictures he'd printed off and twisted the door handle. "I want to see you in two weeks.

Usually it will be every four, but since I put you on a new medication, I want to check your weight."

Meg looked at the little picture of her baby while Dr. Wilkes talked. She glanced up at him as he opened the door to leave the room. He stepped outside, and then almost as an afterthought, he stuck his head back in the room.

"Congratulations," he said with a smile that took her breath away.

She blinked back sudden tears at his words. So far, he was the only person to congratulate her for being pregnant. *Of course, he doesn't know the situation*, she reminded herself. But she couldn't deny that it felt good to have someone be positive about her pregnancy.

"Thanks," Meg managed to say through a tight throat. Dr. Wilkes's smile faded at her reaction, but he turned and walked down the hall.

Meg knew she was going to have to get over his looks. He seemed like a good doctor. She actually felt excited to have this baby now. She looked down at the ultrasound picture as she walked to the receptionist's desk to make an appointment to see Dr. Wilkes in two weeks.

Chapter Six

Matt rubbed the back of his neck as he unlocked the door to his house. It had been a long day, and because of paperwork, he'd missed dinner again. It had been a difficult and busy process buying the medical practice. He felt a knot in his neck and wondered once again if the move had been worth it. He shook his head at the question and forced himself to relax the stress from his face.

He heard little footsteps running down the hall as he pushed opened the door.

"Daddy!" Lilia squealed about two seconds before she threw herself into Matt's arms. Matt held her close for a moment, breathing in the familiar scent of her shampoo. Coming home to Lilia was the best part of his day.

"Daddy, you gotta see what we made," she said excitedly, pulling back from him. Sarah Roberts, Lilia's babysitter, walked from the back of the house with a damp towel in her hands. She looked exhausted.

"Hey, Matt."

"Sarah, sorry I am so late. I can't thank you enough for staying and giving Lilia a bath. I hope you didn't have to miss a class." Matt reached out and took the towel from her, throwing it over the back of the couch.

"I don't have class on Friday nights." She folded her arms. "I did have to cancel a date, though."

Matt groaned and looked down at his watch. Seven-thirty—still early in the young, single world.

Sarah followed his gaze and seemed to read his thoughts. "He gets up at four-thirty in the morning for work, so we were planning on catching an early dinner and movie. By the time I make it home and get ready, it'll be too late for him to go out."

"Sorry. Why don't you try to reschedule for next week, and I'll pay for your date. Go anywhere you want."

Sarah shook her head. "Nah, I didn't like this guy very much anyway. It gave me a good excuse to cancel."

"If you don't like him, why did you say yes to a date?"

"Free food," she answered. "I *am* a college student."

"I don't pay you enough if you have to say yes to dates with guys you don't like just so you can eat."

Sarah laughed. "I love watching Lilia, and you pay me enough."

"Daddy." A very impatient Lilia pulled on his hand. "You need to come see."

Sarah bent down to give Lilia a hug. "See you Monday, Lils. Thanks, Matt."

"Bye, Sarah," Lilia waved as the young woman walked out the door.

Matt closed the door and then turned to his little girl, who was trying in vain to drag him down the hall. He had to laugh at her determined expression.

"Okay, okay. I'm coming," he said.

They walked into Lilia's bedroom, and she proudly held up a craft that consisted of popsicle sticks, feathers, a few scraps of cloth, and even a little tinsel.

"Do you like it?" Lilia looked up at him with big green eyes that resembled his so much.

"It's great," Matt said, scrambling to think of what it could be. Finally he gave up. "What is it?"

Lilia pouted. "You don't know?"

Matt hesitantly shook his head.

"It's a bird." She pointed at one stick that Matt could now see had feathers glued to it. "This is the daddy bird and this," she said, holding up another feathered stick, "is the big girl bird." She stuck her hand inside a homemade popsicle stick box and moved it around. When she couldn't find what she was looking for, she started to panic.

"What are you looking for, sweetie?"

"The mama bird." Tears welled in her eyes. "I can't find her."

"Did you make a mama bird?" Matt asked gently.

"Yes."

"She's not in the house with the other ones?"

"No, I took her out when me 'n Sarah played together."

"I'm sure she'll show up somewhere," Matt tried to console his daughter.

"I need her now," she wailed.

After several minutes of searching yielded no results, Lilia's tears turned to sobs. "I want the mommy bird, Daddy. Where is it?"

Matt took his daughter into his arms. "I don't know. Can't we just play with these birds for a while?"

"No," she said, pulling away. "I want the mommy. I want the mommy." She ran to the middle of the room and threw herself against the bed as she released her tears. Matt put his head in his hands and tried counting to ten to calm down. Her cry too closely resembled his thoughts.

He finally calmed Lilia enough to put her to bed and shuffled toward his own bedroom in exhaustion. These long days at work were killing him. Lilia was affected as well. She was a lot more emotional when he came home.

He pulled off his shoes and lay on the bed, too tired to even get undressed. As his mind ran through the patients he'd seen that day, his thoughts lingered on his last one. Something about her struck him as sad. He'd seen her somewhere before, and he tried to place it. It was that last smile she gave that triggered the memory.

He forced his thoughts away from work, got up, and went into the kitchen to unwind by buffing the kitchen counter, grateful that his daughter was such a heavy sleeper. After several minutes, Matt ran his tingling hand over the smooth section of granite. He still had three more feet to go, but he needed a break from the constant whine and vibration of the buffer.

So far, he'd replaced the carpet and the appliances, and now he was working on the counters before the new cabinets arrived. He'd never fixed up a house before and was surprised at the satisfaction he felt at the completion of every task. Caught in a constant deluge of events he couldn't control, purposefully working on the house and seeing the results was his form of therapy.

The phone rang as Matt put a bowl of macaroni and cheese into the microwave.

"You never called my daughter," Sister Forrester accused when he answered.

Matt sighed. "I'm sorry, but I probably won't call her. I told you I'm not interested in dating anyone." His gaze drifted to the framed picture of him and his wife standing on a beach in Oregon, Lilia sandwiched between them. It was the last picture they'd taken of all three of them together.

"That's because you don't know her. If you would just give her a chance—"

"I'm not interested," Matt interrupted. He swallowed and turned away from the image of his wife's smiling face. The microwave dinged that his food was ready, and his stomach growled. Matt sighed and stirred it. "I need to go."

He hung up the phone, his macaroni and cheese holding even less appeal now than it had before his conversation with Sister Forrester.

A flip through the channels while he ate showed nothing on television worth staying up to watch, so he rinsed out his bowl and took a shower. Once in bed, he fought against the urge to feel the empty space beside him. It had been almost a year now; he needed to stop torturing himself. Clasping his hands behind his head, he stared at the ceiling, wishing he didn't have to reject girls he had never met, wishing he knew what to do about his daughter's tantrums, wishing he could have his wife back.

Chapter Seven

Three days before Thanksgiving, Meg's mom invited everyone to her house to give them their Thanksgiving food assignments and feed them dinner. Meg suspected that her mom mainly invited everyone as an excuse to check up on her. Because of her nausea, she'd missed more days of work and hadn't been to church again. She'd holed up in her house and hadn't seen her mom in several weeks.

As they ate dinner, Meg offered to bring the stuffing for Thanksgiving (but not the boxed kind because Missy would rather eat paste than boxed stuffing). Missy wanted to bring Jell-O (but not with any kind of vegetable in it because Meg argued that there are some things that just don't belong in Jell-O). Their mom happily assigned herself everything else.

Meg felt a twinge of guilt when she thought of all the work her mom was sure to do. Meg had an OB appointment the day before Thanksgiving and planned to stop at the grocery store on her way home. She would just transfer the stuffing into a casserole dish and claim she'd made it.

"Guess who I ran into," her mom said to Meg after they'd cleared dinner from the table. Her dad was working on his Sunday School lesson in the kitchen, and Missy and Tom had cuddled up on the couch in the corner to watch a Christmas movie on TV.

"Who?"

"Oh, just an old friend of yours that we haven't seen around here in a while."

Meg was helping Kaitlyn cut out turkey feathers from construction paper. They were using kid-proof plastic scissors, which meant that it would have been easier for her to just rip the paper. She took a break from the frustrating task and looked over at her mom, who had gone back to crocheting.

Meg sighed. "Mom."

"Hmm?" she murmured, not looking up from her afghan.

"Who did you run into?"

"Johnny Peters."

Meg let her breath out in a whoosh. Johnny was back in town. Although she'd heard updates about him occasionally, she hadn't seen him since high school. They'd written to each other a few times while he was stationed in Iraq, but their letters tapered off after a few months. She tried to picture how he would look now. In her mind, he still looked as handsome as he did when she and Missy took that picture kissing him, but maybe he was more muscular from his military service. She hoped he hadn't lost his heart-thumping, confident smile.

A sudden bout of nausea took her thoughts away from Johnny's attractiveness. With a hand on her stomach, she reminded herself that she was in no position to care what he looked like. Anyway, chances were slim that she'd even see him. "I thought he moved to California. He got a big-time architectural internship or something."

"His dad's not doing well, so Johnny's taking off work until the new year to help him out."

"Has Brother Peters gotten worse?" Meg asked with concern. Brother Peters's health had been in steep decline since his wife died of lung cancer a few days after Johnny graduated from high school. He'd had a stroke a couple of years back.

"He's having a harder time lately. I think it will do him good to have Johnny home. Nothing's ever been the same for them since the cancer took Deanne."

"Yeah." Remembering those days sifted sadness into Meg's emotions. "Hopefully having family here will help him."

"Johnny asked about you."

"Did you tell him about the divorce?"

"I don't air our dirty laundry in public, Meg," her mom said.

Meg felt an odd combination of relief and shame that her mom felt like she had to hide news about Meg's life.

"I'm glad he's here to help his dad." Meg shook off her hurt feelings. "He hasn't been home in so long, I figured that he'd forgotten where he was from."

Her mom's head snapped up. "He came home about as often as you did while you were in school."

Meg knew she hadn't come home enough in college, especially after she met Austin. Then again, her parents had only made the two-hour drive to Tempe twice in the four years she lived there, so she didn't feel overly guilty. And it wasn't like her parents were lonely and sick. They had their health, and they had each other.

Missy interrupted the conversation when she threw her arms around Meg's neck. "I've missed you!"

Meg patted the thin arms that nearly strangled her and looked around Missy's back. Tom had changed the channel to some sports game.

"I just saw you." Meg pointed to the couch. "Over there. With Tom. Watching a premature Christmas movie."

"I know that." Missy pouted with her perfect pink lips. "I mean, we never do anything fun anymore. Not since—" She stopped suddenly, as if rethinking her words. Not since Meg got married, got pregnant, and got divorced. All three would be true.

Meg felt much better with the medication Dr. Wilkes had prescribed, so she felt brave enough to ask, "Do you want to get together sometime?"

"Yes! Let's go out to dinner tomorrow night. We can go into Tucson and get Italian."

"Uh, I don't know if I'm up for a restaurant yet," Meg said, feeling a little guilty for bursting Missy's bubble. She knew she would feel worse later, though, if she went to a restaurant with all the different aromas assaulting her.

"We'll get takeout and go to the park. I'll get you some bread sticks. You can eat bread."

"Missy, it's fifty degrees outside. This isn't picnic weather."

"C'mon," Missy cajoled. "You can bring Cliff. I bet he'll love being outside."

Cliff. Meg felt bad about keeping him cooped up in the house so much lately. Since finding out about the pregnancy, she'd only taken him on sporadic, short walks.

"Okay," Meg conceded with a sigh. "But I don't want to be outside for very long. Maybe we can just eat and catch a movie."

Missy squealed. "Oh, this will be great. You'll see."

Missy ran out of the room, calling Tom's name. He got up from the couch and followed her, glancing back at the TV a couple times on his way out of the room to catch the score.

Meg couldn't help but smile at her sister's enthusiasm, even though the thought of a night alone with her made her stomach twist into a knot. Missy had a problem understanding the meaning of personal space—physical and emotional. Missy would probably pepper her with questions about the divorce that she had been dying to ask.

Meg picked up the worthless plastic scissors and tried to cut another feather from a piece of pink construction paper. The feather ripped in half as she turned a corner.

Why does everything need to be so hard? she thought as she took a fresh piece of paper and started over again.

☙❧

Missy called Meg the next day and told her to come to Arrowhead Park at six. Meg pulled her car into the parking lot at five after and put Cliff on his leash. He pulled her forward, his excitement barely restrained.

The chilly air nipped at Meg's nose and fingers when she stepped out of her warm car. Sahuarita was having an unusually cold winter this year and had broken the state record for the amount of rainy days in a row. The skies that night were relatively clear, considering it had rained most of the morning, but a chill wind raked through Meg's loose hair.

Meg blew on her fingers, but Cliff's pulling made it difficult to keep them by her mouth for long. She didn't have time to put on her gloves before she had to speed walk to keep up with Cliff.

As they entered the darkening park, Meg wished she had insisted that she didn't want to picnic. Eating outside was okay in the afternoon, but not after sunset. A shiver slipped down her back, and she snuggled her chin into her jacket.

"Meg!" Missy stopped in front of Meg, just slightly out of breath, her cheeks a pleasant, rosy color from jogging. "We're over here," she said, pulling Meg's arm.

"We? Who's we?"

Instead of answering, Missy took Cliff's leash and ran toward some shadowed figures at the picnic tables.

Chapter Eight

"Hey, Meg," Tom called out as she followed Missy. Meg saw an unfamiliar man next to Tom as she got closer. He was the same height as her with dark hair that looked like it hadn't seen a comb, or a shower, in days. He bounced on his heels in a chaotic rhythm, his hair flopping with his enthusiastic movements.

"I'm Larry," he said, extending his hand.

"Meg," she felt obligated to respond. An ugly suspicion sprouted in her chest. She glared at Missy and mouthed, *We need to talk.*

Missy ignored her. Meg ripped her hand from Larry's grasp and stomped over to her sister, who had put her arm through Tom's and was resting her head against his shoulder. Meg felt a ping of jealousy in her stomach but quickly shook it off.

"I need to talk to Missy for a minute," she told the group.

"Later," Missy said. "The food will get cold if we don't eat it soon."

"No."

Tom put his free arm around Meg. "Can it wait?" He looked down at her with his big brown eyes, and she felt herself melting. "I'm really hungry."

"Please, Meg," Missy pleaded.

"Fine," Meg said, shaking Tom's arm off of her.

She tied Cliff's leash to a pole and sat at the table as far away from Larry as physically possible. Unfortunately, he scooted toward her until their arms touched.

"Body warmth," he justified with a toothy smile.

"Hmm," Meg mumbled.

They all pulled their food out of the to-go containers sitting on the table. True to her promise, Missy had ordered Meg bread sticks for dinner.

Larry got a spaghetti and sausage plate that Meg probably would have loved before she got pregnant, but looking at it now, her stomach turned. Worse, Larry liked to speak with his mouth full of food.

"So, you and Missy don't look anything alike," he commented as sauce dribbled down his chin.

Meg swallowed her disgust to give him a confirming nod. Missy looked back and forth at them before jumping into the conversation.

"I look more like our mom, while Meg looks like Dad."

"Your mom must be pretty," Larry said, his gaze resting a little too long on Missy's face.

"But Meg is gorgeous, don't you think?" Missy asked Larry. Meg tried to kick her hard under the table, but it was Tom who made a pained face. Oops.

"Definitely," Tom replied quickly. Meg rolled her eyes as Larry looked over at her with new appreciation.

"Thanks, Tom," she drawled. "You sure know how to make me feel good."

Tom reached down and rubbed his shin, "Yeah, same here."

Larry watched the interchange with confusion, taking large, messy bites from his spaghetti plate. Missy beamed as if she'd won an Emmy. She always beamed. Rumor had it, she had beamed while in labor. Meg didn't know for sure because she was away at school when Missy had Kaitlyn, but it wouldn't have surprised her if it were true.

Meg looked over at Cliff pulling on his leash, trying to move as far away from the pole as he could. She knew how he felt.

"Do you want to try this?" Larry stuck a loaded fork in Meg's face.

She leaned away and shook her head. "Get that away from me, please."

"Missy mentioned that the pregnancy is making you feel sick."

"Yep." Meg stuffed a good portion of her bread stick in her mouth so she would be spared any more talk on the subject.

"You know, I'd make a great father," he said.

Meg nearly choked. She started coughing so hard she had to spit out her bite of bread stick on the ground and drink half her soda.

"Food didn't sit well with you?"

"Something didn't sit well with me," she rasped. Meg saw a movement out of the corner of her eye and discovered Tom trying not to laugh. Sometimes she really hated him.

"Oh." Larry belatedly pounded on her back, knocking her head forward. She jerked away, and he picked up his fork with a shrug.

"As I was saying," he began again, "I wouldn't even care who the baby's father was. I would raise it as my own."

Meg gave Missy a threatening look. She was about two seconds away from grabbing Larry's plastic fork and skewering his mouth closed.

Missy popped out of her seat with a clap. "All right, that's enough of that. Tom and I have a rule that we can't talk about Kaitlyn on our dates because we need to focus on us." She stopped to smile at Tom, before raising an eyebrow at Larry. "That rule applies for all kids, born or unborn."

Larry drank in Missy's lecture as if she were a preacher telling him how to gain salvation. Meg jumped up, eager to get away from the smell of Italian food and this dating ambush.

"I need to take Cliff for a walk."

Larry stuffed one more bite of spaghetti in his mouth and stood up as well. "I'll go with you," he mumbled through the food.

"Good idea." Tom gave Larry a thumbs up. She *really* hated him sometimes.

Meg walked away from the table without looking back. She heard footsteps behind her before a clammy hand took hers. Larry grinned and swung their hands back and forth. Meg had an almost irrepressible urge to wipe her hands on her pants. Instead, she untangled their fingers and pulled her mittens out of her pocket.

"My hands are cold."

"Oh," he said, stuffing his hands in his pocket. They walked for a while before Larry cleared his throat. For a moment, Meg thought he was preparing to spit, but instead he rushed forward with a comment. She wished he would've spit instead.

"So, Missy tells me that you just got a divorce." He said it like she just got a car or a home. She was going to have to talk to Missy about discussing her personal life with strangers.

"Yep."

"That stinks. Do you mind if I ask why?"

"Yep," she repeated. Cliff tugged harder on the leash, and Meg complied with his urging to walk faster.

"Oh," Larry said into the uncomfortable silence. "Missy says that your ex got remarried."

"Look, Larry." Meg stopped walking. "I don't want to be mean, but this is none of your business. I didn't even know that this was going to be a date. I thought that it was just going to be me and Missy eating dinner together. I don't feel like I'm even ready to date yet; my divorce was just finalized."

Larry opened his mouth, but she held up her hand. "I don't want to talk about it."

"Okay. Sorry I brought it up." Larry sounded a little hurt. Meg didn't have the energy to deal with all her problems and Larry's hurt feelings, so she sped up. The sooner they could get back to the table, the sooner she could leave.

"So how do you know my sister?" Meg asked as a peace offering when guilt began to needle her for the way she'd spoken to him.

"I met her at work. She's the teller I go to at the bank" he said distractedly. Meg followed his gaze to Missy and Tom. They were chasing each other around the table, laughing. Tom caught up with her and pulled her body against his. Missy laughed with Tom until they suddenly quieted when he dipped his head toward hers and kissed her. Meg turned away from their antics, hating herself for feeling jealous of Missy.

A rush of light-headedness struck Meg, and she grabbed Larry's arm.

"Hey, are you okay?"

Meg blinked her eyes to clear the black sparks in her vision. "I'm fine. This just sometimes happens to me. I think we walked too long."

Missy and Tom noticed them and ran their way. Either the way Meg's body swayed or the terror in Larry's face must have alerted them that something was wrong, because the next thing she knew, Tom and Missy hovered next to her.

"We were just standing here when her face went really white, and she started swaying," Larry explained.

"I'm okay," Meg breathed, her vision already clearing.

Tom took her free arm. "Do you need me to carry you to the car?"

"No, just give me a minute to rest." Meg leaned against him, closing her eyes.

Missy came around to her other side, gently pushing Larry out of the way. "Do we need to take you to the hospital?"

"No, this happens all the time."

Missy's grip around her waist tightened. "This has happened other times?"

Meg shrugged. "It's no big deal. Whenever it happens, I just sit back for a minute and close my eyes. It passes quickly."

"Have you told the doctor?"

"No, I forgot," she admitted.

"Meg, you need to take care of yourself."

"I have an appointment in a couple days. I'll tell him then."

"Promise?"

"Promise." Meg tried to untangle herself from Missy and Tom's arms, insisting she could walk on her own, but they wouldn't hear of it.

They got to her car, and Tom ushered Cliff into the backseat. Missy wanted Meg to come to their house and stay the night, but Meg knew she would sleep better in her own bed. They argued over Meg's ability to drive home while Larry checked his watch.

"Meg, you're not driving," Tom said with finality. He grabbed the keys out of her hands. "Missy will drive you home, and I'll follow so I can take Missy home."

Meg wanted to argue, but Tom already had the driver's door opened, and Missy sat in the car.

"This is ridiculous," Meg grumbled, walking to the passenger side.

She opened the door and was stepping into the car when Larry put his hand on her shoulder. "Can I call you sometime?"

"That's probably not the best idea." She shook off his hand. Missy's stare burned a hole in the back of her head.

"Oh." Larry stepped back.

"Good night." Meg closed the door. Through the window, Tom flashed her a disapproving look. When she turned, Missy had the same one on her face. Meg sighed and leaned back in her seat.

"You could've been nicer," Missy admonished. "He came on this date as a favor to me. You never used to be that rude."

"I didn't ask to be set up on a date. I thought it was just going to be me and you."

"I should've told you, but that didn't give you a right to take it out on Larry."

"Missy, he kept bringing up the divorce."

"So?" Missy shrugged.

"It's none of his business!"

"I guess it's none of my business, either," Missy replied quietly. Her words stung Meg. They spent the rest of the drive in a thick silence.

Missy pulled into Meg's driveway and shut the car off. She turned to Meg and wrapped her arms around her. Meg slowly brought her hands up and patted Missy on the arms.

"Sometimes I really hate Austin," Missy's voice broke.

"Lucky," Meg whispered.

"He took something away from you," she continued. "You changed after you got together with him. You used to be so much happier. Remember all those songs you used to make up? It seemed like every time we were together, you were singing something new or playing something you wrote on the piano. I haven't heard you do that since you met Austin."

Meg turned away. "I grew up, Missy."

"No, you grew apart from our family, from me," her voice dropped, "and yourself."

Meg opened the car door, and the cool night air mingled with the warm blast of the heater. She grabbed Cliff and ran to the front door without a backward glance at Missy.

Tom's headlights shone on the house as he pulled into the driveway. Meg waved at their car and then walked into her cold, dark house. She must have forgotten to turn the heater up before she left.

She shivered and went down the hall to turn up the thermostat. Cliff followed her into the bedroom as she reluctantly pulled off her warm coat. She climbed into bed and curled into a ball.

Hot tears slipped down her cheeks and fell onto her white pillowcase until it grew moist against her face. Missy's words ran through her mind. She wanted to reject them, but a part of her wondered how much truth they held. Had being with Austin really changed her?

Chapter Nine

Dawn brought a furious rainstorm on the day before Thanksgiving. Meg awoke to the creepy sound of wind whistling through the little cracks in her roof. Her clock read 4:45, which meant she could sleep for another forty-five minutes before she had to get up for work. The noise of the wind grew louder and higher in pitch until Meg finally groaned in frustration. She threw the bed covers off and walked groggily toward the bathroom.

A hot shower helped her feel alive again. She wrapped a thick robe around her and stuck her cold feet into warm slippers before padding down the hall. She walked into the kitchen but stopped as something cold and wet seeped through her slippers. A thin layer of water covered her tile floor.

The leak came from a crack between where the wall and the ceiling met. Meg hurriedly grabbed a pot to catch the flow, but the water drizzled down the wall in a steady stream. After grabbing several hand towels out of the drawer next to the sink and running to the bathroom for some more, she sopped up most of the water.

It took her several minutes to get the floor completely clean and dry, and then Meg sat down at the table with a small cup of apple juice and a couple of crackers. She tried to figure out how to fix this problem.

Someone needed to come take care of the leak before it did

more damage to her kitchen. She didn't want to have to replace the entire ceiling. Her gaze swept over the pile of wet towels stuffed in the corner of the kitchen. The towels needed to go into the washing machine before they made the house smell like mildew.

Meg set her empty cup next to the sink and leaned against the counter. She didn't want to deal with this, but there was no one else. A strong yearning for Austin nearly blindsided her, and she wrapped her robe more firmly around her body as if to protect herself from her longing. She needed to figure this out on her own.

Her first class started in twenty minutes. She considered calling in sick but worried that she'd already done that too many times this semester. Thunder roared overhead, reminding her that the leak could turn into a flood if she didn't take care of it immediately.

Tackling her problems one at a time, she pulled out the phone book to call someone to come fix her roof. The only place open that early was already booked with people who had a similar problem because of the night's storm.

She closed the book and tried to think of anyone else she could call. The minute hand ticked in rhythm with the dripping water, both mocking her need to get to work.

She would have to swallow her pride and call Tom. It still irritated her that Missy and Tom had accosted her with that nightmare date, and she'd wanted them to wallow in the silent treatment.

In retrospect, she realized she hadn't treated Larry very well. But it was rotten that Tom and Missy set her up without her knowledge.

Finally she gave in.

"Hello?" Kaitlyn's voice chimed into the phone.

"Hi, sweetie. This is Aunt Meg."

"Meg!" Kaitlyn called out before plunging into the retelling of a movie she had watched. Meg heard shuffling in the background before a groggy sounding Tom came on the phone.

"Meg?"

"Hey, Tom."

"Hey."

"I have a problem," she began hesitantly.

"Just one?"

"Well, no. But this one's pretty big. You can say no if you want to, but I can't find anyone else to help me. I know you and Missy are probably still upset with me, and I'm still a little bugged with you, but I don't know who else to call." It all came out in one breath.

"Whoa, you sounded just like Missy there. What do you need help with?"

"I have a leak in my ceiling," Meg explained reluctantly. "I need to be at work in fifteen minutes."

"I'll be there in ten," he said before hanging up the phone.

Meg pushed aside her guilt at asking Tom for a favor after being rude to Missy just a few nights before. Her family really was good to her—most of the time.

She hurriedly dressed and then ran a brush through her wet hair before calling the school to tell them that she was going to miss most of first period. They grumbled, but someone agreed to go into the classroom for her until she could get there. Once she was off the phone, she had just enough time to put on some mascara and lip gloss before she heard a knock on her front door.

Meg opened it, and Tom stepped in with a toolbox.

"Where's the leak?"

"In the kitchen."

She led him there, and he climbed onto a chair to touch the ceiling.

"Thank you for coming."

He nodded and continued with his inspection.

"I'll take care of it," he finally said.

"Are you sure?"

"Of course," he growled teasingly. "That's what family's for."

"I'd better go," she said, looking at the clock. First period had just started. She backed up toward the door.

"Hey, Tom," she called out before leaving.

"Yeah?"

"Is Missy still mad?"

Tom poked his head around the kitchen wall. He looked at Meg, studying her face. "Are you?" he asked.

"I'll get over it."

He winked. "So will she."

Meg's day only got worse. The students wanted to focus on the few days they would soon get off school and the food they planned on eating rather than on one of the few remaining rehearsals they had before their winter concert. She tried to channel their energy into the music, but their minds remained elsewhere.

Every off note, piercing sharp or dull flat, penetrated her skull. Her head was throbbing by the end of second period and didn't let up the rest of the day.

She had lunch duty and a progress meeting with the principal during her prep hour, so she didn't get the chance to call Tom until after school. He told her that he had patched up the hole for her and found two more holes while crawling around in the attic. He patched those as well, but she needed to get someone to look at the drywall.

After school, Meg sat in the music closet and went through songs her classes could sing in the spring, but even hours later she was still fuming over the ultimatum the principal had given her that day. He'd told her that she had called in for substitutes too many times and that if she missed any more days of work, he might not renew her contract for the next year. She needed job security now more than ever. Mentally she threw sharpened batons at his face as she picked out all her songs. Finally, while restacking the boxes, her eyes roamed past the clock on the wall.

"Oh, no," she said, leaving the rest of the boxes and running to her car. She had an appointment in ten minutes with Dr. Wilkes, and it would take twice that time to get to his office.

She headed toward the highway and pulled out her cell phone

so she could call the office and realized her cell phone battery was dead. Of course. She threw it into her purse and increased her pressure on the gas pedal.

Arriving at the medical complex in record time, Meg whipped into a parking spot and ran to the office. She welcomed the calm of the empty waiting room and exhaled while sitting. A few minutes after checking in, the nurse called her back.

"It's so quiet in here," Meg said as the nurse weighed her.

"It is now, but you should have been here an hour ago. It was a madhouse."

"Is it usually busy in the afternoons?"

"Sometimes," the nurse replied. "Dr. Wilkes had to deliver a baby this morning, so his appointments all got pushed back about two hours. We cancelled most of his afternoon appointments, but it was still pretty busy."

"Did you try calling me?" Meg asked, thinking of her dead phone.

"Yes," she confirmed. "We left you a message but we figured since you had the last appointment, it would be okay for the doctor to see you."

Once the nurse left the room, Meg sat in the exam chair and leaned her head against the pillow. The paper on the chair crackled as she shifted to make herself more comfortable. She closed her eyes and let the soothing music playing over the speakers relax her.

❧

Matt shot his receptionist, Cindy, a frustrated look.

"I wanted all of the afternoon appointments cancelled. I need to be home by five."

Cindy looked flustered as she dropped several papers she was trying to place in a worn folder. "Sorry, Dr. Wilkes. I thought that since she had the last appointment, it would be okay to leave her."

Matt rubbed his fingers over his eyelids and sighed.

"I'll go tell her that she needs to come back another time," Cindy suggested.

"I'll see her this time," Matt barked. "In the future, though, when I tell you to cancel all my appointments, please do it."

He walked away from Cindy, his annoyance blocking out any guilt he might've felt when he saw her eyes water. He normally wasn't so irritable with his office staff, but his patience had worn thin over this long and trying day.

It started at four that morning when Lilia wet the bed while lying next to him. Sarah arrived and informed him that she needed to leave at five that evening because she had family flying in for the holidays. Then he got a flat tire on his way to work and had to change it in the rain. He had been behind all day in his appointments, consequently driving his already uncomfortable patients to irritation.

He opened the door to the exam room and saw his patient asleep in the chair. Her chest rose and fell evenly with deep breaths, and her curly brown hair splayed wildly over the pillow. He envied her peaceful moment and sat softly on his stool to review her chart. There was no reason to wake her up before he needed to talk to her.

Matt opened her chart to read through it again. Megan Sanders. He remembered her from several appointments over the past few weeks for weight checks. He scanned through the chart, trying to commit any significant medical notations to memory. The baby's father's side was empty except for the father's name and date of birth. This would be her first child. He looked over the notes from her last couple of visits before softly speaking her name.

Her eyes flittered open.

"How are you feeling?" Matt gave her a warm smile.

"Hmm?" She shook her head as if to clear it.

"Would you like a drink?"

"Sure," her husky voice replied as she pulled her head off the pillow. Matt filled a small paper cup with water and handed it to her. Her hand shook when she took it from him.

"How have you been doing these past couple of weeks?"

"Um, better," she replied, sitting up taller in the chair. "Sorry I fell asleep," she added, her face turning pink.

"Hey, if I could lay down in one of these chairs right now, I'd fall asleep too."

"Busy day?"

"You could say that. It just hasn't been my best day. It started with a urine-soaked bed, compliments of my daughter, and continued with a flat tire and a crazy office, and well, the day isn't over."

"That can almost compete with my day," she said as she handed him the paper cup. He threw it in the trash can next to the sink and turned on the water to wash his hands.

"Oh?"

"I woke up this morning to find out that I have three leaks in my roof. Then I was late for work, I nearly murdered several of my students today, missed lunch, and had to meet with my boss, who told me if I miss any more days of work that I can consider myself unemployed next year. And then I rushed over here to this appointment, which I was about fifteen minutes late for." She took a deep breath and bit her lip. "But I probably shouldn't have mentioned the last part."

Matt laughed at her sudden look of chagrin. "Probably not. So other than having a bad day, how are you feeling?"

"I'm still feeling a little sick to my stomach. It's not as bad as it was in the beginning, though." She paused for a moment and then hesitantly asked, "Do we get to listen to the baby's heart beat again?"

Matt hadn't intended on doing that at this appointment. He'd planned to ask her a few quick questions about the nausea and then check her weight, but her hopeful expression stopped him from saying no. He opened the cupboard over his head and pulled out the heart monitor. He purposely avoided looking at his watch.

"So you can't miss any more days of work?" he asked her while he searched for the heartbeat.

"Yes. The principal told me that some of the parents had complained about how many subs their students have had this year because of my 'condition,' as he put it. One parent even told him that I'm a bad moral example for their kid."

Matt shook his head. "Really?"

"Never mind that I was married when I got pregnant, and I had no control over my husband leaving . . ." Her voice drifted as the sound of the baby's heartbeat thumped through the room. As they listened to it, Matt's heart went out to this young woman and the long road she had ahead of her. He knew too well how lonely single parenthood could be.

"Do you have someone you can talk to?" He pulled the monitor away from her stomach. It sounded like this woman had a lot to deal with and would need a good support system.

She blushed. "I know, I'm a mess. Yes, I have my family around if I need to talk."

Matt allowed himself to glance at his watch as he put his monitor in the cupboard. Sarah was going to be late picking her parents up from the airport. He wrote a few notes in the chart before closing it.

"The baby sounds great, and your weight stayed the same, which is a good sign, but I'd like you to eat more. Eat as much as you can anytime you feel hungry. I want to see some good weight gain at your next appointment. Okay?"

"I'll try," she said.

"Do you have any questions for me?"

Ms. Sanders hesitated. Matt could tell she had something on her mind. He hooked his doctor's chair with his foot and rolled it over to him. He sat down and faced her expectantly.

"I don't know if this is normal or not," she began, "but sometimes I feel like I am going to faint. I get really light-headed, and I see black spots in my vision. My family says that my face goes pale."

"How often does this happen?"

"Several times a week. It happened once while I was teaching, and I had to sit down. Last time it happened after I'd been outside for a while."

"This is something that we'll want to keep an eye on, but it sounds to me like it may be related to your diet. Your body might not have the energy to go through your day with the small amount of food you're giving it."

"Okay."

"Next time it happens, just sit down and close your eyes. You can put your head between your legs if you need to. If you black all the way out, give the office a call." Matt paused to glance at her chart again. "Since you're doing so well, I think you'll be fine coming in every four weeks from now on. Call me if you have any problems, though." He capped his pen and put it in his pocket. "Happy Thanksgiving."

"You too," she answered, following him out of the room.

Matt handed Cindy the chart, and she flashed him another apologetic smile. He nodded before walking toward his office. It was already a couple minutes past five. Sarah would be calling him any minute to see if he forgot. He'd really wanted to be home early for her tonight.

He grabbed his coat and ran down to his car, waving to Cindy and Ms. Sanders as he left the office. He drove home faster than he wanted to admit and came breathlessly into the house. Sarah sat by the door with her jacket already on and her cell phone pressed to her ear. She jumped up when Matt walked in and put the open phone against her chest.

"Sorry, Sarah, I had a delivery and—"

"It's fine, Matt," she interrupted. "I really need to leave. My parents just called from the airport to say that their plane landed. Lilia was great. She's in her room putting her jacket on because she says you told her that you would take her to the store."

She put the phone back to her ear and rushed out without a backward glance.

Matt groaned and went to find his daughter.

"I'm all ready to go, Daddy," she said when he walked into her room.

"Honey, Daddy is so tired. Can we go in a little while?"

She stuck out her lower lip. "You said we'd go when you got home from work. You're home from work now."

"I am home from work now, and I'll still be home from work in half an hour."

"Half an hour is forever. I've wanted to go to the store right now my whole life." She looked pleadingly up at Matt and took his hand to lead him toward the door.

"Your whole life?" he asked, a smile tugging at the corner of his mouth.

"Yes." She nodded her head.

"Well," Matt said, caving into his daughter's charms, "since you've waited so long, I guess we should go now."

"Okay, let's go." She pulled his hand with all her strength.

Matt cast a longing glance at the couch as he locked the door behind him. Tomorrow was Thanksgiving. He didn't know how Lilia found out about it or even knew what Thanksgiving entailed. He knew that he'd never talked about it with her. If it were up to him, he would let this year's holidays just pass by them.

But whether Sarah had told her about it or she heard it from a television show, Lilia wanted to celebrate Thanksgiving. She had caught Matt in a weak moment the previous night after he got home from work and told him that she wanted to have a big dinner "with turkey and everything." All day he had hoped she would forget about his promise to take her to the store to buy food.

He should've remembered that even at four years old, his daughter had a great memory. Lilia chattered all the way to the store and kept up a steady stream of stories as they walked inside. Once they passed through the sliding glass doors, Matt stopped for a moment to get oriented. He reminded himself to occasionally say "hmm" or "yes" so that Lilia would know he was listening to her.

Matt and Lilia found the frozen food section and studied the five remaining turkeys in the freezer. He picked up the smallest one and decided that it could feed him and Lilia for about two weeks. He set it back down and nearly walked away, but Lilia looked so excited. He loved turkey at Thanksgiving too, but he'd never had to cook it. His mom always took care of it except for last year when she had her hip replacement. Last year, Lydia had cooked it for the first time . . .

He shook his head to dispel the thoughts of his wife. He didn't want to think about her right now. He needed to focus on this year, his daughter, and the turkey.

"Dr. Wilkes," a soft, lilting voice said.

Matt turned and forgot his thoughts when his eyes locked on Megan Sanders.

Chapter Ten

"Hello, Ms. Sanders." Matt cleared his throat. "Getting some last-minute shopping done for Thanksgiving?"

Ms. Sanders held out a package of pre-made stuffing. "Yeah, but don't tell my mom. In about an hour, this stuffing will be sitting in my fridge in one of my own dishes."

Matt couldn't help but laugh. "Passing it off as your own?"

"Yes, and I feel terrible about it."

"I can tell."

"Are you my daddy's friend?" Lilia pulled on Ms. Sanders's hand.

She bent so she was eye level with Lilia. "Your daddy is my doctor."

"Oh." Lilia nodded. "What's your name?"

"Meg. Not Ms. Sanders." She looked up at him with a quirked eyebrow and a smile.

Meg. It suited her.

Meg turned her attention back to Lilia. "What's your name?"

"Lilia Marie Wilkes. I'm four years old, and we are getting a turkey for Thanksgiving. Daddy didn't even know that it was Thanksgiving tomorrow. Sarah told me all about turkey and mashed potatoes, and Daddy said we could come to the store and get some food for tomorrow so we can eat a lot."

"Wow." Meg looked up. "You didn't even know it was Thanksgiving? What would you do without Lilia here to help you?"

64

"He'd starve to death," Lilia said dramatically.

"Probably," Meg answered.

"Hey," Matt defended. "I took care of myself pretty well before you came along, Lils." He tugged on her ponytail. "But I didn't have nearly as much fun."

"That's for sure," Lilia agreed.

Meg laughed. Lilia smiled, basking in the attention.

"Well, I should probably let the two of you finish picking out a turkey." Meg stood, and her long, wavy hair fell over her shoulders.

"Do you know anything about cooking a turkey?" Matt asked her impulsively before she could turn away from them.

"Not really. My mom always cooks the turkey. I think there are directions on the packaging." She handed Matt her stuffing and leaned over the freezer to grab one of the frozen birds. "The cooking instructions are right here. It all seems pretty easy, besides the part where you pull out the innards."

"Innards?" Lilia repeated.

"Uh . . ." Meg looked to Matt for help.

"It's the stuff that's inside the turkey," he vaguely explained.

"Oh, okay." She leaned into Meg's leg.

"If you can get through medical school, I have a hunch that you'll be able to cook a turkey without a problem."

"I hope so," Matt said, unconvinced.

Meg handed him the iced bird. "How many people are you going to have over for dinner? The size of turkey you'll want to get will depend on how many people."

"It's just going to be me and Lilia," he answered, eyes focused on the turkey.

"Well, in that case—" She turned from him and looked into the freezer again. "—the turkey you have is the smallest one. I'd also buy some bread if you don't have any at home because you're going to be eating a lot of turkey sandwiches next week."

"Are you sure you want a turkey, Lilia?" Matt asked, trying to sway her to say no with his tone.

"Of course, Daddy. Sarah says that it isn't Thanksgiving without a turkey."

"All right, it looks like we're going to get this fifteen-pounder then." He turned back to Meg with poorly concealed hope. "Where'd you get your stuffing? Were there any other pre-made dinner foods there?"

"Go straight until you get to the wall and then turn right. There's a whole section of pre-made food that would make my mom gasp in horror." She leaned a little closer to whisper, "They may even have pre-cooked turkeys."

"Really? Lils, let's go check it out." He reached down and grabbed her hand, setting the turkey back in the freezer with a loud thump.

"Thanks for your help."

"No problem. Good luck."

Lilia pulled away from Matt and went over to Meg. "Do you want to come over for turkey tomorrow?"

Meg must have seen the look of panic on Matt's face because she had to cover an obvious laugh with a cough.

"Thanks for thinking of me, and I'd love to eat with you, but I already told my mom I'd go to her house." Meg tucked some of Lilia's hair behind her ear.

"You can come over after."

"Lilia," Matt warned. "Ms. Sanders has other plans."

Lilia pouted. "Please?" she tried one last time. Meg's coughing could not hide the laugh this time.

Sorry, Matt mouthed.

"Is this what you deal with every day? This girl must have you wrapped around her finger."

"That is truer than you know," Matt said under his breath.

"I think that your dad has his heart set on having a Thanksgiving dinner with just the two of you."

"Yeah, Lilia. We're going to have a lot of fun tomorrow playing games and eating turkey and pie."

"Can we play Candy Land?" Lilia clapped her hands eagerly.

"Sure," Matt promised.

"Yes!"

"I can see I'm no match for Candy Land." Meg smiled.

"Well, it is one of the best games ever made," Matt said as Lilia nodded her head in firm agreement.

"I'd better get this stuffing home before my mom drops by unexpectedly and discovers my secret. It was good to meet you Lilia. Happy Thanksgiving, Dr. Wilkes."

"Bye, Meg. See you later." Lilia waved.

"Bye, Ms. Sanders. Remember to rest," he counseled, once again in doctor mode. "Happy Thanksgiving."

Matt reached down and grabbed Lilia's hand.

"My friend Meg is nice," she said as they walked in the direction of the pre-made foods.

"She is nice," Matt agreed. "Now let's go find some turkey."

Meg cringed when her mom decided to taste-test the stuffing before putting it out on the table. She glanced sideways at Meg after she took her bite. "There's a surprise for you in the family room."

Meg backed out of the kitchen before her mom could ask her any detailed questions about her stuffing. She turned around and walked into the living room, hoping her surprise would be something that could cheer her up. She halted when she entered the room, realizing her hopes had been in vain.

"Meg!" Johnny Peters jumped up from the couch and grabbed Meg in a bear hug.

"Johnny," her muffled voice said into his solid chest.

"Wow," he said, holding Meg's shoulders and stepping back. "You look great. Even better than you did in high school, if that's possible. I really like your hair. Remember how crazy it used to be?" He pantomimed a bush around his head.

Meg self-consciously ran her fingers through her freshly straightened hair.

"You look good too," she said, noticing that he did indeed have more muscle than the last time she saw him. Even through his sweater, she could feel his toned arms and stomach as he hugged her.

"What's going on in here?" Tom asked with a suggestive lift of his eyebrows as he walked into the room.

Meg jerked out of Johnny's arms and punched Tom in the stomach. Tom pretended to bend in pain but grabbed Meg instead and wrestled her to the couch. "Johnny, she's ticklish on her sides," Tom called out over her yells.

"Johnny, stay away," she warned, trying to squirm her way out of Tom's stronghold. He ignored the warning and tickled Meg in the ribs. She laughed until she could hardly catch a breath and tears rolled down her cheeks. The boys didn't listen to her pleas and begging, and since she couldn't free herself, she called for Missy.

Missy jumped on Tom's back and wrapped her legs around his waist, trying to tickle under his arms. Tom let go of Meg and tickled Missy instead. Johnny helped Meg sit up while she caught her breath.

"You're going to regret that." Meg poked his side.

"Really?"

"You'd better watch your back, Mr. Peters."

Johnny leaned in close to her. "But it's so much more enjoyable to watch yours."

Meg's face warmed to a shade that resembled the crimson pillows she leaned against. Thankfully, her mom came in just then to announce that she had dinner on the table.

Meg shot up from the couch and darted to the kitchen like she hadn't eaten in weeks. Actually, she *hadn't* eaten much in weeks, but she didn't think that she'd be making up for it today. Just looking at the all the food twisted her stomach.

Meg's dad said a blessing, and everyone filled their plates. Meg took one roll and a small scoop of mashed potatoes. Her mom eyed her plate in disapproval but didn't say anything.

Meg couldn't help but think of Dr. Wilkes and his daughter as the turkey platter passed by her. It was a little weird seeing Dr. Wilkes outside of the doctor's office. She knew that he had a life outside of work, but she had never stopped to think about it before.

He'd specifically mentioned that only he and Lilia were having dinner the next day. She had mulled over his wife's absence the night before but hadn't examined why she cared about what happened to his wife or why he still wore a wedding band.

"Mrs. Pierce, this food is excellent," Johnny said. Her mom responded by offering him some sweet potatoes.

Johnny looked over at Meg's plate as she took the serving plate from her mom's hands. "You're not on a diet are you? If anything, you look like you could stand to gain a few pounds. I could feel every rib when I tickled you."

Meg stopped chewing her roll, all thoughts of Dr. Wilkes's absentee wife gone from her mind. Johnny had to know that she was pregnant. Everyone in this town seemed to know, even though the only people that had heard the news from her own mouth were Tom and Stan.

"I haven't felt well lately," she finally said.

"Do you have that flu that's been going around? You probably get sick more being at the school."

"I don't have the flu. I'll be fine soon."

"Maybe you just need to eat more. Do you want some of my turkey?" Johnny angled his fork toward her, and Meg held her breath and pulled away.

"That little one she's carrying must be a real picky eater," Tom offered.

"Little one?" Johnny asked.

The conversations around the table fell silent.

Everyone looked at Meg like she needed to say something, but she took another bite out of her roll. It seemed that the only good use for food these days was to get her out of contributing to uncomfortable conversations.

"You know Meg is pregnant, right?" Tom asked.

Johnny whipped his head back toward Meg. "You're pregnant?" He looked at her flat stomach.

"I'm only about three months along, and I haven't been feeling very well, so I'm not showing yet," she explained reluctantly.

"You always seemed so—I don't want to say prude, but—innocent in high school. How did this happen?"

"Do you really need her to explain how it happened?" Tom asked.

"No, thanks," he shot back shortly. "I've got the logistics down."

"Just tryin' to help you out, man."

Meg's mom dove into the terse silence that followed. "Who needs a drink refill?"

"I'll help you, Mom." Meg grabbed the cups and refilled them in the kitchen. She took a deep breath before returning to the dining room.

Meg handed Johnny his water and sat beside him. His troubled eyes kept looking over at her until she felt like she needed to give him an explanation. He acted almost like he was disappointed in her.

Yeah, she wanted to tell him. *Join the club.*

"I was married until just a few months ago," she said once everyone had turned back to their own conversations.

"What happened?"

"We got a divorce."

"That much I figured. Why?"

She shrugged.

"I never even heard you got married."

"You were in California. We got married last spring."

"So, this was a long marriage."

"Long enough."

"What's his name?"

"You don't know him," she answered.

Johnny leaned back in his chair. "Wow. And now you're pregnant." He went back to eating and remained quiet for the rest of dinner.

Missy excused herself and came back into the dining room holding a photo.

"What's that?" Meg asked Missy cautiously.

"Only the best picture ever." She held it up. Meg groaned when she saw that it was the picture of her and Missy kissing Johnny. Johnny let out a loud laugh.

"I can't believe you still have this!" he said after Missy handed it to him. "What are the chances that I can get this to happen again?"

"Slim to none." Meg tried to grab the picture out of his hands. "Missy is married now, in case you forgot. I don't think Tom would like her kissing some other guy."

"What are my chances of getting just you to kiss me again, then?" He leaned closer to Meg.

"Less than that." She plucked the picture out of his hand and stuck it in her back pocket.

❧

"How do you like California, Johnny?"

"I love it. I live about a mile from the coast. It's great. The only thing I don't like lately is my job. I'm having some problems with my boss." Johnny's fists clenched. "She drives me crazy sometimes."

Everyone had left the living room except for Tom, who had fallen asleep watching a football game. Missy and Kaitlyn had gone into one of the bedrooms, and Meg's parents clanked around in the kitchen.

"How's your dad doing?"

"Not great," Johnny replied. "I don't know if he's going to make it past Christmas."

"Oh, no."

"Dad's been sick since Mom died." His tone was flat. "I knew it was coming eventually. It gets boring being at home with him all day long. Your mom's invitation to dinner gave me something to look forward to."

"I'm glad you came."

"You are?" Johnny teased.

"Well, I wasn't at first, I'll admit. My family keeps bombarding me with dates every time I turn around. It's a little unsettling."

"So, this is a date?"

Meg sputtered, her face heating up. "No, of course not."

"I wouldn't mind if it was."

She clamped her lips together, like a dam holding back a flood of awkward responses.

"You look really great, Meg." Johnny leaned closer to her. "I have a hard time believing that you're pregnant. It's a little weird to think that you're having some guy's baby." He shook his head.

"It's not 'some guy's baby.' It's my ex-husband's."

"Okay, okay." Johnnie held up his hands in surrender. "It just takes some getting used to. I'm trying to wrap my mind around how much you've changed."

Meg's heart dropped at the reminder that she had disappointed yet another person's expectations of her. She blinked back the sudden tears of frustration that rose to the surface. "I need to go," she said, standing.

Johnny grabbed her arm before she could walk away. "Meg, I didn't mean that the way it came out. I wasn't thinking. You have to admit that things have changed since we took that picture in high school."

"Believe me, I know," she finally said.

"Trust me, I've changed too. And I'm not sure if it's for the better. Please don't take every stupid thing I say to heart. With everything that's going on with my dad, I need a friend here."

Meg softened under his sincere gaze, understanding loneliness very well.

"Okay. Friends?" she held out her hand. Trepidation stirred in her heart when saw desire flicker in Johnny's eyes.

He clasped her hand in his and brought it to his lips. "For now."

Chapter Eleven

eg took a deep breath and looked in the mirror a final time before she walked out the front door. Her knee-length cotton dress hung loose around her waist, and her once form-fitting sweater drooped across thinned shoulders.

It had been over a month since Meg's one visit to church. Between feeling ill and her suspicions that people were whispering about her, she hadn't wanted to go back. Yet, with her mom's pestering and the goodies from a new set of persistent visiting teachers, she contemplated giving it another try.

When she awoke that Sunday morning, cold and lonely, with even Cliff hiding somewhere in the house away from her, she figured she didn't have anything to lose by going.

Organ music filled her ears when she walked inside the chapel. Meg scanned the rows, noticing that the widow's bench had an open space in the middle.

Meg read the lyrics of the opening hymn and let the melody find a home in her mind, wondering if it would ever find a home in her heart again. The meeting ended before Meg could decide whether or not to stay for Sunday School. In the midst of her decision making, she felt two hands clamp onto her shoulders, manacling her to the bench.

"Hey, gorgeous."

Meg turned when she heard Johnny's voice close to her ear. She'd enjoyed their talk after Thanksgiving dinner, but her heart wasn't ready for what she saw in his eyes. She didn't know if she ever would be. His timing definitely left something to be desired. Why hadn't she seen that look directed toward her in high school?

"Do you want to get out of here?" He held out his keys.

Meg considered her options. She could leave and spend the rest of the day with Johnny, who seemed interested in being more than just friends, or she could stay at church and face everyone. "I want to stay," she replied.

"Okay," Johnny said slowly. He spun his keys around his finger and looked out the chapel doors. Turning back to Meg, he stuck the keys in his pocket. "Maybe Sunday School won't be so bad if you're with me."

They walked into the Sunday School room and sat near the back. Meg sat between Johnny and a woman she recognized from the widow's bench.

Throughout the lesson, Johnny continually found excuses to lean so that their arms touched. He'd whisper in her ear and linger close enough that she could feel his breath on her neck. Her muscles tensed, one by one, taut with wariness, poised for escape.

By the end of the closing prayer, Meg was ready to rip out of her seat and run to her car. She'd decided that being lonely at home might actually beat being uncomfortable at church.

"I guess I need to get to elder's quorum," Johnny said reluctantly. He squeezed Meg's shoulder. "I'll see you after church?"

"Hmm," she murmured.

"Great." He winked before exiting the room.

Meg stood and grabbed her purse. She needed to make a break for it now.

"Are you leaving so soon?" the woman from the widow's bench asked.

"Yes?" she asked guiltily.

"You should stay, Meg. Your sister is teaching today. She always gives wonderful lessons."

Meg had no idea how this woman knew her name. She only knew her as the plump widow's bench woman with the short blonde hair.

Meg hesitated, part of her wanting to hear Missy teach. "Okay." She looked around, waiting for the Relief Society president to accost her with a perky smile and pile of clipboards, ready to make Meg the next ward project. "I hope they don't try to introduce me today," she whispered.

"Why?"

"I don't like people making a big deal that I'm coming back to church."

"We're just glad to see you here. People aren't trying to make you feel uncomfortable," she assured Meg.

"Well, I don't want to hear phrases like 'prodigal son' or 'the folly of youth' in regard to me this week."

The widow's bench woman laughed quietly. "I can only imagine." She shook her head and surprised Meg by putting her arm around her shoulders and giving her a squeeze. "I'll be right back."

She stood and walked to the front of the room to talk to someone for a minute. While she talked, her mom and Missy came into the room. They both saw Meg and smiled the same big smile.

Her mom gave her a hug. "Come sit with me in the front."

"I'd rather sit back here. You can sit by me." Meg patted Johnny's vacated seat. Her mom nodded hesitantly and sat next to Meg. She probably felt like a rebel for sitting in the back.

"I'd like to welcome everyone out to Relief Society," the widow's bench woman surprised Meg by saying in a strong voice.

She gave the announcements, and then it got to the part where visitors and new move-ins introduced themselves. She skipped over Meg as she pointed out all the visitors and welcomed them. Relief tingled down Meg's spine.

Once the widow's bench woman turned the time over to Missy and sat down next to Meg again, Meg whispered, "Thanks."

The widow's bench woman smiled and offered Meg her manual. Meg declined but looked over her shoulder throughout the lesson.

Missy's lesson held Meg's attention, making her glad she decided to stay. Her sister's teaching captivated her and drew her into the fold of women that listened and participated. Warmth pricked and then filled her chest, momentarily dispelling the awful emptiness. She held a hand over her heart to press in the feeling that had eluded her for so long. The warmth that had rushed in like a flood trickled out as the room emptied, and she realized that church had ended.

Johnny waited for her somewhere out in the hall. Her family would have numerous questions for her. She wanted to make a break for it out the window of the Relief Society room. She could probably squeeze through one, but it would be indecent. People at church already talked about her. There was no need to add gasoline to the flame.

She resigned herself to walking quickly out the door. Her mom went to talk to Missy, so Meg made her break while she could. She kept her eyes focused straight ahead, knowing that eye contact was the arch nemesis of antisociality.

"It's my friend Meg!"

The little voice came from her left side. The doors to freedom called to her from ten feet away, and despite her resolve not to get sidetracked, she looked down to see who had called her name.

A young girl threw her arms around Meg's legs and buried her face in Meg's skirt. Meg rested her hand on the head of blonde hair that was pulled into a knotty ponytail and looked around for who she belonged to.

"Lilia," a deep voice called out. A handsome man in a suit stepped over to where they stood. His black suit contrasted with his stark white shirt. Meg found herself looking in his eyes for a moment, seeing an emotion flash briefly in them.

Pain. She knew that look well.

"Dr. Wilkes?"

"Meg," he answered in surprise, masking his haggard expression with a strained smile.

"Daddy, I was walking, and I saw my friend Meg, so I came over to say hi and to give her a hug." She kept her arms around Meg's legs.

Dr. Wilkes adoringly mussed Lilia's hair.

"How long have you been in this ward?" Meg asked him, amazed she'd never seen him there before.

"About two months," he answered.

"Oh." Meg cringed with the reminder of how long it had been since the last time she came. "Where'd you move from?"

When Dr. Wilkes hesitated, Meg kicked herself for prying.

"I used to live in Washington," Lilia inserted into the conversation. "Did you live there?"

"No, I've lived here almost all my life. This is the ward I grew up in," Meg answered, looking at Dr. Wilkes. Something in his appearance today struck her as looking so sad.

Lilia stopped hugging Meg but pulled lightly on her skirt until her attention turned to the little girl again. "We had turkey."

"Did you end up cooking one?" Meg asked Dr. Wilkes with a raised eyebrow.

"Yes. It was a disaster. It took a lot longer than I thought it would, and we didn't end up having any turkey until about eight that night."

"And we played Candy Land six times," Lilia broke in proudly, holding up five fingers.

"Wow," Meg said, stifling a giggle at the look of pain on Dr. Wilkes's face that verified the statement. "That must be your favorite game."

"Oh, yeah." Lilia's head bobbed. "Do you want to come over and play Candy Land? We're eating turkey sandwiches for lunch. Right, Daddy?"

Meg kept silent, letting Dr. Wilkes handle his daughter's impromptu invite.

"Today's not a good day, Lilia."

"Why not?" she whined.

"Lilia," he warned.

"Please, Daddy. I want to have fun. You're no fun today. All you do is cry," Lilia accused her dad with a quiver in her bottom lip that indicated she might join him.

Dr. Wilkes tensed, and Meg let her gaze shift to her hands. She tried to pretend like she hadn't heard what Lilia just said, even though it was completely obvious she had heard every word. Meg assessed Dr. Wilkes from the corner of her eye while he looked down at his daughter.

His eyes did seem red. She couldn't even imagine Dr. Wilkes crying.

He finally looked up from his daughter. "Would you like to come to our house for lunch today?"

Meg tried to read his expression. Did he want her to say yes or no? Was this an obligatory invite to get his daughter off his back, or did he really want her to come? His tortured eyes shifted from Meg, to Lilia, to the floor, to somewhere behind Meg's shoulder.

"I don't know," she hedged, trying to figure out what she should do.

"Please, Meg," Lilia pleaded. "We can play Candy Land together."

She wanted to cave in to the sweet girl when she started to beg. Dr. Wilkes wasn't helping anything by staying silent, staring at the wall.

"I should probably get home." This moment was uncomfortable enough. She didn't need an entire afternoon of this.

Lilia's earnest expression crumpled, but Dr. Wilkes looked relieved.

Meg squatted down in front of Lilia as best as she could in a dress. "I'll come over another day for lunch. I promise."

"I wanted you to come today." She leaned forward like she wanted to tell Meg a secret. "Daddy's sad."

"I know," Meg said, pulling the little girl into a hug.

"I'm sad too," Lilia wailed into Meg's shoulder. Meg looked up at Dr. Wilkes for help, and he leaned over and picked Lilia up, holding her tightly in his arms.

Sorry, he mouthed while patting his daughter's back.

"Is everything okay?" Meg asked, mentally willing the words back the second they came out of her mouth. Of course everything wasn't okay. If it was, the Wilkes family wouldn't be looking as though they were ready to fall apart at any minute.

"We'll be fine." He paused and looked as if he was internally wrestling with something.

"Would you mind coming over for just a little bit this afternoon?" he finally asked, sounding almost pained as the words came out. "Just for a sandwich and a game of Candy Land. It's been a hard day for Lilia, and I think this would help her." He sighed and kissed the top of Lilia's head.

"Sure." She leaned close to Lilia's face. "Do you still want me to come to your house and play?"

Lilia lifted her head up from her dad's chest and wiped her eyes. "I want to be the red piece."

"I think that means yes," Dr. Wilkes said. "Do you need to run home first, or do you want to follow us?"

"I'll follow you," Meg answered as they walked out the door. Lilia wiggled out of her dad's arms, her eyes still red with tears. Her sticky hand took hold of Meg's, and she smiled up at her. Meg's heart turned to mush. She could see why Dr. Wilkes had a difficult time denying Lilia anything.

They turned the corner from the church doors to the parking lot, and Meg saw Johnny leaning against her car. He hadn't seen her yet.

"Oh, no," she moaned under her breath.

"What?" Dr. Wilkes asked, following her gaze. "Is he bothering you?"

"Sometimes . . . I mean no. No," Meg tried to be more firm. "He's an old friend." She sighed, trying to think of what to say when she went over there, and Johnny inevitably hugged her or touched her shoulder, or made some other gesture that she didn't want right then.

"Should I go over there with you?"

"No." The offer tempted Meg, but what was Dr. Wilkes going to do? Scare him off with his haunted smile and dark green eyes?

"All right," he said uneasily. He took Lilia's hand from Meg's and started to head toward his car when Johnny spotted them and jogged over. Dr. Wilkes turned around to greet him.

"Hey, Meg." Johnny threw a glance at Dr. Wilkes and then looked back at Meg.

"Johnny, this is Dr. Wilkes. He's new in the ward."

"Doctor?" Johnny asked.

Meg blushed and began to explain when Dr. Wilkes held his hand out to Johnny. "Just call me Matt."

"Nice to meet you."

You okay? Dr. Wilkes mouthed when Johnny turned back to Meg.

Meg nodded.

"See you in a little bit." Dr. Wilkes waved and carried Lilia to his car.

"I'd better get going," she said, walking around Johnny.

"Why is he going to see you in a little bit?" Johnny asked as he followed her to her car.

"I'm going over to his house for lunch." *Not that it is any of your business.*

"Is that safe? You don't even know him."

"I'll be fine."

"I was hoping you could come over for dinner."

"I can't tonight. I've got some other things going on."

"We're not eating until six. My dad would love to see you."

Meg hesitated. It had been a long time since she had seen Brother Peters. Johnny noticed her hesitation. "I'm making home-made lasagna and garlic bread."

"Okay," she agreed reluctantly.

"Awesome, see you at six." He leaned forward to give her a hug. Meg forced herself not to push him away. She closed her car door and let out the breath she'd been holding.

Meg eased behind Dr. Wilkes, and he signaled for her to follow him out of the parking lot. Meg briefly considered bailing on what could prove to be an uncomfortable afternoon, but when she thought of Lilia's large, pleading eyes looking up at her, eyes that looked so much like her dad's, Meg knew that she needed to go. No matter how awkward it might be.

Chapter Twelve

"One more time, please." Lilia clasped her hands together under her chin. Meg sat back in the hard chair and eyed the little pixie that had already convinced her to play the game too many times that afternoon.

"Lils, you've already played four times. Give Ms. Sanders a break," Dr. Wilkes called from the couch in the adjoining living room.

Lilia ignored her dad. "Please," she pleaded.

"One more time." Meg tried to say it firmly in light of the fact that she melted so easily to Lilia's charms. "If your dad plays this round with us." They'd been playing Candy Land for the past hour, and Dr. Wilkes had yet to play with them. He'd made lunch so the girls could eat while they played, and then he cleaned up after them. He'd been really quiet, and he had seemed preoccupied from the moment Meg walked into their house.

At least Lilia hadn't cried since she got home from church.

Meg decided that maybe Dr. Wilkes needed a little distraction himself. Unless studying his abominable walls was a distraction. She stared at them herself for a moment, trying not to speculate over the origins of certain stains that speckled the patchy paint.

"Yeah," Lilia concurred. "Sit by me, Daddy."

"Hmm?" Dr. Wilkes murmured from the couch.

"We want you to play this round, Dr. Wilkes," Meg called over to him. She winked at Lilia.

"I'll make you a deal." Dr. Wilkes looked over the back of the couch. "Bring the game in here, and I'll play it with you two. And it seems strange to have you call me Dr. Wilkes in my own house. It's Matt."

Lilia picked up the game board, and Meg grabbed the small game pieces and brought them into the living room. She wasn't sure if she could really call her doctor by his first name, but he did seem more like a Matt than a Dr. Wilkes as he sat up and dragged the coffee table closer to him so they could all play Candy Land together. Lilia took a pillow to sit on the floor to his right. Meg was grabbing a pillow to do the same on his left when he pulled her down next to him on the couch.

"Pregnant women do not sit on the floor." He took the pillow and put it back on the arm of the couch.

"I'm not that pregnant."

He laughed. "Oh, so you're only partly pregnant?"

"You know what I mean. I'm not showing yet."

"Doesn't matter. You need a comfortable seat, or you'll regret it later."

"That's probably true," Meg admitted, thinking about how her back hurt after just an hour of sitting on the hard chairs at the kitchen table.

❦

"I won!" Lilia exulted at the end of their game. "Let's play again!"

"Oh no, that's enough for today." Matt picked Lilia up and threw her on the couch next to Meg. He tickled her for a few minutes and then looked over at the clock. "Time for your nap."

"No!" she wailed. "I'm not tired. I don't want a nap."

"You need to rest for a little while."

"Will Meg still be here when I'm done resting?"

"Probably not. Say good-bye to her now. She'll come over another time."

Lilia gave Meg a hug accompanied by a pathetic sigh. "Bye, Meg."

"I'll be right back." Matt led Lilia down the hall.

Meg let her body sink into the couch. She followed a particularly nasty gash in the wall as she listened to the soft murmurs of Matt telling Lilia a story.

Meg let her eyes drift closed for a moment, every part of her body feeling worn out. She always seemed to be tired lately. Meg's mom blamed her exhaustion on the fact that a significant amount of her body's energy went into developing the baby. Sometimes she wished it didn't take so much energy, because at the end of the day there was none left for her.

Whispers and a soft clanking noise filtered through Meg's sleep-dulled senses. She blinked her eyes a few times and looked around the room, feeling disoriented. Sitting up slowly, she pulled at the blanket covering her and let her groggy gaze search the dim room. Where was she?

She stretched her arms out and heard a young voice yell, "Meg!"

The memory of that afternoon filtered into her mind, and she realized that she'd fallen asleep at Matt's house. Lilia jumped onto the couch and rubbed her small hand over Meg's hair.

"Your hair is funny," she said with a giggle. Meg touched her hair self-consciously, already suspecting that it stood up and swirled out. Matt walked into the room and handed her a glass of water.

"Did you sleep well?"

"I can't believe I fell asleep," she croaked. "How long have I been out?"

"Four hours," he answered reluctantly.

"Four hours?" The last of the fog cleared out of her mind with a cold drink of water and the realization that she'd been sleeping at their house for most of the afternoon. "I am so sorry. You should've woken me up."

"Daddy said that we needed to be really quiet," Lilia said, still talking quietly. "You need sleep to make your baby."

"Are you sleeping well at night?" Matt asked.

"I sleep okay, I guess." Sleep eluded her most nights with stress and loneliness as her consistent nocturnal companions.

Matt looked at Meg as if waiting for her to say something more. When she didn't, he sat next to her on the couch. "You must have been exhausted. When I got back from putting Lilia in bed, you were out. You didn't even wake up when I put a blanket on you."

Meg wished she could bury her flaming face in the back of the couch.

"Try to drink the rest of that water," he ordered. "Lilia and I were just making tacos for dinner. Would you like one?"

"Dinner? What time is it?"

"It's a little after six."

"Oh, no." She jumped up too quickly from the couch and immediately felt light-headed. She reached out and grabbed Matt's arm to steady herself until her vision cleared.

Matt grasped her elbow and made her sit down. He looked concerned as he lifted up her eyelids and looked at her pupils.

"I'm fine," she said, letting him take her pulse as he counted against his watch. "This happens all the time. I just stood too fast."

"Did you eat breakfast?"

"Um, a couple crackers and a glass of water."

"And you just picked at your lunch. You only ate part of your roll. You need to eat a little something before you can drive home."

"I'm going somewhere for dinner," she argued. "I was supposed to be there at six."

Matt pulled his cell phone from his pocket and handed it to her. "Call whoever it was and tell them you'll be late. You can't drive like this. I'll go find something milder than tacos for you to eat."

Meg knew that it was pointless to argue with him, especially when she realized that her hands shook as she ran her fingers over the keypad on his cell phone. She could already hear cupboard doors opening and closing in the kitchen.

"Do you have a ward phone list?" she called out to him.

"Yeah, hang on." Matt came into the room and opened up a

backpack. He pulled out a folder with the list.

Meg took it from him and looked up the Peters' home number.

"Hello?"

"Is this Johnny?" she asked.

"Meg? Why are you calling from Wilkes's phone?"

Caller ID. Johnny sounded like he was accusing her of something.

"I'm still over here."

"Dinner's ready. I've called your cell phone five times, and you haven't answered. I tried calling your mom, but she said she hadn't heard from you all afternoon either."

Meg groaned. Great. Now her mom knew she had planned to eat with Johnny. She'd never hear the end of this.

"I left my phone in the car," she answered. "I'm sorry this is such short notice, but I'm not going to make it for dinner tonight."

"What's going on?"

"I'm just not feeling that great."

"But you're still at Wilkes's house."

"I'll be heading home soon," she replied, hating that she felt like she had to explain her actions to him.

"Do you need me to come get you?"

"No, I'm fine," Meg said empathetically. "We'll have to reschedule for another time."

"If you're sure . . ." He paused. "I'll call you later, then."

Meg ended the conversation and handed the phone back to Matt. He had a funny look on his face. "Was that the 'old friend' that was by your car earlier?"

"Yes."

"And you said you would go to dinner at his house even though you didn't want to talk to him this afternoon?" he pressed.

"Yes." She cringed. Why did he have such a good memory?

"What is up with you women? Why do you say yes to dates with people that you don't like?"

"It wasn't a date. We're just friends."

"Did it have something to do with a free dinner?"

"Not exactly," she hedged. "It had more to do with the fact

that I didn't want to sit at home by myself, and I haven't seen his dad in a while. And he said he was making lasagna and garlic bread. It sounded good for some reason."

"You and Sarah would get along great," Matt muttered under his breath as he walked toward the kitchen. Meg heard some cans hitting the counter and the sound of tap water falling into the sink. Who was Sarah? Was that Lilia's mom?

"Daddy says we can put on a movie while he makes us some dinner." Lilia danced into the living room with a package of crackers in her hands. "This is our apple-izzer."

"Appetizer?"

"Yep. Daddy says that we should eat some of these crackers." She held the package out to Meg for her to open. Lilia put a movie on, and Meg tried to relax. She'd already imposed on Matt's entire day. Now her visit was stretching into the night.

Lilia cuddled next to her, and Meg wrapped her arm around Lilia's shoulders. She rubbed her hand over her stomach, wondering what her own baby would be like, if everything would go okay, if she could do this alone.

As the movie lulled her body toward sleep and her eyes drifted shut, Meg forced herself to stand. The last thing she wanted to do was fall asleep again.

"I'll be right back," she whispered to Lilia. Meg walked into the kitchen and stood behind Matt.

"Is there anything I can do to help?"

He started when she spoke and dropped his spatula on the floor. Red sauce splattered on the floor.

"Sorry," he said, grabbing a towel. "I'm not used to having another adult in the house." He wiped up the floor and handed Meg the towel to wipe off her leg and shoe. "You can help me by sitting down and resting," he said after he rinsed the spatula off.

Meg looked around the kitchen and took in the ingredients he had set out as she sat on a backless stool. "I thought you said you were making tacos."

"I was," Matt said, turning back to his sauce. "But then you said that lasagna and garlic bread sounded good. I was going to have Sarah make lasagna for us tomorrow, but I thought I'd make it for us tonight so that there is more of a chance that you'll actu-ally eat."

There was that Sarah again. Who was she? Meg felt like it would be prying for her to ask, so she just left it alone. She couldn't believe he was making lasagna for her just because she said it sounded good.

"Thank you," she murmured.

"You're welcome," he answered with a smile that made the corners of his eyes crinkle. The heat of the kitchen started to get to her, and her face turned warm.

"You're going above and beyond the call of duty as a doctor," Meg teased.

"I'm just a saint." He stuck his finger in the sauce and licked it off. Then he grabbed a small spice canister and added another sprinkle of something.

"So, Saint Matthew, now that we're on a first name basis . . ." Meg began.

"Yes?"

"I have to know, what in the world is going on with your walls? Is this like a new decorating trend? Because, if it is, I need to save you from your sorry lack of taste."

Matt looked at the walls and then back at Meg with a raised eyebrow. "You don't think the stained and destroyed look is appealing?"

"Um, no. What happened?"

"A nightmare. I walked into an even bigger mess than these walls. I've spent almost all my free time and money since moving here to fix up this house after the previous owners destroyed it with a 'foreclosure party.'"

"Ah." Meg nodded her head.

"You know what that is?" The skillet sizzled as Matt dropped a pound of ground beef on its heated surface.

"Of course. The news has covered foreclosure parties around here for a while. There are so many houses being foreclosed, espe-cially out here. People wield revenge on the bank by destroying the house that they're losing."

"Well, then I'm apparently the only person who didn't know

what that was. I just thought I was getting a great deal on a house."

"You didn't know it was going to be trashed?"

"Unfortunately, I walked into this blindly. It was even worse before professional cleaners scoured the place. There's still a lot of work to do, but at least it's livable now."

Meg watched his back as he broke the meat up with a wooden spoon and pushed it around the skillet. She couldn't believe the smell wasn't bothering her too much. Still, it could come and go at times. Cresting the nausea hill would make this already difficult journey a lot more pleasant.

"Lilia seems to be doing a little better," Meg ventured cautiously. The silence that followed her comment expanded between them. She leaned her elbows heavily on the counter, still feeling groggy from her extended nap and debated saying something else.

"I think so," Matt finally said, his back still to Meg. "Thank you for coming over. This had the potential to be a very emotional day for us, so I was willing to do just about anything to keep her happy."

"Why? Are you missing your family?"

He didn't say anything right away, and the heat from the kitchen made Meg dizzy. She buried her head between her crossed arms and tried to clear the fuzz from behind her eyes.

"This is a rough time of year for us," he answered. Meg hoped he'd say more. He didn't, and she felt his warm hand on her back a few seconds later. "Are you okay?" he asked. She wondered if he'd ever asked a guest that as many times as he'd had to ask her that night.

"I'm fine," her muffled voice responded. Her head felt heavy, and she didn't want to lift it.

"You need to go lie down for a few minutes. I'll come and get you when dinner is ready."

"Okay, just give me a minute." Meg took a deep breath. "Aren't you glad you invited me over to your house today? So much for your day off."

"Don't worry about it. You were a bigger help than you'll ever know. Do you need to lean on me?"

"I'm fine," she insisted, mortified that she was such a high-maintenance visitor. But although she had most likely overstayed her welcome, she did not feel up to driving right then.

She dragged herself the few feet into the living room and collapsed next to Lilia. Lilia snuggled right up to her again, and Meg rested her cheek against Lilia's hair.

"You almost missed the best part," she scolded Meg, before turning back to the movie. Meg closed her eyes and savored the darkness and comfort behind closed lids. She fought sleep for a few minutes before giving into it. She'd already been a nuisance and embarrassed herself. She couldn't make things any worse by falling asleep again.

Chapter Thirteen

*N*early a week later, Meg's piercing alarm startled her awake.

"No," she groaned, throwing her arm over to the night table and trying to feel her way to the snooze button. She'd had another rough night—one of those ones where she saw every hour on the clock ticking slowly by, mocking her. She'd finally managed to fall into a deep sleep about an hour and a half before she needed to get up.

She pressed *snooze* and lay in bed for another two minutes, vainly trying to fall asleep again. It was no use; the alarm had done its job.

She sat up and grabbed the package of crackers she'd begun stashing next to her bed. Several crumbs fell onto the blankets, and Meg pulled the covers over them. She'd deal with the mess later.

Johnny was picking her up at eight.

What in the world had possessed her to agree to drive with him up to Phoenix this early on a Saturday morning? His company had a branch in Phoenix that he wanted to transfer to so he could be closer to his dad, and he needed to go up there for an interview. He'd hinted that he wanted some company for the two-hour drive when he called her on Sunday night after she got home from Matt's. Meg's guilt for missing Sunday dinner prompted her to tell him she would go with him.

While Meg got ready, she thought about how she looked when she finally got in front of a mirror after coming home from the Wilkes's.

After napping on the couch, her hair certainly did look funny as Lilia had said. It had come halfway out of the clip that had been holding it back and was stuck up like a tangled ocotillo. Based on her crazy-lady appearance and the fact that she'd imposed on most of his day, she figured Matt regretted inviting her over to his house. He probably thought her life was a wreck.

Oh, well. He wouldn't be the only one.

A hard knock sounded at her front door, and she opened it a moment later to see Johnny with a paper bag in his hands. He wore a suit that complemented his well-built torso but contrasted with the rugged stubble on his face. Meg fought a nervous tremor in her stomach when he brushed by her.

"I can put this in the kitchen while you go change." Johnny shook the bag in front of Meg like she was a puppy he was enticing with a treat.

Meg looked down at her jeans and green cashmere sweater. "You think I need to change? I thought I was just along for the drive."

He looked Meg up and down and squinted. "I guess it's okay."

"Why are you doing this on a Saturday, anyway? Is it a normal business day for them?" Meg complained, irritated that apparently she didn't pass inspection.

"No. One of the uppers in the company is leaving on vacation next Monday. This was the only way they could get me in for an interview before the new year. It's really important for me to make a good impression. I need this job transfer. I can't work in California anymore."

His vehemence took Meg aback. "I'll change if you really think it will make a difference."

"I don't know if it will. But could you change, just in case?"

"Sure," she said slowly.

Why did I agree to go again? Oh, yeah. I don't know how to say no.

"Hey." He grabbed her wrist as she walked out of the room. Meg turned toward him. "Thanks for going with me."

"I'll be right back." Meg left Johnny standing in the doorway. She exchanged her jeans for a denim skirt and ran her fingers through her hair. Johnny's little touches were making her tense. She'd forgotten how touchy-feely he was.

"I brought muffins," Johnny's voice traveled down the hall. Meg took a deep breath to fortify herself before walking into the kitchen. Several muffins sat on the counter next to him. She picked one with blueberries and took a small bite. Needing something to wash it down, she grabbed a couple of glasses from the cupboard and filled them with milk from the fridge.

"So this was the house you lived in with your husband?"

"Yes," she said once she'd swallowed, hoping to nip any personal questions in the bud with her brisk tone.

"It's hard for me to think of you married." He shook his head. "What was his name?"

"I'd rather not talk about it."

"I just wanted to know his name," he pressed.

"Austin Sanders."

"Your name is Meg Sanders then?"

"It is."

"So what happened? I always pictured you as a 'for time and all eternity' kind of girl, not a 'till death—or the first bump in the road—do us part' kind."

Meg turned away from Johnny, upset that she hadn't been the eternity kind of girl and even more upset that he'd point it out. She accidentally knocked her cup of milk onto the floor. The glass shattered on the tile, and milk splattered over all the cabinets. Meg held back tears as she grabbed a towel to clean it up.

"It's not like I planned on getting a divorce," she said from the ground, angrily sopping up the milk. "Maybe you should just go to Phoenix without me."

"Meg, I'm sorry." Johnny crouched in front of her and took her hands. She yanked them away and turned her back to him to wipe up more of the milk. "We should probably go before it gets too late."

"I don't know, Johnny."

"Friends? Right?" He held out his hand.

Meg sighed. "I remember. Do you?"

He left his hand out, and she took it and let him help her stand up. She rinsed the milky rag in the sink and leaned down to wipe the floor one more time. "My divorce is off-limits as a conversation topic, Johnny."

He nodded and pulled her toward the door. "I get it. I promise I'll try to mind my own business. Let's go."

Meg followed, wondering if he was always going to want more than she was ready to give.

❦

Meg pulled at her sweater and straightened her skirt as she and Johnny walked into the plush lobby of Longman and Brant Architecture. Tan leather chairs lined one wall, and a flat screen television hung on the opposite side. A soft butter tone coated the walls and blended into the lush cream carpet. Next to a set of paneled wooden doors, a lovely young woman sat behind a large walnut desk. She smiled at them as the door closed behind them.

"I have an appointment at ten-thirty."

"Jonathan Peters," the receptionist murmured as she typed something into the computer. "You are meeting with Mr. Terelli today. I'll let him know you're here."

Moments later the receptionist got off the phone and asked Johnny to follow her through the paneled doors.

Meg looked through old magazines and watched the news while she waited for Johnny. Time ticked by slowly, and after forty minutes of reading celebrity news, Meg asked herself again why she'd agreed to come along. She kicked herself for not getting Johnny's truck keys so she could visit some college friends she hadn't seen in a while. Maybe it was better that she couldn't see them; she and Austin had known all the same people.

She must have sighed too loudly because the receptionist came and stood in front of her a few seconds later. The woman handed her a soda. "These interviews don't usually go over an

93

hour. There's a bookstore around the corner. I can tell him you went over there when he gets out."

Meg jumped at the opportunity. "That would be great."

She walked outside and breathed in the fresh air. She wished, not for the first time, that she had come up with some excuse not to come. Her panty hose pressed against her stomach, and she longed to slip them off and throw them in the nearest trash can.

Walking in her safety-pinned skirt only allowed for small steps, but she didn't dare give Johnny an excuse to look at her more than he already did.

Meg wandered around the bookstore before finding the parenting section. She perused the pregnancy and baby books and picked one that answered some of the questions she'd had but hadn't asked the doctor.

Johnny walked into the store just as she handed her book to the clerk. "They're going to let me transfer," he said excitedly, pulling her into a hug.

"Congratulations." She patted his back and pulled away to sign her receipt.

"What did you buy?" he asked, lifting the book up. He studied the title and flipped through the pages. "It's still weird to think that you're pregnant." He held out a picture toward the end that showed a woman in labor getting ready to push.

"You get used to it." She snatched the book out of his hands and put it in the bag. She didn't even want to think about labor, much less discuss it with someone else.

"Where do you want to eat?"

"I'm not really hungry. You pick." Her body ached for food, yet rejected the idea at the same time. The sugary soda she'd sipped at Johnny's office pitched and rolled in her stomach, eating away at her insides like acid.

"Let's go to Lupe's." Johnny grabbed Meg's hand and led her toward his truck. She let him hold it, unsure if she let him because his enthusiasm at getting the job influenced her or because she felt sick and welcomed the extra support while she walked. Or, most likely, the baby had taken needed nutrients from her brain, leaving her to act in an unexplainable manner. Whatever the reason, she enjoyed the warmth of his hand in hers and the feeling of belonging with someone.

Johnny helped her into the truck and then got in on his side, shedding his suit coat and loosening his tie before starting it up. He reminded her of a model posing for a business shot. He looked at himself in the visor mirror and straightened his hair before starting the car.

Johnny talked about how the interview went for the entire drive, and Meg tried to nod her head in the right places. She only half listened. The other part of her vacillated between berating herself for wanting to stare at Johnny and convincing herself that she really didn't need to throw up.

Lunch at Lupe's didn't help anything. The smell of Mexican food wafted to her nose with a stomach-clenching clarity. After their food arrived, she excused herself and stumbled to the bathroom. She lost the contents of her angry stomach in the toilet and tried not to think about how many germs she had attracted by leaning over a toilet in a public restroom.

She rinsed her face in the sink and steadied herself to walk back to the table.

"Do you feel better?" Johnny asked, chewing the last bite of his burrito.

"A little," she rasped. "I think I'm ready to head home."

"Got it." Johnny took a final drink from his cup before standing. "I paid the check while you were in the bathroom, so we can leave now."

Meg rested her head against the door of his truck when they reached it.

"You don't look so great."

"Thanks."

"You just need to think about something else. Sometimes feeling sick is all in your mind."

"This is not just in my mind."

"Well, if you dwell on being sick, you're going to continue to feel sick," he responded in an irritatingly calm voice.

"Who made you a doctor?" she snapped.

"Never mind," he said as he started the truck. They drove

most of the way home in silence. Meg pretended to fall asleep, but she couldn't get comfortable enough to actually do so. Her neck hurt from being bent, but she was afraid if she stirred too much he would know she was awake and want to talk to her.

Meg opened her eyes into a slit at one point and saw that they were in Tucson. She pretended like she was just waking up and stretched out her arms.

"Sleeping Beauty's awake finally?" Johnny smiled at her.

"Sorry." She put her hand over her mouth to cover a real yawn, still tired because she hadn't really slept. "I'm a little worn out, I guess."

"We're almost home."

"Thanks for coming with me." Johnny leaned his arm against the door frame.

"It was fun," Meg fibbed. She felt obligated to say something nice as she searched for her keys in her large leather purse. She rifled through all the junk she'd accumulated in her bag, finding them stuck between her wallet and a pile of old receipts. "I'm glad you got the job."

"Me too." He intertwined his fingers with hers. "My dad isn't the only reason I wanted to move closer."

Meg felt panic start to form in the pit of her stomach and explode from her mouth as he bent his face closer to hers.

"Stop. I'm not ready for anything," she blurted out. She pulled her hand away and pushed her front door open.

"I can wait."

"Please, don't. Doesn't any of this bother you at all?" Meg saw his eyes follow her hands to where she placed them on her stomach.

He shrugged. "I haven't thought much about it."

"Really?" She lifted her eyebrows.

"Okay. It bothers me a little. How could it not? But it's not enough to make me not want to see you again." He leaned toward her, and she put a firm hand against his chest before his lips could reach hers.

"I don't understand why you're doing this, Johnny."

"Does there have to be an explanation for everything, Meg?" Irritation laced Johnny's voice. "Sometimes you feel something, so you go for it. Or sometimes you just need a distraction, and you go for it."

"So do you feel something right now, or is this a distraction?"

"Does it matter?" Johnny pressed closer.

"No, it doesn't." She turned her head and pushed him away from her.

"Are you going to be at church tomorrow?" He sounded annoyed.

"Probably," she said warily.

"I'll save you a seat."

"Johnny—"

"It's a seat, Meg. Not a marriage proposal."

Cliff's barking warned Meg of his approach to the door. "I've got to go." Meg struggled to keep Cliff from running around her to the front yard.

Meg walked into her house and closed the door to Johnny's stiff, retreating back. She needed a plan for tomorrow that would keep her away from Johnny. Skipping church was not an option, especially considering the guilt that pricked her when she considered it. She'd missed church enough over the years and had made a huge step in the right direction last week by staying for the entire meeting. She didn't want to go backward now. She sighed and pushed away from the door. There had to be a way out of this mess.

Chapter Fourteen

*M*eg awoke on Sunday morning with a risky plan already forming in her mind. It was just chancy enough that it might work—or it could blow like a milkshake in an open blender. If all else failed, she would fake sick and leave church early. And really, she wouldn't be faking because she felt sick most of the time.

She pulled into the church parking lot a couple minutes after sacrament meeting started, walked to the door, and listened to the congregation sing the opening hymn. She stood just outside the line of vision from anyone in the chapel until the song ended, waiting for the prayer.

Normally, she would agree that it was in bad taste to walk into the chapel during a prayer, but she knew that it was her best opportunity to enter undetected because everyone's eyes would be closed. If she played this right, no one would see her coming into the room.

She hoped the person praying was long-winded.

A brief silence followed the end of the hymn. Papers shuffled and books closed before an elderly man's voice came through the microphone. Old people always seemed to pray longer—it was her lucky day.

Meg did a quick scan of the room, zeroing in on Johnny. Front, left side. Tell-tale space beside him. He was definitely saving her a spot. She let her eyes drift over to her family, sitting just an aisle away from him in the middle. They were too close to each other for her to be able to realistically fake that she hadn't seen him.

She glanced back at the widow's bench. Full. Apparently she needed to get to church early to get that coveted spot. She scanned the room with rising panic. Even an old-timer's prayer had to end eventually.

She felt uncomfortable sitting next to any families she didn't know, and no one had opened up the accordion curtain to the overflow for the convenient folding chairs. She looked longingly at the couches in the foyer but vetoed it. If Johnny had to go the bathroom, he'd spot her.

Finally, her eyes rested on Lilia's head sitting on the right side of the chapel, three rows from the back. Lilia leaned against her dad with folded arms. Meg couldn't sit by them. Dr. Wilkes—Matt—was probably still sick of her after last week. She looked at the praying man to gauge how much time she had left when she made eye contact with the bishop.

Eye contact during a prayer. There must be some kind of rule against that. She panicked and only let herself think about it for half a second before she sat next to Lilia and Matt. Lilia opened her eyes and smiled at Meg right as the old man said "amen." Meg slouched down on the bench and tried to ignore the smile on the bishop's face. She kept her eyes averted from the side of the chapel where Johnny sat, so she didn't know if he saw her or not.

She lowered her body further down the bench just in case.

"Are you feeling okay?" Matt's warm whisper made her ear tingle.

"I will be in a minute." She stayed hunched down the bench. Matt picked Lilia up and put her on the other side of him. He slid his hand over Meg's forehead as though feeling for a fever. Meg's face heated up, and she knew he'd feel the warmth there.

"What's wrong?" he persisted.

She sighed, embarrassed. She didn't want to tell him; she had some dignity she wanted to have stay intact. On the other hand, she talked to this man about urine samples and throwing up. Did she really have any dignity with him?

Of course, they didn't talk about those things at church.

He continued to look at her as people around them shuffled through the pages of their hymn books.

"Can we switch seats?" she asked.

"Sure," he said. She felt vulnerable sitting on the aisle. Plus, now that she had time to think about it, she realized that sitting next to Matt and Lilia was probably sending the gossips in her ward into spasms of joy, trying to figure out what was going on between them.

He stood up so she could scoot over.

"Now will you tell me what's going on?"

Meg grabbed a hymn book and found the sacrament hymn. "Remember Johnny Peters?" she asked, holding the hymn book up so the bishop wouldn't see her talking when she should be singing. It was probably an unnecessary procedure, but she couldn't be too careful.

Matt leaned in closer to her. "Your old friend, right?"

"Yes. He's saving me a seat."

Matt looked around the hymn book and scanned the room for a moment. He stopped when he saw Johnny.

"And that's a problem because . . ." Matt's eyebrows creased together like he was trying to figure out a complicated puzzle. Meg squirmed under his stare. She suddenly became very aware of how close their heads were so they could talk quietly. She could smell a distracting combination of soap and toothpaste that had her mind fighting to concentrate on the conversation.

"I don't want to sit by him."

"Then why is he saving you a seat?"

"Because we went to Phoenix together yesterday. He wants to move a little faster than I'm ready for and decided to save me a seat—to claim me? To make a move? I don't know, and really, I don't *want* to know. I didn't make it a secret that I'm not ready for anything." She ended her explanation with a heavy sigh and looked into Matt's eyes. She bit her lip and pushed her back into the cushioned seat to try and put a little space between them. It was too hard to think clearly when he was so close.

Matt shook his head and rolled his eyes. She couldn't believe her doctor, a thirty-something-year-old man, had just rolled his eyes at her. She gave him a dirty look and tilted the hymnal away from him, refusing to share.

She was bugged at him but not bugged enough to move. She let her eyes wander for a minute and made accidental eye contact with Johnny. She darted her glance away and pretended that she hadn't seen him, which was stupid because they both knew she had.

Meg started singing the hymn just so she would have something to concentrate on, hoping that would keep her from looking around the room and making eye contact with people.

Matt's low voice sang in a heartfelt manner that put Meg's barely audible singing to shame.

Lilia leaned her small body against Meg's side and looked up at her with an impish smile. Meg kept her arm around Lilia all through sacrament meeting, holding her like a lifeline.

It was testimony meeting, and every testimony seemed catered to her and what she needed to hear. She risked looking at the bishop to see if he was telling people what to say in their testimonies, but he wasn't even looking at her.

One of the most touching testimonies was given by Sister Crafton, previously known to Meg as the widow's bench woman. Meg's mom had later informed her that Sister Crafton was the Relief Society president. Things must have changed since the last time Meg went to church actively, because Sister Crafton hadn't even tried to make her the ward project.

"Can you keep an eye on Lilia for me?" Matt whispered, interrupting Meg's thoughts.

"Sure."

He walked to the front to bear his testimony. Meg held her breath as he stood in front of the microphone, her annoyance at him melting away as he spoke. He bore a simple testimony, getting choked up once when he vaguely mentioned some struggles he'd had. Then he closed.

Lilia dug her face into Meg's neck and murmured, "I miss Mommy."

Meg ran her fingers gently through the little girl's knotted hair. "It's okay," she murmured back.

When Matt sat down, Lilia moved from being cuddled into Meg's side and rested her head against Matt's chest. He put his arm around Lilia, and his hand accidentally brushed Meg's shoulder. She felt a cascade of goose bumps travel down her arm. Disconcerted at her reaction, she tried to focus on what the rest of the speakers said. If she could concentrate on the meeting, she could keep her mind away from things that she did not want to contemplate. Like Johnny, her mother, her past, or most important, the reason she was currently hoping Matt's hand would accidentally touch her shoulder again.

PART THREE

The Second Trimester

Chapter Fifteen

"Hi, Meg."

Meg looked up from her grade book to see Johnny Peters leaning in the doorway of her classroom.

"You're back," she said.

He took this as an invitation and came into the classroom to sit on the edge of her desk.

"Just got into town a few hours ago," he confirmed.

"How did everything go?"

"Better than expected."

"Did your company understand why you needed to transfer?" Meg closed her grade book and sat back in her chair. In the three weeks he'd been in California wrapping up business, she hadn't heard from him.

"Yeah." He leaned closer, his tie touching her hand. "They understood that I got reacquainted with a gorgeous girl that I want to get to know better and it would be easier to do that if we lived in the same state."

"Johnny! You did not say that." Meg felt panic well up in her chest.

"No, I didn't. But it's true."

"You moved to Phoenix to be closer to your dad."

"Sure, that too."

Johnny stood and grabbed her hands so she had to stand in front of him. He tried to pull her into a hug, but she backed up a step.

"Johnny," she said firmly. "I'm not ready for any kind of relationship right now." She pulled her hands from his and put one hand against his chest to keep him from coming any closer.

"I'm not asking for a relationship," Johnny countered. "I just want a hug."

Meg let him pull her into a hug and felt his phone vibrate in his pocket. She glanced at the screen as he pulled it out. Samantha.

"You can answer it," she said.

"Nah. It's just someone from San Diego." He looked at his phone one more time before putting it away. "Go to dinner with me."

"I'm going to be here until late tonight getting my semester grades ready to turn in."

"We'll go out after. I have a bunch of things I need to get done as well."

Meg hesitated, hating herself for not being able to just give him a firm no that he would listen to.

"Great," he said, interpreting her silence as an acquiescence to his request, or order actually. "I'll be by at seven."

"Wait," she forced the words from her mouth. "I'm already worn out, and I have an early doctor's appointment tomorrow morning. Tonight isn't a good night."

"Doctor's appointment. With Wilkes?"

"Yes."

"Isn't it a little weird to you that he's your doctor?"

"No," she said with supreme patience.

"You have to admit that it's strange to go to a man who is in our ward and single."

"What's that supposed to mean?"

"Look, the Meg I remember wouldn't have married someone and then gotten a divorce a few months later. It seems like you only married him for one reason. And the guy wasn't a member, so I can only imagine how things went while you were dating. Then there's this doctor . . ."

Meg fought angry tears from showing up in her eyes, but they came anyway. "You don't know anything about me, Johnny."

"Look, Meg, I'm sorry. That came out wrong."

She stepped back when he reached toward her. His phone rang again, and he pulled it out of his pocket.

"I need to get back to work," she said stiffly.

"We'd better skip dinner together tonight. I'll come by your house tomorrow at seven."

"No, Johnny—" she began, but he already had his phone pressed to his ear as he walked out the door. His "Hey, Sam," drowned out her response.

A deathly quiet hung in the doctor's office. The secretary wasn't at the front desk, the phone wasn't ringing, and Meg couldn't even hear the gentle hum of a running computer.

"Hello," she said timidly, leaning over the front counter. The computers hadn't even been turned on yet. She wondered if she'd come on the wrong day, but the door had been unlocked, and the lights were on. She sat for a few minutes, waiting for someone to come to the front desk. Ten minutes passed before Meg decided to try and find someone.

"I'm here for an appointment," she called out as she opened the door that led to the exam rooms. She walked toward the door in the back that had Dr. Wilkes's name on it.

"Dr. Wilkes?"

"Matt?" she tried again.

She heard a noise coming from inside his office, so she started to turn the doorknob when someone's hand dropped onto her shoulder. She shrieked and pushed the person back with all of her strength.

"Meg?"

Recognition dawned, and with it, anger. And more than a little embarrassment. She must have really taken him off guard to push him all the way to the ground.

"What are you doing?" Matt groaned as he pulled himself up from the floor.

"You can't sneak up on people like that," she snapped. "I think you just took ten years off my life."

Matt stared at her. "You're really going to yell at me?"

"I got here about ten minutes ago and no one was in the front, so I came back here to find you. I guess I got a little freaked out when I couldn't find anyone."

Meg saw the beginnings of a smile quirk one corner of his mouth. He stood in front of her in a pair of scrubs and tennis shoes with his dark brown hair mussed, looking like he just woke up and came to work. His smile broadened when Meg relaxed enough to look him in the eye. Unexpectedly his smile made her stomach flutter. Matt started laughing, and Meg covered her face with her hands.

"I'm sorry I knocked you down," she finally managed to say laughingly through her fingers.

"Me too. So what's going on?" he asked, opening his office door. His fax machine hummed, which accounted for the noise she'd heard. He moved around her and walked the rest of the way into his office.

"I have an appointment with you today, but no one's out front yet."

Matt looked at her in surprise. "My appointments don't start until nine on Fridays." He glanced at his silver wrist-watch. "It's only eight. That's why no one is here yet."

"I thought that your secretary said my appointment was at eight." Meg paused to think back to when she'd made the appointment and realized that she couldn't remember.

"Do you mind coming back in an hour?" he asked. "I don't like doing exams unless my nurse is here. She usually doesn't come in until right before nine."

"No problem," Meg said, feeling stupid. It would take almost twenty minutes just to drive home. Then she'd have to turn around and drive back. Maybe she could find a restaurant to stay at until her appointment.

"I'll walk you out to your car in just a second."

"You don't have to do that."

"I want to," he broke in, motioning toward the chair in front of his desk.

Matt dropped his backpack on the floor and pulled a chart

from it. He started to walk toward the door when his cell phone rang. He looked down at it and then glanced up apologetically. "Sorry, this is from home; it'll just take a minute."

"Hello," he said cheerfully into the phone. He listened for a moment, and then his lips tightened into a line and his eyebrows wrinkled together.

"What's wrong, Sarah? Is it Lilia?" he demanded after a pause, his voice laced with panic.

"Oh." He looked like someone had punched him in the stomach. "I'm so sorry. I'm leaving right now; I'll be there as soon as I can."

"Is everything okay?" Meg ventured nervously when he hung up.

"Sarah's sister was in a car accident this morning on her way to school. She's in the hospital, and they're not sure if she's going to make it."

He pulled his keys out of his pocket and left his office. Meg had to jog to keep up with him. "I have to get Lilia and find someone to watch her so Sarah can catch a flight to see her family."

"Matt." Meg put a hand on his arm to slow him down. "Do you want me to come with you? I'll watch Lilia while you help Sarah."

He paused in his rush to leave. "Are you sure?"

Meg walked to the passenger side of his car and opened the door. "The only thing I've got going on this morning is my appointment with you."

"Okay, let's go."

Matt seemed preoccupied as they drove down the highway that led toward his home. He drove about fifteen over the speed limit, and Meg continually glanced behind them to see if Tom was following. So far, so good.

Matt's hands gripped the steering wheel so tightly that his knuckles turned white. His lips were drawn into a tight line, and his eyes took on that haunted look she saw on the Sunday after Thanksgiving. Meg debated saying something, the pressure of the quiet weighing on her. She needed to know what she was walking into.

"Who's Sarah?" Her words punctured the silence.

Matt started and looked at her, as if realizing for the first time that she was in the car with him.

"Sarah is Lilia's babysitter. She's a student at the University of Arizona, but her family lives in Texas."

"So she's going to try to get a flight from Tucson to Texas today?"

"I hope she can get one." Matt's voice sounded strained.

"Does Sarah mean a lot to you?" Meg asked tentatively.

He glanced at her quickly, looking annoyed. "No. Well, yes, as Lilia's babysitter and a friend. She's only nineteen years old, Meg."

Meg shrugged her shoulders, a little confused. He was taking this very personally.

Meg watched the cacti fly by through her window. She tried to count the saguaros along the highway, but there were so many she couldn't keep up. She tired of her childish game and glanced behind her again to check for Tom. He seemed to have an inner Meg-radar. He almost always caught her when she sped.

Just as the thought escaped her mind, she saw the front end of a white Taurus poking out from behind some overgrown mesquite trees in the median of the highway.

"Matt," she warned, but it was too late. The lights turned over, and the hidden car pulled out.

Matt groaned and pulled his car over to the side of the road. He rolled down his window and retrieved his license, tapping his hand impatiently on the steering wheel the whole time.

"What can I do for you, officer?"

Meg frowned as Tom leaned down and looked in the window. He raised an eyebrow at her and started to smile knowingly. She knew an embarrassing remark was about to come from his mouth, so she spoke to cut him off.

"Tom, this is Matt Wilkes from church. We really need to get to town quickly. He has an emergency at home. His babysitter's sister was in an accident, and she needs to fly to Texas, so we need to go get his daughter and find someone to watch her."

"Okay," Tom said, patting the roof of the car. "Just watch your speed. You too, Meg." He winked before turning away from the car and sauntering off.

Meg shook her head, embarrassed, as Matt continued to stare at her.

"He goes to church with us?"

"Yeah, his name is Tom Baker. He works with the Young Men."

Matt restarted the car and eased back onto the highway. "I need to have you with me more often. I've never gotten out of a ticket that easily before, and I know I didn't this time because of *my* good looks." He glanced at Meg from the corner of his eye.

"Good looks had nothing to do with it."

"I saw how that cop smiled at you," he teased.

Meg's face flamed even hotter. "Tom's my brother-in-law. I think he was smiling at me because I'm in the car with you."

"Oh." He looked surprised. "Well, having a cop in the family is even better than having a cop who's an admirer."

"Why is that?"

"An admirer might have wondered why you were in the car with another man and given me a ticket just to spite me."

Meg couldn't help but laugh. "I don't think you need to worry about any spiteful admirers. Or even admirers, period."

Matt raised an eyebrow. "Even Brother Peters?"

Johnny was more like a critic than an admirer these days. "Especially Johnny."

"Did something happen?"

Meg shrugged.

"None of my business?"

"No, it's not that." She sighed. "Johnny just said some things to me yesterday after school that made me angry, but it's not like anything he said wasn't true."

"What did he say?"

"Oh, he just brought up my divorce again—I told you I was divorced." Meg waited for his nod before she continued.

"Part of it is that he's upset because I got a divorce after only a few months of being married, and I don't want to give him any of the details. It's like he's contrived this image of me from when we knew each other back in high school, and now I don't live up to it."

Meg shifted her gaze away from him, out the window. "I

know I shouldn't let my feelings be hurt by anything he says, because he's only saying what other people are thinking. I wish everyone would drop it. It's like I'm the poster-child for irresponsibility in my generation. I'm sick of it, but I don't want to spread my business around any more than it already has been, so I just have to take it."

"Why do you stay here then? You can go somewhere where no one knows you or anything about you."

"Matt, I'm pregnant. I have a life here. Wherever I go, people are going to see that I'm an unmarried pregnant woman. If they ask where the father is, I'll have to see the pity when I tell them that he's in Hawaii honeymooning with his new wife."

"So you stay here because you're afraid of what people will think of you?" he asked quietly.

"I stay here because it's home, and after everything that's happened to me, I just need to be home," her voice cracked.

Matt didn't say anything for almost a minute. "You have enough pressure just dealing with everything you've got going on right now. Don't add more to yourself by worrying about what other people are thinking or trying to live up to some impossible standard. You'll get through this."

Meg filed his words away in the back of her mind, hoping that they might silence some of Johnny's words that still poisoned her thoughts.

"Thanks," she said with a sniffle. "It's embarrassing that I'm so emotional."

"Well, it sounds like life hasn't been very easy lately. And it's completely normal for a woman to be more emotional during a pregnancy."

"Yeah, I read that in one of my books. Believe me, I'm using that to explain all of my awkward outbursts."

Matt laughed weakly, and Meg noticed that he still clutched the steering wheel as if it alone held him together. She wished that there was some way for her to comfort him, but she didn't know him well enough to give him a hug or even a pat on the arm. She still couldn't decide if she should call him Matt or just stick to Dr. Wilkes.

They pulled into his driveway a few minutes later. Meg started to open the door when Matt put his hand on her arm to stop her from exiting.

"I don't know what we're going to find in there, how much Sarah's told Lilia." He released a shaky sigh. "Lilia's mom—my wife—died in a car accident a little over a year ago. Sarah doesn't know that, but Lilia remembers it. This may bring back difficult memories for her."

He tore his pain-filled eyes from Meg's and jumped out of the car. She absorbed Matt's hurried revelation about his wife before following him. It seemed that Lilia wasn't the only person having bad memories resurface because of this accident.

"Daddy," Lilia cried before throwing herself into her father's arms.

"Where's Sarah, honey?"

"In the bathroom. Sarah's sad," Lilia whispered. "She let me watch a movie this morning even though I'm not supposed to watch movies until the afternoon, and she cried."

Matt set her down and walked down the hall to the bathroom.

"Meg!" Lilia threw herself at Meg's legs.

"Hey, cutie." She knelt in front of Lilia, thinking all the while about what Matt had just told her.

"Sarah's sad," she repeated. Meg gave into the urge to pull Lilia into a hug.

"Are you okay?"

Lilia shook her head. "Why is Sarah crying?"

Meg scrambled for an explanation. She wished Matt was here to answer his daughter's question, but he was down the hall, talking on the phone.

"Someone in her family was hurt," she finally said, hoping it was the right thing to say.

"Are they dead?"

"No," Meg answered, half-panicked. She did not want to have this conversation with Lilia.

"Oh," Lilia played with the ends of her hair. "My mom is dead."

"I know." Meg blinked her tears back. Lilia didn't need to see her crying, too. "Let's go pack your bag."

"Why?"

"We need to get some of your favorite things together so you can go to someone's house today. Sarah is going to see her family."

"Okay." Lilia grabbed Meg's hand and pulled her down the hall.

They had to pass Matt and Sarah in the hallway. Matt had one arm around Sarah and was saying something quietly to her. She had buried her head in his chest, and her shoulders shook with emotion.

Meg's stomach pulled at the sight of them so close together. Lilia walked past them like it was no big deal to see them hugging in the hall. Matt had to be more than ten years older than Sarah. There was nothing going on. Besides, her sister might be dying. Sarah needed someone to comfort her. It was none of Meg's business anyway.

"All right, let's get this bag packed," Meg said, diverting her dangerous thoughts. She saw through the open bedroom door that Lilia had already begun piling clothes and toys on her bed.

Matt's free hand grabbed Meg's when she walked past them. His bloodshot eyes crinkled with worry. "I need to run Sarah to the airport. Is there any way you can stay with Lilia for just a little while?"

"No problem."

Matt gave her a weary smile and let go of her hand. Sarah lifted her head up from Matt's chest to reveal mascara and tear-stained scrubs.

"Thanks, Matt," Sarah whispered. "I'll get my things."

"Is she going to be okay?" Meg asked quietly as Sarah walked down the hall.

"Eventually."

Chapter Sixteen

$\mathcal{L}$ ilia fell asleep with her head in Meg's lap. The movie Lilia had been watching continued to play as Meg ran her fingers through Lilia's soft hair. She wanted to cry when she thought about what this little girl had been through.

Meg's hand drifted to her own stomach without thought. What would happen to her baby if she died? There was no way she would let the baby live with Austin.

The best people to leave the baby with would be Tom and Missy. They had a stable household, a daughter who would not be too much older than her child, and a love of the gospel. They had everything Meg couldn't give her baby, but it was everything she wanted.

Meg was so lost in thought, she didn't hear the front door open.

"How'd she do?" Matt spoke quietly, but he still startled Meg. Her heart hammered wildly for the second time that morning. Lilia stirred, but Meg held as still as she could until Lilia settled back down.

"You've got to stop doing that," Meg scolded.

"Sorry." Matt lips turned up a little. The smile quickly faded as he slumped next to Lilia. He let his head rest against the back of the couch and rubbed a hand over his eyes.

"Lilia did fine," Meg answered once he was settled. "She doesn't know what happened to Sarah's sister, only that she was hurt."

"Good." Matt's relief was evident in his tone. "I need to find someone who can watch Lilia for me today. Thanks for staying. I know you probably need to get to work."

"Actually, we're out for winter break. Yesterday was my last day of teaching until the first week in January."

Matt's eyes closed, and his breathing deepened in the few seconds' pause after Meg finished speaking. She considered letting him fall asleep but knew that there were patients waiting for him back at the office.

"Matt." She leaned forward and gently shook his shoulder. "I'll watch Lilia for you today."

He opened his eyes a crack and turned his head toward her. "Are you sure?"

"Lilia and I will have a lot of fun together. I'm going to put up my Christmas decorations today. She can help."

"She'd love that." Matt blew out a long breath and continued to sit on the couch.

"Do you feel up to working today?"

"No, but I will. I've been up since four this morning because of a delivery. Then to get that phone call from Sarah. . . . It just brought everything back to me. It was like it was Thanksgiving weekend last year all over again."

"What happened?" At first Meg didn't think he'd heard her. Then he started speaking.

"Last year, the Sunday after Thanksgiving, I received the worst phone call of my life—it was the most horrible day of my life. Lydia, Lilia, and my dad were all in the car." He shuddered. "My mom was in the hospital following a total hip replacement, and we had all dropped by to visit her. Lilia was tired and needed to go to bed, but I had a few more things that I wanted to talk to my mom about. Dad offered to drive them home so I could have some time with her.

"They were making a left turn when the other car flew through the intersection. The guy was distracted, didn't see that the light had turned red. Completely totaled the car.

"When they called me, Lydia was already gone." His voice broke, and he paused to rub a hand over his eyes again. His fingers came back wet.

"Sorry," his thick voice finally said. He laughed derisively. "I was so worried about Lilia having a hard time with this, but I should've been worried about myself."

"Was Lilia hurt?"

"Just bruising from her car seat straps. It's a miracle the force of the crash didn't kill her. The impact broke my dad's back."

Lilia stirred on Meg's lap but remained asleep. Meg wiped her eyes and noticed Matt do the same. He cleared his throat.

"I'm going to change my clothes and call the office. Will you be ready to go in about fifteen minutes?" Matt stood. His voice sounded rough from emotion.

"I packed a bag for Lilia while you were gone." Meg eased Lilia's head from her lap to the couch. She snuggled into the cushion. "She sleeps through anything," Meg said in amazement.

"It's a blessing now because I have to leave in the night every once in a while for deliveries, and she doesn't wake up. When she becomes a teenager . . . "

Meg's laugh eased some of the tension that still lingered from Matt's story.

"Matt," she called as he walked down the hall. "Why don't I call your office for you? That will buy you some more time. You could even take a shower if you wanted."

One side of Matt's mouth lifted slightly. "Are you trying to tell me I need a shower?"

Meg's face flushed. "No, I just thought that after a delivery and everything else this morning, you might want one."

"Hmm, a shower would be nice." He seemed to debate for a minute. "Well, for the sake of my patients . . . Tell Cindy I'll be there in about thirty minutes."

Matt woke Lilia up when they got to his office. His hair was still wet from his shower, and he smelled like fresh soap. His tie fell over Lilia's forehead as he picked her up from the backseat.

Meg grabbed her bag and walked to her car. She unlocked it and threw Lilia's bag in before she realized Matt wasn't next to her. She saw him walking toward the office with Lilia still in his arms.

Meg jogged toward him. "Hey, my car is over there."

He turned around and walked backward. "I know. You have an appointment this morning."

"I thought—"

"We're going to listen to the baby's heartbeat today. Don't you want to hear it?" He pushed open the doors, not waiting for her answer.

Meg hurried after him. He held the elevator door for her and set a now-fully-awake Lilia on her feet. She gripped her dad's hand.

"Where are we?"

"We're at Daddy's work," Matt answered.

"We are?" Lilia jumped and clapped her hands. "Do I get to see any babies?"

"Not today, honey."

"But if it's okay with your daddy, you can listen to one." Meg smiled.

"You have a baby, Meg?"

"Right here." Meg took Lilia's hand and placed it on her barely bulging stomach.

"Oh," she breathed. The elevator doors opened and Lilia took off down the hallway.

"Lilia," Matt warned. She slowed her running to a skip. "Are you sure you want to watch her?"

"I don't know," Meg teased. "Maybe she could stay here and help you with your patients."

Matt laughed. "They'd love that." They both watched as Lilia started singing once she realized that her voice echoed.

Six pregnant women looked up at Matt and Meg when they walked into the office, some with thankfulness and some with ire. It made Meg very glad that she wasn't Matt. This morning was not going to be pleasant for him.

She grabbed Lilia's hand, and they followed Matt to the exam rooms. While Matt dropped his bag off in his office, the nurse weighed Meg and took her blood pressure. Meg had gained half a pound since her last appointment.

Matt and Lilia walked into the exam room just as the nurse

left. Matt sat Lilia on his lap and rolled his stool next to the exam table. He placed the heart monitor on Meg's stomach and moved it around until they heard a faint thumping noise.

"That's the heartbeat," Matt told Lilia.

"Cool." She studied Meg's stomach. "How will the baby come out?"

Meg held her breath to keep from laughing. Thank goodness Lilia had asked Matt this question now and not her later.

"Well, Meg's body is making the baby. It's not ready to come out yet. It will still be a few more months. But once the baby is ready to come out, Meg will know, and she'll come here, and I'll help her."

"But how do you get the baby out?" she pushed. "Is it through her belly button?"

Matt looked a little uncomfortable. "I'll tell you about it later, Lils."

Meg wiped her stomach and pulled down her shirt to hide how her shoulders were shaking with repressed laughter.

"Is there any way you can explain how a baby comes out to Lilia today?" Matt asked as he led them out of the exam room.

"Not a chance, Dr. Wilkes."

"Oh, you're going to pull out the 'doctor' title now? That's low."

"Hey, I could pull out the 'daddy' title."

"Fine." He sighed. "But I'll warn you. I know my daughter. She is not going to let it drop until she gets her answer."

Meg made an appointment to come back in a month while Matt reminded Lilia to be good and said good-bye. Meg sketched a map to her house and wrote her phone number on the top before he left to go see his next patient.

"Here you go," she said, handing it to him. "Don't worry about her. We'll have fun."

"Thanks, Meg. See you tonight," he called as he opened the door for his next exam.

Chapter Seventeen

"What happened here?"

Meg surveyed the mess that she and Lilia had made throughout the day and tried to picture it through Missy's eyes. Boxes and tissue paper were strewn everywhere. The plastic Christmas tree was scattered in its different pieces all around the room. Decorations spread across the furniture. Tree lights unstrung and piled in messy bunches—one pile for the tree and one for outside the house.

Meg had planned to place all her Christmas decorations around the house and assemble the tree, but she soon realized that she didn't have very many ornaments to hang. Lilia helped Meg pull out and sort her pitifully small pile of balls and bells and then decided that they needed to go shopping.

Meg didn't realize how many things a four-year-old could throw into a cart without a person seeing. She noticed when she paid that there were a few items she didn't recognize, but she got sidetracked when Lilia started begging for a candy bar. Meg spent the next few minutes trying to explain to Lilia why she could spend money on a cartful of decorations but not fifty cents on a bar of chocolate.

Her argument rang lame in her own ears, and the next thing she knew, she had promised Lilia a visit to McDonald's. The candy bar would have been cheaper—and probably healthier. Meanwhile, the Target worker beeped her items along, the numbers climbing higher and higher until Meg nearly fainted at the $124 total. That was a lot of money for a schoolteacher, but there was a line behind them, so she paid it without complaint.

The upside of it was that Meg wouldn't have to buy decorations for a long time. Or so she thought. Because for all the decorations they bought, they forgot to get ornaments for the tree. Too tired to go back to the store—and too broke to risk another trip with Lilia—Meg decided to count it as a loss. This year her tree would be bare. Or, maybe she could string up some popcorn or something. Her mom would probably cry with pride if she did that.

"Are you going to stand there and ask questions, or are you going to help?" Meg growled.

"I'll help." Missy had to step over several boxes to get to where Meg sat between masses of crumpled tissue paper. Kaitlyn squealed and jumped into a pile of boxes. "So, why are you in the Christmas spirit all of a sudden?"

"I'm always in the Christmas spirit. My wallet, on the other hand, not so much."

"Meg!" Lilia called from the bathroom.

"Who's that?" Missy asked as she followed Meg down the hall.

"Lilia Wilkes. I'm watching her for the day."

"As in Brother Wilkes's daughter? The same Brother Wilkes you were with this morning?"

Meg looked at her sharply. How did she know? *Oh, right. Tom.* Sometimes she hated him and his big mouth.

She knocked on the door and avoided her sister's question. "What do you need, Lils?"

"I got water on my pants. Can you get me new ones?" she yelled from the other side of the door.

"You don't have any more pants." Meg sighed in frustration and turned to Missy. "She's gone through two pairs already. Every time she gets something on them, she wants to change into a new pair. I put the dirty ones in the wash, but they're still drying."

Missy knocked on the door. "Lilia, this is Missy, Meg's sister.

We have a surprise out here for you."

Within seconds Lilia stepped out of the bathroom. There were no more than two or three little spots of water—at least Meg hoped it was water—on the little girl's pants.

"What's the surprise?" She looked around the room.

Missy took her hand and led her into the family room. "Kaitlyn, do you know Lilia from church?"

Kaitlyn popped up from inside the empty tree box and cheered.

"I'll take that as a yes," Missy said, leading Lilia over to Kaitlyn. "Why don't you two go outside and play with Cliff." She opened the sliding back door and let them run around outside, the wet pants forgotten.

Meg cleared a place on the floor with her foot and slumped onto it, resting her back against the couch. "I can't do it."

"Can't do what?" Missy started piling all the boxes together in the corner of the room.

"I can't be a mom."

"Are you applying for the position to be Lilia's mom? Is this a trial run?"

"No." Meg turned toward her, annoyed. "I'm being serious, Missy. I'm totally exhausted after just a few hours of babysitting. I don't know what I'm doing."

"When you have your own it's different. They start out as babies, not four-year-olds. You learn with them."

"So it won't be this exhausting with my own child?"

"It'll probably be worse."

Meg groaned.

"But you adjust. You do what you have to do," Missy tried to assure her.

"I hope so." Meg pulled herself up to help Missy clean the family room.

"So," Missy began a little too casually. "Why are you babysitting Brother Wilkes's daughter?"

"I offered."

"When?"

"This morning. His babysitter had a family emergency, and

he needed someone who could watch Lilia with no notice, so I volunteered."

"He had an emergency, so he called you?"

"Not exactly."

Missy stopped cleaning to glare at Meg.

"I was with him this morning because I had an appointment. He got a phone call about the babysitter's sister that upset him. I offered to go home with him to help out with Lilia."

"Hmm," she responded.

"Don't read too much into this. Matt is still grieving his late wife, for heaven's sake. And I am sworn off all men for now, thanks to Austin."

"Really? Sworn off all men? That's not what Johnny says."

"What is Johnny saying?" Meg asked with dread.

"He ran into Tom at the store last night and told him that he moved here in order to be closer to you."

"He moved here so that he can be closer to his dad." Meg gritted her teeth. "Your husband is a worse gossip than some of the women in the ward."

Missy shrugged. "He only tells me. He doesn't spread it around. It's not his fault that people tell him things."

"Well, Johnny was just teasing him. He's trying to get to know me better, but I'm not interested in a romantic relationship right now. If he wants to be friends, then fine."

"So what is Brother Wilkes, then?"

Meg continued to stack boxes and thought about that morning. "I would say that Matt is more than an acquaintance. He's starting to be my friend."

"And that's all?" she pressed.

"Yes, Missy. I don't want to get close to someone again for a long time, if ever. I have too much baggage."

"In that case," Missy said with a smile, "let's figure out what in the world possessed you to buy this?" She held up a hideous-looking plush monster that wore a red-and-white striped scarf and grunted along to the tune of "We Wish You a Merry Christmas."

"Lilia must have put that in the cart when I wasn't looking."

"This is a great gag gift. Have you gotten anything for Johnny yet?"

"Are you crazy? I'm not getting him anything for Christmas!"

"What if he gets you something?"

"He won't."

"He might. He's telling people he moved here for you."

Meg turned her eyes up to the ceiling and sighed. "If he gives me something, then I guess he'll get our grunting monster. But, he won't."

"If you say so."

Missy helped Meg straighten the family room until it finally looked somewhat presentable. They found a few other surprise purchases, including six bags of candy bars. For the life of her, Meg could not figure out how Lilia got them into the cart without her seeing. The girl was a mystery.

None of the decorations actually decorated anything but the floor, but at least they sat in respectable piles instead of cluttered masses all over the room.

Missy and Kaitlyn left about half an hour before Meg expected Matt to come and get Lilia. She threw a frozen lasagna in the microwave, and it finished cooking a few minutes before she saw Matt's car pull into the driveway. His homemade lasagna put this pre-made offering to shame, but she'd never been much of a cook.

Meg let Matt into the house, and Lilia ran to him for her hug. Matt enfolded his daughter in his arms and straightened with a moan. His rumpled clothes and shadowed eyes spoke of a difficult day.

"Do you and Lilia want to stay for dinner?"

"Are you sure you're not sick of us?"

"C'mon." Meg led them to the table that sat in a little dining nook. She laid out three plates. "There's not too much space in here, but it should be enough."

Matt volunteered to bless the food and then dished everyone's plate. Meg couldn't remember the last time anyone blessed the food in her house. She didn't think it had ever happened before, at least in the time that she'd lived there. It was kind of nice.

Meg ate over half of her serving of lasagna before she realized that she wasn't nauseous at all. She continued to take small, cautious bites, unable to trust this newfound ease.

"How was work?" Meg asked once they'd all eaten a little.

"Busy. I ran nonstop from the time we got there until the time I left. I didn't even get a lunch, so this is the first time I've eaten all day."

"It sounds like you're on my diet," Meg joked.

"Are you still feeling sick?"

"I'm doing better," Meg assured him.

Matt sized her up with his doctor gaze before finally coming to a satisfactory conclusion. He turned to Lilia. "What did you do today?"

"We went to the store and got Christmas stuff. Then we went to McDonald's, and Kaitlyn came over, and we played with Cliff."

"Wow." He looked at Meg with a raised eyebrow. "Is Cliff one of your admirers?"

"Yes. He's my favorite one."

"Oh, so you have favorites?"

"Of course," she smiled. "Would you like more lasagna?"

"Sure." He held out his plate, and Meg put another large portion on it.

Matt began to speak when they heard a knock at the door. Cliff started barking like crazy from the backyard. Meg reluctantly got up from the table to answer it.

"Are you ready to go?" Johnny asked when she opened the door.

"Go where?"

"We're going out." He looked over to her driveway. "Whose car is that?"

"I told you I couldn't go out with you tonight." Meg pushed her hair out of her face in frustration.

"No, you said that you couldn't go out last night. Can I come in?" He pushed passed Meg. "Do you have people over?"

"Matt and Lilia Wilkes are in the kitchen."

"Matt Wilkes? Is he in the habit of eating at all his patient's homes?"

"No, just at my friends' houses," Matt answered from behind Meg.

"Is this why you wouldn't go out with me tonight?" Johnny waved his hand toward Matt.

"No, I didn't want to go out with you because you were being a jerk yesterday."

"How convenient that you also happen to have a date with Wilkes tonight."

Meg wondered if she even needed to justify that with a response. She didn't want Matt thinking that she thought they were on a date, so she wanted to correct Johnny. Yet, at the same time, if Johnny thought she was on a date, maybe he would leave her alone.

Meg sighed and walked into her living room to sit on the couch. Johnny followed her while Matt went into the kitchen. Meg closed her eyes, and Johnny sat down next to her on the couch a few seconds later.

"It seems like every time I turn around you're with him. This is the second time you've broken a date with me to be with him."

"Sorry," she said, rubbing her temples. She didn't have the energy to argue again that they didn't in actuality have a date for that night.

"Are you okay, Meg?" Meg heard Matt come up behind her. She opened her eyes and turned over to look at him. His concern for her was obvious.

"I'm fine," she answered. "I'm just tired."

"I think you've overstayed your welcome," Johnny said to Matt.

Meg stood and took a step away from the couch, fortifying her nerve. "Johnny, stop. If you can't be civil, then please leave."

"You would choose Matt over me?"

"I'm not choosing anybody. Matt is my friend. I would like to have you as a friend too, but I've told you I'm not ready for a relationship right now." Meg felt self-conscious having this conversation with Matt standing there. She glanced at him, and he took her cue to leave the room.

"I'm just trying to be your friend, Meg. You're not making it very easy."

"It seems like you want more."

"I just want to be friends. If it turns into more, then great."

"See, there's always that pressure."

"I'm not trying to pressure you. Let's just get to know each other better. No pressure. We'll just take it easy and see where things go."

Meg sighed, starting to give into him a little. "Okay, we can hang out together as friends sometime," she conceded, emphasizing the friend part.

"Starting tonight?"

"No, starting another night. I'm too tired to hang out tonight."

"But you're not too tired to hang out with Wilkes?"

"Lay off it, Johnny," she burst out in irritation. "I watched his daughter for him because his babysitter had a family emergency. He had a hard day at work, and we ate dinner together. I don't even know why I'm explaining this to you." Meg walked toward the front door. "I'll talk to you later."

"Is he staying?" He nodded his head in the direction of the kitchen.

"Bye, Johnny." Meg ignored his question and shut the door. She put her forehead against the cool wood and breathed out a sigh of relief.

"Hey." Matt put his hand on her shoulder. "We should probably get going soon so you can rest."

"I'm sorry Johnny was a jerk to you."

Matt pulled her shoulder so she had to turn and look at him. "You should be sorry that he was a jerk to you. Why do you keep letting him come around?"

"He's persistent. He wears me down."

"Don't let him wear you down too much. Tell him to get lost."

"Get lost?" Meg's mouth curved up. "I haven't said that to anyone since junior high."

"So when was that, a couple of years ago?"

Meg put her hands on her hips. "How old do you think I am?"

"I know exactly how old you are. I have your medical chart, remember?"

"Oh, that's not fair. I don't know how old you are."

"Old enough to be your dad."

"Yeah, right. If you fathered me when you were five."

"I would have been eight."

Meg laughed at his tone of mock offense and quickly did the math. She was twenty-four, so that would make him thirty-two. That wouldn't be too old for her—if she was looking. Which she wasn't. Yet, when he yawned, Meg couldn't help but notice his strong jaw and discarded the unwelcome urge to run her hand along it.

Matt leaned over and ruffled her hair like she was a little girl, putting any thoughts of his five o'clock shadow out of her mind. "Let's go find Lilia."

Now she knew why Lilia's hair was always in knots. Mildly irritated, Meg tried to smooth out her hair as she followed Matt to the family room. Lilia's nose was pressed against the glass door. Cliff barked and tried to lick Lilia's face through the clear barrier.

"Time to go, Lils," Matt said.

"Can I say good-bye to Cliff?"

Matt nodded, and Meg opened the door to let Cliff come inside.

"Cliff is your dog?" he asked as Cliff sniffed his hand.

"Of course."

"I should've guessed."

Chapter Eighteen

eg winced when Bishop Miller extended his hand as she came into his office for her appointment. He'd wanted to meet with her for some reason, and she had the irrational thought that her sins could transfer from her palm to his, like a flesh-information network. At least meeting with Bishop got her out of going to Sunday School with Johnny.

"Sister Sanders," he began. "Have a seat."

Meg wiped her sweaty hands on her skirt as she sat. He sat down behind his large mahogany desk and rested his folded arms on the top.

"It's been awhile since I've talked to you. How are you doing?"

Did he want the honest answer or the easy answer? Probably the honest, but she wasn't sure if she was ready to unload herself yet.

"Fine."

He arched his eyebrows. "Really," he stated. Apparently he was going for the honest answer.

"Most of the time," she tried again.

"What about the other times?"

Meg shrugged, already feeling the tears burning behind her eyes. She fought them back valiantly.

"What can we do for you, sister?" he asked.

Meg looked into his caring eyes and tried to shrug again. She felt like a sullen fourteen-year-old. All she needed was greasy skin, frizzy hair, and a piece of gum to chomp. "Turn back time."

Bishop Miller chuckled. "You're not the only person who has wished I could do that, including myself. Unfortunately, we can only move ahead."

He paused for a moment, looking at her intensely. "And fortunately, we have the Atonement to help us overcome our sins and heartaches and carry us forward."

Meg stayed silent. She'd never really understood too much about the Atonement. She knew about the Garden of Gethsemane and Christ dying for everyone's sins, but she didn't really know how it all worked.

"You're probably wondering why I want to talk with you."

Meg nodded, feeling a little anxious.

"First, I want to ask you if you would attend the Gospel Essentials Sunday School class for a few months. I know your dad teaches Gospel Doctrine, but I think that you would really like the Gospel Essentials class. It could be beneficial for you."

Relief flowed through Meg. Perhaps he was an inspired man. His request gave her a way to legitimately get out of having to go to Gospel Doctrine, and more important, she wouldn't have to sit by Johnny Peters.

"What's Gospel Essentials?" she asked, perhaps a little too eagerly.

"It's the class that new converts usually take. The ward missionaries teach it, and it goes over basic gospel principles. They meet in room seventeen, next to the kitchen."

"Okay, I can do that."

"Great." He smiled and leaned back in his chair. "Sister Sanders, I would also like to extend a calling to you at this time."

"A calling?" Meg was stunned. This was the last thing she thought he'd say when he called her into his office.

"Yes. My counselors and I have been praying about this particular calling for a couple of weeks, and your name keeps coming to our minds. Let me ask you, how do you feel about music?"

"I love it."

"Good. We'd like to ask you to be the ward chorister."

"The one who leads the music in sacrament meeting?" Meg clarified.

"Exactly. You would prayerfully pick the hymns for us and arrange any musical numbers that would take place."

"Wow. Are you sure?"

He laughed softly. "I am very sure. Sister Sanders, I don't know why, maybe you do, or maybe you'll find out, but I feel very strongly that you would be the best person for this calling."

"Can I think about it?"

"Sure. How long do you need?"

"I'll let you know after church. I just need time to let this settle."

"That's fine."

He stood, and Meg followed suit. "I'd like to meet with you again. Can you come by my office right after church next week?"

"I think so," she said.

Meg left the bishop's office and walked toward room seventeen, her mind reeling from the calling. Ward chorister. It meant that she would have to stand in front of everyone every Sunday. There would be no hiding her pregnancy.

Why did she feel like she needed to hide it? She wasn't ashamed of her baby. She was ashamed of the baby's father and what had become of her life. She would be on display week to week, smiling, singing. Could she really do that?

Yet, the music. She loved the hymns. She felt the melody in her soul when she sang. It was an incredible feeling she hadn't been able to capture in years. Would the feeling come back when she was forced to sing the hymns she led? Was that feeling worth standing in front of everyone every week?

Questions rolled through her mind as she arrived at room seventeen. Meg looked down at her watch. The interview with Bishop Miller had only taken about ten minutes, so she wasn't walking in too late.

She slipped into the classroom and looked up at the teacher to apologize.

Matt Wilkes stood at the front of the small room, a folded-back manual in his hands. There were four other students in the class, as well as the full-time missionaries.

"Hello." Matt smiled at her.

"Hi," Meg answered, still standing by the door.

"What can we do for you?" he asked.

Meg glanced around the room and realized that everyone was looking at her. She felt her face heat up. "Bishop Miller asked me to come here."

"Does he need one of us?"

"No." Meg walked further into the room and pulled a folding chair away from the wall. "He wants me to take this class."

"Great." Matt leaned against the chalkboard and actually did look happy that she was going to be in the class. "We just started a few minutes ago, so you haven't missed too much,"

Matt reopened his manual and dove into his lesson. Meg couldn't help but be captivated by his animation as he taught about having faith in Christ. She could picture him as the type of missionary that was very enthusiastic. It was a contagious excitement.

It felt like only a couple minutes had passed when Matt asked one of the Elders to give the closing prayer. Meg closed her eyes, reveling in the feeling of contentment she had at that moment. She'd never been so interested in a Sunday School lesson before. She usually ditched Sunday School when she was a teenager and was bored to death when she couldn't find an excuse to skip it as an adult.

She thought that the bishop might actually have been inspired to send her to this class—and for more than just the reason of keeping her away from Johnny. *And if he was inspired in this, could he also be inspired about calling me to be the ward chorister?*

"So, did I bore you to death?" Matt took Meg's folded chair from her hands and leaned it against the wall as everyone filed out of the room.

"Nearly," she teased. "I had to keep thinking of everything I have to live for just to get through."

"Ouch. Maybe I'll have you teach next week, so I'm not endangering your life." He held the manual out toward her.

Meg laughed and pushed it back. "I'm just kidding. That was a really good lesson. I've never heard some of that stuff before."

"So you liked it?" Matt's smile widened.

"I can honestly say that was one of the best Sunday School lessons I've ever heard."

Matt shrugged. "This is a really good class."

"Well, this may be a good class, but it has a good teacher as well."

Matt looked a little uncomfortable, so Meg flicked his tie before walking toward the door. "Just don't let it go to your head."

Meg heard him chuckling behind her as the door closed. No, this class wasn't going to be bad at all.

Chapter Nineteen

eg rooted around her night table until she finally came in contact with her ringing cell phone.

"Hello," she croaked.

There was silence on the other end of the line.

"Hello," she said again, clearing the sleep from voice.

"I'm so sorry, Meg. This is Matt Wilkes. Did I wake you?"

"Don't worry about it." She sat up in bed, still trying to piece everything together.

"I know this is last minute, but I'm trying to find a babysitter for Lilia. Sarah's going to be gone until after the new year. I thought I remembered you saying you were out of school for a little while . . ." His voice trailed off.

"Bring her over."

"Are you sure? I've tried calling other people we know, but they're all busy or not answering their phones."

"So, I'm your last resort?" she teased, finally waking up all the way.

"No, I just hate asking you to work on your days off. And I know you haven't been feeling all that great with the pregnancy."

"I'm feeling a lot better lately, Matt. We'll have fun." Meg pushed away thoughts of their chaotic day on Friday.

"I'll pay you. It won't be as much as you usually make, I'm sure."

"Well, you know teachers usually bring in the big bucks. You don't need to pay me."

"Yes, I do."

"I'm not taking your money."

"We can argue about this later. Is it okay if we come over now?"

Meg looked at the clock and realized that she had slept in until almost 7:30. Rehearsals and the final Christmas concert and play for her choir and drama classes wore her out more than she thought. At least she didn't have to think about students, festivals, or auditions for another two weeks.

"Come on over."

She knew she wouldn't have time to shower, so she pulled on a pair of worn jeans and a T-shirt and threw her hair in a ponytail. She was pouring a bowl of cereal when the doorbell rang.

Meg drank in Matt's weary appearance when she opened the door. He wore his usual slacks, but this time with a rumpled button-up shirt and an undone tie that hung around his neck. His tousled, uncombed hair gave her a glimpse of how he must've looked as a little boy, but the whisker stubble of a few days' growth reminded her that he was anything but that.

"Meg, thank you so much," Matt said as Meg let them into her house.

"It's no problem. Have you eaten breakfast?" she asked Lilia, looking at her for the first time. Lilia still wore her nightgown, but she had a pair of jeans on underneath it. Her hair was in a very messy ponytail, and she dragged a bag behind her. The bag was so stuffed with toys and clothes that it couldn't even be zipped shut.

"No, I'm hungry," she complained.

Matt turned to Meg. "It's been a hectic morning."

"Well, I was just going to have cereal for breakfast. Would you like pancakes instead?"

"Yeah!" she cheered.

Matt leaned over and gave Lilia a hug, telling her to be a good girl.

"Thank you," he said to Meg as he followed her into the kitchen. "I'll pay you back for anything she eats."

Meg ignored him while she grabbed her pancake mix and poured a bunch of it into a bowl. She stuck the bowl under the sink, added some water, and began to mix the soupy batter. "Did you eat breakfast?"

"No," Matt hesitated. "Uh, have you ever made pancakes before?"

Meg glanced up from her batter and laughed at his concerned expression. "Yes. Let me guess, you make it from scratch."

"Sometimes. I've made it from the box before, but I still have to add milk and eggs. And use measuring cups."

"Let me introduce you to the world of Meg's cooking." Meg grabbed the box she had poured from and handed it to him. "'Just add water,'" she read. "It really doesn't matter how much water you add to the mix. It pretty much tastes the same no matter what. It just changes the thickness. For me, this is about as homemade as it gets."

"I *almost* wish I could stay and try it," he said.

"Sure you don't have a few minutes? These won't take very long to cook." Meg plugged her electrical skillet into the wall.

"No." He chuckled. "As tempting as this looks," he lifted the spoon and the runny batter dripped back into the bowl, "I'd better get to work. I don't want to start off today behind."

Meg grabbed the spoon from him. "I know it doesn't look as good as 'homemade' pancake mix, but trust me, with a ton of butter and syrup on top, it still tastes pretty good. You're missing out."

"Fortunately, I'll just have to take your word for it," Matt said, backing out of the kitchen.

"You can't mock a chef in her own kitchen. You're just lucky that I'm a nice girl, and you're on your way to work, or else you'd get the opportunity to taste a pre-cooked pancake, as it's dripping from your hair to your mouth." Meg smiled sweetly as she walked toward him with the bowl in her hands.

Matt held out his hands. "Truce. I can't go into work looking any worse than I already do or else my patients will lose all faith in me."

"What?" Meg asked innocently as she tucked the bowl under her arm. "I'm just walking you to the door."

"All the same, I'd feel better if you were in front of me, so I can keep an eye on you."

"See you tonight," she called after him as he slipped out the front door.

He stopped and smiled at her before he got into his car. Meg's heart jumped into hyperdrive at the happy curve of his lips. She hurriedly turned back inside the house. These pregnancy hormones were going to be the death of her.

The day of babysitting Lilia went a lot smoother than the prior week's escapade.

They started off the morning by putting Lilia in the bathtub and finding an outfit in the overfilled duffle bag. Meg brushed out Lilia's hair and discovered that it fell down in smooth waves between her shoulder blades. As Meg pulled it into a neat French braid, she wondered if Lilia's mom had had similar hair.

The rest of the day was pretty mellow. They played Old Maid and Go Fish for a while, went for a walk, watched a movie, and Lilia took a short nap. Meg took a shower and changed into a nicer pair of jeans while Lilia slept.

Once Lilia got up, Meg thought that maybe they were up for a more challenging activity.

The bare Christmas tree begged for decorations. She cringed at the thought of another trip to the store and instead decided to attempt homemade ornaments. Lilia helped her gather paper and markers, cut string and yarn, and pop the popcorn. Once Meg's favorite Christmas music filled the room, they worked on their separate creations. Meg glanced at her chattering companion as she stuck her needle through a piece of popcorn and pulled it down the string. Her spirits lifted when Lilia held up a picture of a family and pointed Meg out as a part of it. She'd worried about depression sneaking in over the holidays and welcomed the love this little girl offered.

She tried to forget that she had expected this to be her first Christmas married and instead she would have to spend it all alone. She'd said yes to her parents' invitation to do Christmas at their house, but it just wasn't what she'd imagined this Christmas to be. Every time she went to her mom's it was just another reminder that she was alone. Mom had Dad, Missy had Tom, and Meg had no one.

When a knock sounded at the door, Meg looked up at the clock and realized that she and Lilia had been working steadily on Christmas tree decorations for the past hour and a half. Time had flown, especially with Lilia's constant stories.

Meg hopped up from the floor to open the door. Matt stood there, looking even more tired and disheveled than he had that morning.

"Rough day?"

"You could say that."

"Come sit down for a minute. I'll find us something for dinner."

Matt gently grabbed her wrist as she started to walk toward the kitchen. "Let's go get something to eat. I'll take you out."

"I can make us something."

"I know you could, but wouldn't it be nice to have someone else make it for us and then clean it up?"

"Yes," Meg said. "But are you sure you want me to come with you two? I'm fine just eating something here."

"We want you to come." He walked into the family room and looked around him at the mess. There were strings of popcorn and Lilia's colored papers everywhere.

"You two have been busy."

"We're decorating the tree," Lilia explained.

"Well, it's going to look good. Do you want to take a break and get something to eat?"

"Yeah!" She jumped up from the floor and ran over to the adults. Matt ruffled her hair and mussed the smooth French braid.

"Let's go."

They went to a little pizza place located right behind Matt's work. Meg tried to convince Matt to let her take her car and follow them over so he wouldn't have to come all the way back to drop her off at home, but he wouldn't hear of it.

Meg ate more pizza than she had been able to eat for months. It felt good to have a full stomach. She hoped this meant that the sickness was finally starting to wear off permanently. Lilia kept them entertained for most of dinner with her stories.

Matt drove Meg home once they finished dinner. Matt and Lilia hopped out of the car and followed Meg to the door.

"Thanks for dinner," she said, feeling a little weird.

"You're welcome."

"Well," she shifted her feet, "good night, I guess."

"You're not going to let us help you finish decorating your tree?" Matt asked.

"You want to help me?"

"It sounds like fun. We haven't had the time to get a tree yet, and I'm not sure if we will."

"Well, sure. Great. Come in." Meg opened the door and let them into her house. Unexpected relief filled her when they entered. She hadn't looked forward to being by herself for the rest of the evening.

Matt sat down on the floor with his back against the couch. "So what are we doing here?" He picked up a string of popcorn and ate a kernel off it. "Is this our after-dinner snack?"

"No." Meg snatched the string from his hands. "This is one of the decorations. I'm going homemade this year."

"Okay. Just show me how to do it, and I'll help you string up some popcorn."

Meg sat down next to him on the floor with the big bowl of popcorn between them. "First you put the string in the needle. Then you just stick it carefully in the popcorn and pull it down the string. I want them all to be about ten feet long."

"Sounds easy enough." Matt worked on the popcorn while Meg turned the Christmas music on and helped Lilia cut out a few of her drawings. Meg found Lilia more paper to draw on before sitting next to Matt again. She grabbed her own string and got to work.

"Thanks again for watching Lilia."

"It's no problem. I like watching her. It gives me something to do in the day besides think about my life."

"Is your life so bad that you can't stand to think about it?"

"Not all of it, but certain parts." She nodded her head decisively. "Yes, sometimes life stinks."

"How so?"

Meg laughed shortly. "How about the fact I'm going to be a single mom?"

"I know what you mean."

"Oh, I'm sorry." Meg could've kicked herself.

"Why?" he asked, pulling another piece of popcorn down the string. "It's true. I hate being a single parent. There's not a day that goes by that I don't wish that Lydia was still here with us. It's not easy doing it all by myself. I have Sarah to help, but it's not the same as if her mom were still here with me."

"You're doing a great job. Lilia's a good kid."

"Thanks. I wish I could take most of the credit, but she has a lot of her mom's personality in her."

Lilia ran over to Matt to show him the picture she'd finished drawing. He praised it, and she left to go color more.

"You're going to be a great mom." Matt picked their conversation back up. Meg looked into his green eyes and had a hard time pulling her gaze away. "It's going to be hard sometimes to do it all by yourself, but you'll make it. You'll be amazing."

Meg felt tears burn behind her eyes. "I hope so."

"You will," he said firmly.

Meg realized she was leaning dangerously close to him and jumped up from the ground. "I bought candy bars at the store last week. Do you want some?"

Matt looked startled at her quick outburst. "Sure."

Meg nearly ran into the kitchen and leaned against the counter. She needed to get control of her senses. She took a few deep breaths to steady her nerves and grabbed one of the six bags of candy bars Lilia put in the basket. Matt had finished his ten-foot length of popcorn garland and carried it over to the tree. He looked at the bag in Meg's hands before setting down the popcorn.

"Those are my favorite."

That explained why Lilia had put six bags of them in the basket.

"Help yourself. I have plenty more in the kitchen."

Matt did help himself. In between wrapping lights and the popcorn strings around the tree, he ate an entire bag. For the final touch, they cut out Lilia's drawings, and Meg punched a hole in the top of each paper so she could tie a string through it. Lilia was proud to see her drawings all over the tree.

"Well, I think this is the best tree I've ever seen," Matt said as he, Meg, and Lilia stood on the other side of the room to look at their masterpiece. Meg switched the lamp off so they could get the full effect of the glowing white Christmas lights.

"Definitely," Meg agreed. The tree looked a little ragged and droopy in some parts, but they'd had so much fun decorating it that it really did look good in a charming sort of way.

Lilia yawned and leaned against her dad's side.

"I guess we need to be getting home. Thanks for letting us crash at your house tonight."

"I liked having you over."

"See you tomorrow?"

"I'll be here."

"Good night."

Meg leaned against the door and thought about her evening with Matt Wilkes. It felt good to spend time with someone who thought she was going to make it.

Chapter Twenty

Since it was Christmas Eve day—and feeling a need to prove that she did have some cooking skills—Meg decided that she and Lilia should make cookies for Santa Claus. Matt probably didn't have time to make any, though Meg had a suspicion that if he did, his cookies would taste better than hers.

Meg pulled out her recipe book and looked through it for the one cookie recipe she knew how to make—chocolate chip.

"Flour?"

"Here it is."

Lilia wore one of Meg's aprons and stood on a chair so she could reach the counter to stir. Matt only had to work a half day, so she expected him in about twenty minutes. So far it had taken almost thirty minutes just to mix the dough together.

"Chocolate chips," Lilia requested.

"Just a minute." Meg walked into the pantry. She looked in the area where she theoretically stored her baking supplies—it was pretty sparse for lack of ever actually baking—and realized that she didn't have any chocolate chips. She suddenly recalled a craving for chocolate a few weeks earlier that led her to open the bag and graze on the sweet morsels for several days. She had no chocolate chips but a whole bowl of chocolate chip cookie dough.

She turned to tell Lilia that they were going to have to go to the store when her eyes passed over the bags of candy bars. They were Matt's favorite. What if she cut them up and put them in the cookies? It was worth a try.

Meg grabbed a bag and took it over to Lilia. "Help me unwrap these, please."

"Okay." Lilia wiped her hands ceremoniously on her apron and began unwrapping candy bars.

Meg chopped the bars and threw them in the dough. Then Lilia helped her shape little balls and put them on the cookie sheet. The doorbell rang two minutes after the first pan went into the oven.

"Daddy," Lilia yelled, throwing the door open and taking Matt's hand. "We made cookies!"

"I can tell." Matt ruffled Lilia's hair and straightened her apron. "You look like a real cook."

"I *am* a real cook," Lilia giggled.

"Hey, Meg." Matt's smile grew as he looked at Meg.

"What?"

"I like the new makeup you're wearing."

"I'm not wearing makeup," Meg said, blushing in spite of herself.

"Really?" Matt walked over to her and touched her nose lightly. Her nose burned where his finger ran across it, and her breath caught in her throat. Matt seemed wholly unaffected by the whole thing.

He held his finger out to her; it was covered in white flour. Meg wiped her hands across her cheeks, feeling the soft powder against her palms, wishing that she had at least checked her reflection in the fridge before answering the door.

"The cookies smell done," she said, going back into the kitchen. She groaned as she removed the cookie sheet from the oven. The candy bars had melted, and the caramel had clumped.

"Did they burn?" Matt leaned over her shoulder and looked at the pan.

"No, but they look horrible."

"Can I try one?"

"Go for it. We made them for Santa, but if you don't like them, Santa will have to settle for store-bought cookies."

He took the spatula and lifted a cookie off the pan. "I love hot cookies." He took a bite. "These are awesome."

"Yeah, right."

"Seriously. What kind of cookie is this?"

"It was supposed to be chocolate chip, but I found out too late that I didn't have any chocolate chips, so . . ." Meg gestured to the counter filled with candy wrappers.

"No wonder I like these so much. How many bags of that candy do you have?"

Meg opened the pantry door and showed him the four remaining bags on her shelf. He whistled between his teeth. "Were you craving chocolate or something?"

"No. Does Lilia know this is your favorite candy bar?" Meg asked him.

"Yeah. I get one almost every time we go to the grocery store together. I let her have the first bite."

"Lilia snuck all these bags into the grocery cart when I wasn't looking."

Matt shook his head, his mouth full of his second cookie. He swallowed it down. "How much did it cost? I'll pay you back." He pulled out his wallet.

Meg took a firm grip on his arm. "No. You can pay me back by taking these cookies home with you."

"That's not much of a deal for you."

"Trust me. You'll be doing me a huge favor by taking them off my hands. If you don't mind hanging out here for another hour or so, I'll have all the cookies made."

"We don't have anything else going on today," he answered.

"Do you want to put a movie on while I get the next batch in the oven? The DVDs are in the cabinet next to the television."

"Sure." Matt's arm snaked around Meg, and he grabbed another cookie from the pan.

⊗⊗⊗

Meg walked into her parents' house for Christmas dinner, half expecting to see Johnny Peters sitting at the table. Or worse, Larry. She was relieved when the only men she saw were her dad and Tom.

"Hey, Meggie-girl," her dad said from his recliner.

Meg sat down next to Tom on the couch and looked around for the rest of her family. "Where are Missy and Kaitlyn?"

"Your mom went with them back to our house so Kaitlyn could show off her gifts."

"Oh." She was a little hurt that they didn't wait for her to go with them. It must've shown in her voice, because Tom put his arm around her and hugged her to him.

"They'll be back soon. Kaitlyn was so excited about the bike we got her that she couldn't wait to show Grandma."

"It's fine," Meg said into his chest.

Tom let her go and smiled mischievously. "So, I haven't seen you since I pulled you over with Brother Wilkes."

"Brother Wilkes?" Her dad popped into the conversation. Meg shot Tom a glare.

"I've been doing well since then," Meg said, skirting around the implied question. If she had reacted, Tom would have mercilessly teased her until she walked away or Missy stopped him. She had nowhere to go and Missy wasn't there, so she was low on options.

"Yeah." Tom ignored her and turned to her dad. "Meg was in a car with Matt Wilkes. You know him; he's the ward mission leader."

Her dad nodded. "Why were you in a car with Brother Wilkes?"

"He had a family emergency. I was helping him out."

"How much were you helping him?" Tom waggled his eyebrows.

Meg punched him in the shoulder. "Not that much. I'm watching his daughter until school starts back up. I know Missy told you."

"She told me." He nudged her ribs.

"Tom, we're just friends."

"What happened to that nice Peters boy?" her dad interjected.

Meg sighed. "Sometimes he isn't so nice, Dad."

"Now, Meg, that wasn't a very good thing to say about your friend," her mom lectured from the doorway. Missy and a pink-cheeked Kaitlyn were right behind her.

Missy walked in and gave Meg a hug before sitting on Tom's lap. Her mom kissed her dad on the cheek. The familiar well of jealousy sprung up in Meg's chest, and the ache in her heart started to come back full force. She thought this feeling was gone for good. It had been weeks since she'd even let herself think about Austin, much less miss him.

It was a relief when the doorbell rang.

"I'll get it."

No one argued with her. Meg looked back into the living room before she answered the door. She noted with irritation that Missy still sat on Tom's lap. Meg had moved, so now there was an extra couch cushion. There was no reason to stay packed together on the couch—except to rub it in her face that she didn't have anyone.

"Hey, Meg," Johnny said when she opened the door. He looked really good in a deep blue sweater and brown slacks. His dark hair fell just right over his forehead in an endearing way that made Meg want to reach up and brush it out of his eyes.

She shook her head and tried to remember that she was angry at him. If not for the things he said to her, then for how he'd treated Matt.

"Hey."

"How have you been?"

"Fine," she answered shortly.

"Look, I've had some time to think this week while I was setting up my new office, and I realized what a jerk I was to you. Is there any way you can forgive me?"

Part of her wanted to say no, just to be spiteful. Another, bigger part of her wanted to say yes. It wasn't because of the way her lonely heart jumped when he smiled at her. And it definitely wasn't because of the way her ears burned when he pulled her into a hug and whispered, "Come with me."

Meg called into the house that she'd be right back. Johnny grabbed her hand and took her across the street to his dad's house. She walked into the musty-smelling home and spotted Johnny's dad asleep on the couch. His head was tilted back against the headrest, his mouth slightly open.

Johnny indicated that they should be quiet as he led Meg back to his bedroom.

"Should we be back here?" she asked.

"Does this really bother you?" Johnny raised his eyebrow.

The look on her face must have alerted him to his mistake, because he grabbed her hand as she started to walk out of the room. "This will just take a minute. We'll keep the door open. Dad is just in the other room. David and his family will be here from Flagstaff soon. You're safe." He sat on the bed and patted the spot next to him.

"I'll stay here," she responded, leaning against the doorjamb.

Johnny sighed. "I'm not going to attack you."

Meg didn't say anything. Johnny got up, walked into another room, and came back with a folding chair. He set it up a few feet from the bed and sat on it.

"Now will you come in?" he asked a little exasperated.

"I'll sit on the chair."

"Great." He pulled her down into his lap.

She wriggled to get away. "Johnny!"

"I'm just teasing you," he said, letting her go. He pushed her gently toward the bed, and she sat down, relieved that she wasn't on his lap anymore. "Tom told me you had great reactions when you were teased."

"Remind me to kill Tom," she muttered.

"Why?" Johnny asked, standing up. He seemed to forget his question quickly as he reached inside his closet and withdrew a wrapped box.

"I got you a present."

"Why?" she asked, panic rising in her chest.

"Because I like you."

"I didn't get you anything."

"That's okay. I didn't get you a present expecting something in return."

Yeah right. Maybe he wasn't expecting a present, but she had a feeling he might be expecting something else.

"Open it," he encouraged when she hesitated.

Inside the box was another box. A small velvet box. She held it in her hands and cursed herself for coming into Johnny's room. She'd always learned that only bad things happen to girls in a guy's room before marriage. Here was proof positive. A small, velvet jewelry box. A square one. She nearly had a heart attack but forced herself to open it.

Inside was a necklace. Not a ring. *Oh, thank heavens not a ring.*

The relief was so great that she found herself telling him how beautiful it was before she could measure her words.

"Wow." She held it up and looked at the teardrop-shaped blue sapphire dangling from a delicate silver chain.

"Let me help you put it on," he said eagerly.

His words pulled her eyes away from the fantastic stone. "This is too much. I can't accept it."

"Turn around," he ordered as he pulled it out of the box.

"Johnny, really, I can't take this."

"Yes, you can. When I saw it I thought of you. It made me think of your eyes. Now pull your hair up."

Meg bit her lip and looked at Johnny. Then, against her better judgment, she turned and pulled her hair up so he could clasp the necklace on her. The gem rested just below her collarbone.

Johnny stood in front of her and put his finger under her chin. He looked into her eyes until Meg stared to squirm at his intense stare. He glanced down at the gem. "Almost a perfect match," he murmured.

He lowered his head and pressed his lips to Meg's. Meg found herself kissing him back, momentarily relishing the feeling of being wanted. Johnny's kiss deepened as he leaned her back and sudden panic struck her. She pushed Johnny away and jumped up from the bed.

"I need to go," Meg said, walking from his bedroom. She berated herself for kissing him. She couldn't afford to get emotionally involved with someone so soon after Austin.

Johnny followed her outside and took her hand. "I'm sorry. I thought you wanted to kiss me. In fact, I know you did."

"I can't do this."

"Please." He pulled her to a stop outside her mom's house.

Meg turned to look at him. "I've said we can be friends. Don't push me for something more. I'm not ready." She pulled away and walked into her parents' house.

"Surprise!" Cathy Wilkes said as Matt opened the front door.

"Mom?" Matt blinked in surprise. "What are you doing here? Where's Dad?"

"Is that any way to greet a guest? Who raised you, anyway?" she scolded as she stepped into her son's open arms.

"You know I'm happy to see you." He hugged her tight, realizing how much he'd missed his family over the past few months.

His mom pulled back and eyed him critically. "Something's different about you. What is it?"

"I got a haircut," he said, running his fingers through his shortened hair.

"No, that's not it. It's something else."

"Nothing else is different, Mom."

"Something is different, young man. Don't tell me that it isn't. I'll figure it out. Now you go help your dad wheel up the luggage, and I'm going to go find my grandchild."

Matt met his dad in the driveway and took the luggage that rested beside his wheelchair. "How did Mom think you were going to get all the bags in the house and wheel yourself up this steep driveway?"

"I imagine she was thinking more about Lilia and less about how I was going to manage that," he said with a twinkle in his eye.

Matt leaned down and gave his father a hug. "I had no idea you guys were coming to see us. You didn't say anything when I talked to you last night."

"Your mom threatened to leave me behind if I ruined her surprise. I hope it's okay that we just dropped in like this."

"More than okay." Matt pushed the words through his tightening throat. "This is going to make Lilia's Christmas."

"Then let's get up this mountain and see my granddaughter. I've missed my little girl."

"She's missed you too, Dad."

Matt hauled the luggage behind his father. By the time they made it to the front door, Lilia had spotted him. Her ponytail swung behind her head as she jumped into her grandfather's lap and wrapped her arms around his neck. Matt's mom leaned over and put her arms around the pair. Matt flexed his jaw and swallowed his emotions down at the picture of his family together again.

Chapter Twenty-one

Meg unclasped the sapphire necklace and held the chain between her fingers. The gem gathered the light from her bedroom and emitted a stunning sparkle. She couldn't believe she'd taken the necklace from him. She couldn't believe she'd kissed him.

Meg ran her fingers over her lips. It had been over two years since she'd kissed anyone besides Austin. She felt like she was betraying Austin by kissing someone else. They hadn't been divorced very long. And she was pregnant with his child. There was no bigger reminder of Austin than her quickly expanding waistline.

Yet, the kiss wasn't bad. Unexpected? Sure. Uninvited? Maybe not as much as she thought. Horrible? Not really. She wondered if she was making too much out of kissing Johnny, but it felt nice to have a handsome man show her some attention. Especially since she'd been so easily discarded by another.

Her cell phone vibrated in her pocket as she was filling a glass with water from the fridge. She didn't recognize the number on the caller ID.

"Hello," she answered, taking her drink into the living room and curling up against the arm of the couch.

"Hey, babe." Meg's heart skipped when she heard Johnny's voice on the other end. *Please, please don't say something stupid*, she wanted to beg.

"Hey, Johnny."

"Can I come over tonight?"

Meg ran her thumb across her bare ring finger, still expecting to feel the ridges of her wedding band. She was too vulnerable to resist Johnny's magnetism if he came over.

"Well, I'm sitting in your driveway. Are you really going to turn me away when I've already driven out here to be with you?"

Meg unfolded her legs and walked to the front door. She peeked out the side window, and saw that, sure enough, Johnny's car was parked in her driveway.

"Okay," she said against her better judgment.

"You're not wearing your necklace anymore," he said when he reached the door.

"I just took it off to wash my face."

"Hmm," he murmured. He stood next to Meg as she closed the door and then leaned into her until she rested her back against the wall. Meg felt a little breathless as Johnny lowered his head and brushed his lips against hers. His kiss was soft at first; then he pressed harder. She started to respond, but thoughts of Austin intruded into her mind.

"I wasn't planning on doing that when I came over tonight," he whispered when she pulled away. "You're just irresistible."

Meg laughed nervously and tucked a stray hair behind her ear. She moved around him and headed into the kitchen. He followed closely behind her. A little too closely for her sanity. Her face flushed with embarrassment.

"Do you need a drink?" she asked without looking him in the eye.

"Sure."

She turned her back to him to grab a glass from the cupboard. As she pulled it down, she suddenly felt warm air on her neck.

"Johnny," she warned.

"You smell so good," he said, wrapping his arms around her.

Meg fell into his embrace for a moment. It felt good to be held by someone again. Johnny started to nibble on her ear, and she yanked her head away as though she'd been burned.

"Don't," her voice cracked.

Johnny's arms tightened. "I can't resist you."

Meg wiggled until he released her. "I've already told you I'm not ready."

"Don't fight this so hard."

"Why did you come over, Johnny?"

"We need to talk."

"About what?"

"Meg, I like you. What do I have to do to convince you to give us a chance?"

Wow. There was no beating around the bush with Johnny. She walked around the counter and sat on a stool.

"I don't know what to say," she finally answered.

"You can't deny that we have chemistry, Meg." He placed one hand on the back of the stool and the other on the counter in front of her, his face inches from hers.

"And what about the baby?" she asked, ignoring his remark about chemistry. She felt it with him, too. But chemistry wasn't everything. She'd had great chemistry with her husband, and look what happened there.

"The baby?" Did he forget already?

"Johnny, I'm going to have a baby in about four and a half months. That time is going to go by quickly," she said with frustration.

"I've told you before, I don't care that you're having a baby."

"I know it bothers you," she argued.

"It bothers me a little, yes. But I can overlook it. I just want to be with you."

"It's never going to be just me."

"I don't know why this concerns the baby." Johnny's knuckles tightened on the counter and he leaned so close that her senses filled with the woodsy scent of his cologne. "This is about you and me. I want to see where this can go. I've got the rest of the week off work. Spend it with me. See how you feel."

"I can't."

"Why?"

Meg didn't want to tell him. "I've got some things going on."

"Like what?" he pressed.

"I'm babysitting Lilia Wilkes until school starts up again," she answered reluctantly.

"It's always Wilkes." He straightened and stepped away from her. "At some point you're going to have to decide, Meg."

"Decide what? I can't be friends with both of you?"

Johnny groaned and ran a hand over his rough jaw. "If I hear the word *friends* one more time . . ." he stopped. "Look, you can't be spending every minute with Wilkes next week. Right?"

She nodded.

"Great." He took her hand and pulled her toward the door. "I'll call you then."

Meg followed him outside, feeling conflicted. She'd just been railroaded into spending most of her free time with Johnny. She wasn't sure if she wanted to deal with the pressure that might entail. Yet, as they stood by his car door, a large part of her didn't want him to go anymore. At least when he was with her she wasn't so lonely.

Meg let Johnny kiss her. "Tomorrow night?"

She could spend some time with him. He was an old friend. And really, was a kiss here or there so bad? Especially with someone who looked like Johnny Peters. The alternative to being with him would be another night alone—unless Matt and Lilia stayed late again. She pushed that thought out of her head. They had better things to do than hang out with her.

Meg nodded. Johnny kissed her again and got in the car, leaving Meg in the driveway as he drove away.

☙❧

"So who is this Meg that Lilia keeps talking about?" Matt's mom asked once they had Lilia down for bed that night.

"Meg's been watching Lilia for me while Sarah's in Texas with her family."

"Is she another student from the university?"

"No. She's a teacher at the high school. She's in my ward and just happened to be with me when I found out about Sarah, so she offered to watch Lilia during her break."

"Oh. Are you two a couple?" she asked directly.

"Mom, no!" Matt exclaimed.

"Well you don't have to sound so horrified. Is she ugly or something?"

"No, of course not. I can't believe you asked that. She's very pretty. We're just friends. She's actually a patient of mine."

"Oh, so she's already taken." She sighed despondently.

"She just went through a divorce with an idiot of a husband who was cheating on her, and I think she's dating some new jerk now." He moved behind his mom's chair and rubbed her shoulders. "I'm not ready to be with anyone else yet. I know it's been over a year since Lydia died, but sometimes it feels like it just happened."

"I know." His mom's eyes closed as he worked out the knots in her shoulders. "When are you moving back home? No one else can rub my shoulders like you."

"That's because you taught me how to do it."

"Dang right I did."

Matt rubbed his mom's shoulders for a few more minutes and then asked how long his parents were staying.

"Until January third," his mom replied.

"I'd better call Meg and tell her I don't need her to watch Lilia for me next week."

His mom followed him down the hall to the guest bedroom. He heard his dad say something to her, and she laughed. Matt smiled at the familiar sounds and went into his own bedroom. He scrolled down to Meg's name in his cell phone.

"Hello," her soft voice came clearly over the phone line.

"Hey, it's Matt."

"Matt! Merry Christmas."

"You too. Did you have a good day?"

"I did," she said with reservation.

"Really?"

"Yes, mostly. I'm just confused about some things, but I'm sure it's nothing you want to hear about. So what about you? How was your day?"

"Well, that's why I'm calling. My parents ended up surprising Lilia and me by flying into town today."

"Wow! I'll bet Lilia was excited."

"She was. It took us almost an hour to get her to bed tonight, she was so wired."

"How long are they in town?"

"Until after the new year."

"That sounds like fun. So are you calling to tell me you don't need me this week?"

"Yes. I'm sorry it's such short notice. Thank you for being so helpful this past week. You were a lifesaver."

"I loved doing it. It was like a crash course in parenthood for me. Of course, I don't think I learned very much, except for realizing there is a whole lot I don't know about having a child."

"You did a great job. Lilia hasn't stopped talking about you all day. My parents asked me who you were tonight because of all the nice things they've heard."

"Well, that's sweet," she replied. "The feeling is mutual. Let me know if you need me again. If I can, I'd love to watch her."

"I will," Matt said. "And I'm going to pay you."

"Matt, we already talked about this. I won't accept any money from you for watching Lilia. I wanted to do it. It helped me as much as it helped you."

"How so?"

"At least when I was busy with Lilia, I wasn't thinking about being so lonely this Christmas."

Matt heard her sniff and felt a sudden, unexpected desire to pull her into his arms while she cried.

"Are you okay? Do you want me to come over?" he asked without thinking and immediately berated himself. What was he saying? He couldn't go over there.

"No. You've got your family there," she responded, partly to his relief. He was unsettled to realize that another part of him felt disappointed. "Don't mind me. Pregnant women are emotional, remember? I'll be fine."

"Well you've got my number if you need to talk. Call me anytime." That was safe.

"Thanks, Matt. Tell Lilia I said hi."

"I will. Good night, Meg."

"Good night," she responded softly. Matt turned off his phone and let his head fall against the pillow, his mind still lingering on Meg. He wondered if her plummeting emotions had anything to do with Johnny Peters.

He pushed down his rising anger when he thought of how Peters had treated her just a few nights previous when Matt was there for dinner. She was an adult; she could make her own decisions. He just wished he could shake some sense into her and tell her to stay away from him. She needed someone who would love her and build her up, not tear her down.

Matt noticed the house was quiet and got up to check the locks on the doors. The light under his parents' door was off as he walked past it. After locking the front door and turning off all the lights in the house, Matt stood in front of the artificial Christmas tree Lilia had begged him to buy. White lights twinkled from the pre-lit branches, casting long shadows across the room. The scent of Lydia's perfume filled his nose, and he could almost feel her come up behind him and wrap her arms around his waist. As quickly as the sensation came, it was gone, leaving him with a sharp ache of longing for his wife.

He stood alone by the tree for a while longer, indulging in memories of past Christmases that hadn't been filled with pain and yearning for something that could never be. Tears tapped against his eyelids, and Matt swiped his fingers across his eyes with a groan.

He decided to leave the tree lights on for the night and went down the hall to check on Lilia. She slept peacefully under her pink bedspread.

Lydia, I miss you, he allowed himself to think the words as he took in his daughter's light blonde hair spread over her pillow, so much like his late wife's. Every time he looked at her, he thought of Lydia.

He remembered when they found out that Lydia was pregnant with Lilia and later how it felt to hold his own baby in his arms. He'd held hundreds of babies in his career, but nothing compared to holding his own little girl.

He'd finally reached a point in his life where he was not

consumed with painful thoughts of Lydia every minute of every day like he had been in the beginning. He thought of her almost every time he looked at his daughter, but the pain wasn't as overwhelming. Except on days like today when he wanted her here with him to share this quiet moment.

I tried to make this day good for Lilia. I want her to be happy, but more than anything I wish you were here.

He kissed Lilia's forehead. "I love you."

Chapter Twenty-two

Meg and Johnny were together every day from Christmas until the day after New Year's when he had to go back to Phoenix to finish moving into his apartment. Meg was no closer to deciding if she really wanted to begin a relationship with him. Perhaps the time of decision had passed. It was a likely conclusion that they were dating. She just wasn't sure if she liked that conclusion. There was still something about him that didn't always sit well with her.

Is it really supposed to be this hard to decide if I want to date someone? she wondered as she walked through her neglected house. Clothes, food, dishes, and Christmas decorations were everywhere. Because she couldn't figure out her messed up and complicated life, she decided that she could at least take care of her messy house.

She threw a load of laundry into the washer, put away the dishes that had been drying on the counter, and decided to tackle a job she'd been postponing for several months—mopping the kitchen floor. She hated mopping the floor, so she put it off until she absolutely had to do it, and after cooking with Lilia the week before Christmas, it was time.

It was in the upper sixties outside, a warm January day even for southern Arizona, and Meg knew she was going to be burning up from pushing the mop around her tiled floor. She went through the house and opened all the windows to get fresh air flowing. She needed music, so she plugged her ancient CD player into a kitchen outlet. Then she found an elastic band and pulled her hair up into a messy bun. Once she'd exhausted all of her stalling procedures, she finally filled the mop bucket with sudsy water and got to work.

Meg pushed the mop steadily over the floor and tuned out all of her thoughts, trying to focus on her task and the music. The upbeat melody entered her body through her skin, gliding past her muscles and over her bones until if became a part of her.

Singing along with Celine Dion, she scrubbed the mop over the tiles that had caked-on flour paste from making cookies. She stopped mopping when her favorite part of the song came on, and she held the mop to her mouth like a microphone. Her hips swayed to the motion of a few clumsy dance moves.

"Hi, Meg!" a little voice called through the window over the sink.

Meg stopped singing and dancing immediately. She looked through the window and confirmed what she already knew— Matt and Lilia were watching her.

She fanned her face as she waved them over to the back door, all the while wishing she could hide.

"How long were you standing there?" she asked.

"About a minute." Matt's mouth curved up in a heart-racing smile.

"You sing good," Lilia said enthusiastically.

"You heard me?"

"We tried knocking on the front door, but I guess you didn't hear us. We heard the music, so we walked around to the back of the house," Matt provided.

"And saw the show," she finished for him.

"I didn't know you could sing like that."

Meg shrugged her shoulders and tried to hide her perpetual blush. There was something about this man that had the blood constantly rushing to her face like it too wanted to have a look at the handsome doctor.

"You blush a lot," Matt commented as his smile grew broader.

Meg's blush deepened, especially as she remembered her last thought. She put her hands to her cheeks. "I can't help it."

"It's sweet," Matt said, pulling her hands away from her face. He dropped her hands after a second and looked around the kitchen. "Busy?"

"Just doing some cleaning that I've been putting off for a few weeks." Or months.

The doorbell rang before Matt could reply.

"Grandma and Grandpa!" Lilia exclaimed. Cliff barked excitedly as the two ran for the door.

"Oh, and my parents are here too," Matt said as Lilia threw the door open. Meg struggled to hold Cliff's collar as he tried to jump up on an older couple, the woman standing just behind a man who sat in a wheelchair.

She dragged Cliff into the backyard and tried to smooth out some of the frizz she knew was exploding from her wild bun before she went to the door to greet her unexpected guests. Of course he had to bring his parents on a day when she looked like a mess.

"I'm Cathy." A thin woman who appeared to be in her early sixties extended her soft hand to Meg. Her blonde hair curved attractively about her small face.

"Paul," Matt's dad said. He took Meg's hand in his rough one and shook it soundly. "Sorry to barge in like this, but Cathy wanted to meet you before we leave for home tomorrow."

"I tried calling," Matt interjected. "You didn't answer, but we were in the neighborhood anyway so we decided to drop by. We can come back later if that's better for you."

"I must've forgotten to plug my phone in last night. The battery's probably dead," she explained. "Now is fine. Would you like to come in?" Meg directed her question to Cathy and Paul.

"We'd love to," Cathy said as Matt helped pull Paul into the house

"I guess my house isn't wheelchair friendly," Meg observed as Matt maneuvered the wheelchair over the curb of the threshold.

"Neither is mine. We're used to this move after doing it all week," he assured her.

Meg led everyone into the house and encouraged them to take a seat. They eased comfortably into conversation; the only sign of Meg's nervousness was that she kept pulling at the threads of the hole in her jeans.

"Well, mostly I wanted to come by to say thank you again for watching Lilia," Matt told Meg when there was a lull in the conversation. "I don't know what I would have done without you."

"It was no problem. Lilia and I had fun."

"I would like to pay you—"

"No," Meg said firmly.

"—but I know you won't let me," he continued. "Instead, how would you feel if I helped you with a few things around the house?"

"Like what?"

"First of all, I could look at your dishwasher and see what's wrong with it. We can take a look at those leaks you mentioned awhile back if no one has permanently taken care of that problem. Then, I don't know. I'm sure there are other things that you need fixed, aren't there?"

"And you can do that?" Meg asked dubiously. She had a difficult time picturing Matt as the down-and-dirty fix-it man.

"Yes." He seemed insulted. "I always work on things around my house. In fact, I've fixed a lot of the problems in the house we just moved into."

"You really don't have to do that. I didn't mind watching Lilia for you."

"I'd like to do something. If you don't like this idea, we'll think of something else."

Meg still thought it likely that Matt was overestimating his handy-man abilities, but she pushed her skepticism aside and decided to give him a shot. *Besides*, the traitorous thought filled her head, *this way you get to spend more time with him.*

"Let's do it. So you think you can fix my dishwasher?"

"It depends on what's wrong with it. I'll have to take a look at it first."

"Right now?"

Matt looked at his parents, and they nodded that it was fine with them. "We'll watch Lilia," Paul said. "Take your time."

"Okay." Meg led Matt into the kitchen and waved her hand

toward the dishwasher. "Have at it."

Matt handed Meg her mop. "Don't let me keep you from your singing."

"Ha, ha." She picked up the mop and dunked it in the water. "I should probably go keep your parents company."

"They'll be fine. We're the ones who interrupted you." He pushed a few buttons on the dishwasher and opened the door.

Meg glared at the mop. She wouldn't even have the benefit of music if she mopped right now, but she should finish, or at least keep an eye on Matt. Hopefully he didn't break the dishwasher even more.

As Meg's eyes continually drifted over to Matt, she discovered that there was even better motivation than music to keep mopping.

Matt and Meg didn't talk very much while he looked at her dishwasher and pulled it away from the wall, but there was something about just watching him. The way his forehead creased, and he ran a hand across his rough chin when he was concentrating. His muscular arms and back pulled on the seams of his shirt, and she wondered why she ever doubted that he could do difficult physical labor. Every once in a while, he'd say something to himself and then fiddle with a part or move to another area. His full attention seemed to be on his job.

Meg, on the other hand, could not rip her attention away from Matt. She did a few token wipes on the floor with the mop for appearances' sake, but really, she was just moving dirty water around. At this point, she needed a valid reason to stay in the same room as him.

"I found the problem." Matt held up a small metal part for Meg's inspection. "This is busted. I can get a new one for you at the hardware store in Tucson, and once we put it in, it should work."

"Really?" Meg doubted it would be that easy, but it was worth a try.

Matt's mom insisted on taking Lilia and Meg out for lunch

while Matt and his dad went to Tucson to get the part for the dishwasher.

"You know, my hair used to be brown," Mrs. Wilkes said while the waitress filled their cups with water and took their lunch orders. "Once I started to get more gray hairs than brown, I decided that was God's way of giving me a fresh pallet to work with. My hair was never as thick and gorgeous as yours, though."

Meg self-consciously ran her hand over her hair and tucked a few stray curls into the bun at the back of her head. "It's usually not so crazy. I've been cleaning all morning, so I just wanted to get it out of the way." She took a sip out of her straw. "Why'd you choose blonde?"

"Well, I'd been a brunette my whole life—several shades lighter than yours—so I wanted something different. The first time I had my hairstylist dye my hair, she did it red. I think my personality changed though, because all of a sudden I was a lot more outspoken and fiery. Since that happened to coincide with the time I was starting to go through 'the change,' you know"—she waited for Meg to nod—"I thought that maybe it was too much."

"Maybe I should go red," Meg said. "I could use a little more feistiness."

Mrs. Wilkes laughed. "Wait till you turn gray. Your hair is too beautiful to touch now. Anyway, I went blonde as another experiment, and I love it. Paul loves it too, and best of all, Lilia and I have the same hair color. Right, Lilia?"

"Right," Lilia said enthusiastically.

An awkward silence fell across the table. Mrs. Wilkes helped Lilia color for a few minutes before she turned back to Meg. "When are you due?"

"June third, give or take a few days."

"Do you know what you're going to have?"

"No. I want to be surprised."

"Does your ex-husband want to know the sex?"

Meg picked at the hole in her jeans for a moment before forcing herself to look up at Mrs. Wilkes, who seemed to be very interested in Meg's life. "Definitely not."

"Oh?"

Meg shrugged. "I didn't find out that I was pregnant until after we were divorced. By then he had moved on." She fiddled with her straw. "If he'd found out before he left, he may have stayed for a few months, but eventually he would've gone. Impetuousness is his strength, not commitment."

"So, Matt tells me you're dating someone."

A server came to the table with everyone's food, giving Meg time to gather her thoughts. Why had Matt told his mom that she was dating someone?

"He probably meant Johnny," Meg said, when Mrs. Wilkes looked at her expectantly. "We went to high school together. But we're just friends.

"I wonder why Matt thought you were dating Johnny."

Meg's felt her face heat up. "Johnny's made it no secret that he wants a relationship with me. He and Matt don't really get along."

"Really? Matt usually gets along with everyone."

Meg shrugged, wishing she hadn't said anything. "Every time we're all together, they argue. They must just rub each other the wrong way for some reason."

A knowing light flickered in Mrs. Wilkes's eyes as she studied Meg.

"So you're only in town until tomorrow?" Meg asked in an obvious attempt to change the subject from her love life.

Mrs. Wilkes nodded. "I've never been to Arizona before, but it's been wonderful. Matt tells us the summers get hot, but the winters might make it worthwhile."

"I think so, but I'm a desert girl—Arizona born and raised—so I'm a little biased."

Mrs. Wilkes lowered her voice and glanced over at Lilia. She was still coloring on the children's menu and didn't seem to be paying any attention to their conversation. "I'd like to try and convince Paul to move here so we can be closer to Matt and Lilia. I don't want to get her hopes up though, in case it doesn't work out."

"I bet she'd love that. Do you have any other children?" Meg asked.

"We have four kids, three girls and then Matt."

"Wow, Matt has three older sisters?"

"He sure does. Oh, the pictures I could show you. . . . Those girls made Matt their little doll. Whenever I show people our family albums, they assume that I had four daughters because Matt's sisters were forever dressing him like a girl." She shook her head. "Poor Paul. He finally got his boy, and we all treated him like a girl. When Matt finally grew big enough to defend himself from his sisters and show an interest in sports, Paul was in heaven."

"What did he play?"

"Oh, anything with a ball. He was on the basketball team all through high school and his first few years of college until he decided he wanted to be a doctor and needed to focus on his grades to get into medical school. He kept up his basketball with his dad, though. They joined a city league and played together for years."

"That's awesome. The league accommodated for players in wheelchairs?"

Mrs. Wilkes paused. "Paul wasn't in a wheelchair then. That, I think, has been one of the hardest things for him to give up. He tries to play in our driveway, but it's hard for him to not get frustrated when the ball bounces off the rim and he can't run after the rebound. It's going to take a few more years for him to get used to playing certain sports in his chair."

Meg's fork clattered against her plate as she wished she'd kept her mouth shut. "I'm so sorry to bring it up. I didn't realize—"

Mrs. Wilkes interrupted her. "It's been over a year since the accident. We're still adjusting, but it's not as hard to talk about as it used to be."

"Accident? Not the one . . ." Meg glanced at Lilia.

"Yes. It was tragic in more ways than one. I'm just so grateful that Paul and Lilia made it."

"Matt mentioned that Paul broke his back, but I didn't make the connection."

Mrs. Wilkes stopped eating and looked thoughtfully at Meg. Meg began to squirm under the scrutiny.

"I'm surprised he told you about the accident. He always said it was too painful to talk about when I tried to bring it up."

"I just happened to be there when he needed to talk," Meg said.

"Thank you." Mrs. Wilkes reached across the table and squeezed Meg's hand. "You seem like a pretty special young lady, and I know that Matt and Lilia think the world of you."

Meg blinked back the emotion that rose to the surface at Mrs. Wilkes's words.

"Enough of this serious talk," Mrs. Wilkes said, and Meg thought she saw her blinking back her own tears as well. "Let's get some boxes for our food and head back to your house. We've got to make sure that dishwasher is coming along."

Chapter Twenty-three

"Good as new," Matt declared as he looked at the dishwasher. He wiped his hands on a kitchen rag and threw it over his shoulder.

"You fixed it?"

He turned around to find Meg standing behind him. "Don't look so surprised. It's not good for my ego."

Meg had the decency to at least feign chagrin.

"I just loaded the dishes you had in the sink and turned it on to see if it will run okay. So far so good."

"Wow." Meg sounded impressed as she inspected her dishwasher. "This will be so much nicer than washing everything by hand."

"So where is everyone?"

"Lilia wanted to take your parents outside to see Cliff. Apparently, Lilia has tricks she can do with him that she wants to show off."

"Is your dog patient?" He could just picture the tricks his daughter would have with a dog. Riding him like a pony? Making him bark when she pulled his tail?

"Cliff's been living with my parents for the last couple of years, so he's had a lot of exposure to my niece, who is about Lilia's age."

"I'm sure my mom will watch her. Did you have a nice lunch?" Matt couldn't help but be curious as to what they talked about.

"It was nice. I really like your mom." She paused and gave Matt a mischievous smile. "So, I hear that you look good in a dress."

Matt groaned. "I can't believe my mom told you about that. Never mind. That was always her favorite story to tell girls I—" *liked*. He caught himself before the word slipped out. He didn't feel that way toward Meg. He liked her, but only as a friend. It didn't go beyond that, no matter how cute she looked in an over-sized T-shirt with her hair pulled back and curls springing out everywhere.

"What?" Meg asked when he didn't finish.

"Uh, people I knew," he finished lamely.

"Oh." Meg nodded like that made sense.

Matt took the towel off his shoulder and put it on the counter. "We'll get out of your way now. Thanks for being a good sport about meeting my parents and letting us drop by unexpectedly."

"You guys can drop by anytime. It was fun."

Matt ignored the way his heart jumped at the idea of coming over again. He grabbed the handle of the mop that leaned against the counter, and the image of her singing popped into his mind. He'd never heard her sing before. He assumed she had a passable voice since she taught choir at the school, but he didn't realize that her talent was so incredible.

"So when do we get to hear you sing again?"

"Every Sunday when I lead the music."

"You don't sing then. You just move your lips."

He loved that he could make Meg blush.

"Do you do that in your high school classes?"

"No."

"Then why don't you sing in church? Don't want to show off?"

"It's hard to explain," she hedged.

Matt leaned against the counter and raised his eyebrows. He knew that he'd taken up too much of her time already, but spending a few more minutes with her felt like a really good idea.

Meg leaned her hip on the counter about a foot from where he was.

"Do you like music?" she asked.

"Yes."

"Me too. Only for me, it's more . . . I don't know," she paused. When she spoke again, she used her hands while she explained. "I do more than hear music. I feel it. Music is everywhere—in trees, wind, people's voices, even their steps. Just the way a person moves is like a melody."

"How so?" Matt was intrigued. He hadn't seen Meg this animated since he met her.

"I don't know if I can explain it."

"Try."

"You, for instance," she finally said. "The way you move, the way you are is calming. I hear a slow, gentle melody whenever I'm with you." She put her hands down and faced Matt. Her voice wasn't as animated and she cringed. "Not literally, though. Ugh. I probably sound crazy, like those people who see auras and colors around people, only I hear them instead."

"It's not crazy. It's beautiful," he said. He didn't know if he was talking about Meg or the way she viewed people. Both, he decided as she bit her lip. She tilted her gaze from the ground to him, and a shy smile broke free. If all it took was a compliment to get her eyes to sparkle like that, he could think of a dozen he'd like to give her, but he knew he shouldn't.

"Anyway," she continued, "this connection, or whatever you want to call it, with music has always been my strongest form of bearing testimony. So when I'm up on stage leading the music, I can't sing. I can't make the words go through my mouth, because then they will go through my body and into my soul," she concluded.

"Why don't you want that?"

"I don't know." She fiddled with the hem of her shirt. "I mean, I *do* want that. But I want it without the guilt. Without feeling like a hypocrite."

"What would you have to feel guilty about?"

"This," she gestured toward her stomach. "My whole life for the past two years. I was willing to ignore my beliefs for a man. A man who left me like I was nothing more to him than a way to pass the time. All my life I couldn't understand why people would turn from God for other pursuits. I looked down on my friends that chose jobs and school over missions. I couldn't understand why people chose immorality over everything we'd been taught." She laughed bitterly. "Yet, look at me. All it took was one good-looking man taking an interest in me, and I made the same decision."

"Meg," Matt started to say before she interrupted. She was carrying too much of a burden that she needed to give away.

"Did I tell you that Austin wanted me to get an abortion?"

Matt shook his head, disliking this man he'd never met even more.

"He tried to send money through his lawyer. Said that it happens all the time. It made me wonder what happened to the man I married. Who was this cold person talking to me through a lawyer? He changed his phone number." Her voice broke suddenly. "I couldn't even call him to tell him I was having our baby." Her eyes focused on the ground again. "That is the man I left everything behind for. That's why I mouth the words in church. I don't deserve to sing to God."

Matt couldn't believe how much guilt Meg felt. He watched her try to furtively wipe away the tears his questions had released. Taking a step closer, he pulled Meg into his arms. She slowly wrapped her arms around his waist and buried her head in his chest. He tightened his grip on her as her shoulders shook, and his shirt grew damp from her tears. The soft floral scent of her shampoo brushed his nose as he held her close.

Meg's crying calmed with a shuddering breath. She sniffled before lifting her head from his chest and letting her arms drop. "I'm sorry." She averted her eyes toward the tile. "I can't believe I'm crying all over you. Like spilling my guts wasn't mortifying enough."

A cold ache replaced the warmth of Meg's body close to his. Matt let his arms slip from around her but put one hand on her cheek and used his thumb to brush away a lingering tear. His heart rate increased when she leaned her cheek into his hand.

"Meg." He tipped her head up until her dewy gaze met his. The softness of her skin against his hand urged him to caress her cheek again. "I felt power—a strength—in you when you talked about music. There was serenity that I haven't seen in you the whole time I've known you. This is part of who you are. Don't let your ex-husband"—his jaw tightened—"take anything more from you than he already has."

"I don't know how to get it back," her hoarse voice caught.

"Sing."

"I don't know if I can."

"You can, Meg. I don't think you realize what an amazing woman you are. Not just what I've heard of your voice, but *you*. How you are with my daughter. With me." His face moved closer to hers, and she closed her eyes. "You are remarkable," he whispered.

Matt's heart hammered in his chest, and Meg's closeness was making it hard to think. He lowered his mouth until it hovered an inch above hers, her sweet breath mingling with his. He barely caught himself before he gave into the desire to let his lips brush across hers.

"I need to go." Matt's ragged breathing moved some of Meg's hair as he worked the words out of his mouth. Meg opened her eyes and studied him for a moment before pulling away. He was glad she did, because he didn't think he could have done it.

His hoarse voice called for Lilia, and he ran his fingers roughly through his hair as he made his way to the door. Meg walked everyone out to the van and said her good-byes to his parents. Matt wanted to say something to her to ease the awkwardness that had sprung up between them.

"Meg." Matt jogged over to where she stood at the door once everyone else was in the car. "Hey, I meant what I said. You're a strong woman who has gone through a lot. You deserve to feel peace again."

Meg looked over his shoulder at some kids playing in the street. Her clear blue eyes finally met his gaze. "I don't know if I can be that person again, but I want to try."

Chapter Twenty-four

"So how long have you been in love with Meg?"

Matt swallowed his hot eggs too quickly and started to cough. His mom slid a cup of milk over to him, which he proceeded to guzzle down in an effort to soothe his burnt throat. He loosened his tie and pushed his plate away.

"What are you talking about?" Matt finally choked out in response to his mom's question.

She calmly cut a small portion of her syrup-slathered French toast. "You heard me," she said before she placed the bite in her mouth.

Matt looked behind his chair to assure himself that Lilia was still in the bathroom. He didn't need her getting any ideas in her head that she might feel inclined to share with Meg when they saw her at church.

"Mom," he said quietly, "I am not in love with Meg. I haven't even known her that long. We're friends. That's it." The memory of her sweet, curved lips just before he almost kissed her crowded his thoughts. He tried to push them away with another bite of food.

"Thanks for breakfast, Mom. This is great."

"Don't try to change the subject. I told you there was something different about you and that I would figure it out. I did." She smiled with satisfaction. "You're in love."

Matt groaned and pushed his chair away from the table. "You're crazy, Mom."

"Look, you can argue with me all you want, but I know what I saw."

"I know you and Meg hit it off at lunch, but that doesn't mean that I'm in love with her. She's going through a lot right now because of the pregnancy and her divorce, and you know the baggage I carry around with me."

Matt's mom stared at him until he felt the urge to squirm in his seat. "Those are all circumstances—unfortunate circumstances, yes—but they are not reasons for not being in love."

"I'm not in love with Meg."

"Matt." Her lighthearted tone turned more forceful. "Yesterday I saw something that I haven't seen in over a year." She leaned closer. "You were happy. Genuinely happy and carefree. I saw how you kept looking over at her while we were talking, wanting her to be in the same room as you while you were working. And I don't know what happened in that kitchen while your dad and I were outside with Lilia, but you both came out of it a little flushed."

Matt put his hand behind his neck and tried to disassociate himself from the words his mother spoke. He liked being with Meg. She was a strong, attractive woman. Who wouldn't want to look at her or work with her near?

As for what happened in the kitchen? Again the memory of that moment filled his mind, and he felt her body close to his, her soft hair between his fingers, her pink lips drawing him closer . . .

"Then there's the little smile you have when I talk about her," his mom finished, ripping him from his thoughts.

Matt loosened his tie a little more before deciding to just pull it off and undo the top button of his shirt. He felt like he was choking to death.

"I am not in love with her," he repeated to himself as much as to his mom.

His mom only smiled and began scooping eggs on a new plate. "How many pieces of French toast do you want, honey?"

"Two!" Lilia called from behind Matt. He turned in time to see Lilia walking down the hall. He waited for the inevitable request for a new dress because he could already see she'd spilled water on this one when she washed her hands. As much as he tried to break her of the habit, they often went through several changes of clothes before the day was done. But today Lilia must have been distracted enough by a breakfast other than cereal or oatmeal.

Lilia's appearance diverted his mom from continuing their conversation, and Matt took the opportunity to leave the table and search out his dad. His appetite was gone now, anyway.

His dad was just placing a bookmark in his scriptures when Matt knocked lightly and then pushed open the guest room door.

"Did your mom send you to get me?"

"No. I left before she could." Matt watched his dad maneuver the wheelchair next to the bed. He transferred into the wheelchair almost effortlessly, only his tightly flexed arms showing evidence of strain.

His dad settled into the seat and took the wheels in his hands. "Kind of miss the electric one when we're on vacation, but this one is easier to pack."

"It's good for your arms," Matt replied. He wasn't sure if he would ever get used to seeing his father in a wheelchair. The days following the accident were all a blur in Matt's mind. From the moment the police officers informed him that his wife was dead, he felt like he was swimming through a fog. He surfaced for a clear breath when he saw for himself that Lilia was alive and only mildly bruised. After that, he just went along with the current, letting it pull him wherever it would.

He didn't even find out that his dad had broken his back and gone through surgery until the next day. Since his mom was at a different hospital because of her hip, no one had been with his dad when he woke up. Matt's sisters all lived in different states and made it there within the next few days. In time for the funeral.

"Seeing me always reminds you, doesn't it," his dad said, reading Matt accurately.

"Not in the way you're thinking." Matt's mom had told him about the guilt his dad carried because of that accident. He had been driving, he'd survived, and he'd nearly killed himself with "what ifs" every day since then.

"You know that if I could, I would've changed places with Lydia in an instant."

Matt moved his dad's scriptures and sat down on the end of the bed. "I know, Dad. I'm glad you're alive—you and Lilia. It's just been a difficult year."

"I need to know something. It's extremely important that you're honest with me. Don't worry about hurting my feelings or any such nonsense."

"Okay," Matt said slowly.

"Was seeing me in a wheelchair every day part of the reason you needed to move down here to Arizona? Did it remind you too much of the accident?"

Matt started shaking his head before his dad even finished the question. "No. That had nothing to do with why I needed to move."

"I told you to be honest with me."

"I am being honest. Yes, it's a reminder. But every day when I look at Lilia, it's a reminder. It reminds me that miracles really do happen. That accident could have easily left me without a wife, a father, and a daughter." Matt paused as the pressure in his throat tightened his words.

"I moved down here because I needed a fresh start with people who didn't treat me differently because they knew what we had been through. When I heard about the opportunity of buying this medical practice, it felt right. Leaving you and mom was the most difficult part of that, not the reason."

His dad pulled a tissue out of a box on the nightstand and ran it over his eyes.

"I'm sorry if I ever made you feel like I was upset with you. I am so grateful that you're alive. Seeing you in the wheelchair doesn't make me think of tragedy. It makes me think of life." Matt leaned back on his hands. "What brought that up? Has it just been on your mind awhile?"

"Your mom wants to move here."

"That doesn't surprise me." Matt knew his mom would have a hard time being too far from Lilia. All of his sisters met their husbands in college and moved around the country for various jobs.

Matt was the only one who married someone from Washington and then moved back there after medical school. As a result, his mom was really close to Lilia.

"We're still in the discussion stage, just seeing if it would even be feasible. I needed to make sure that we wouldn't be chasing you down with the very thing you were trying to get away from."

"Not at all," Matt said fervently. "I would love to have you and Mom down here by us."

"Paul!" his mom called from the kitchen. "Are you going to come eat your breakfast before it's ruined?"

"Coming!" he yelled back.

Matt jumped up from the bed and stood next to the wheelchair. He looked at his dad's head, noticing some spots where hair was beginning to fall out.

"Looking a little patchy up here, Dad."

His dad rubbed a hand through his balding hair. "I used to complain about the gray. Blamed every single one on your sisters. Now I'm starting to lose even those. I've thought about just shaving it all off."

"Why don't you?"

"That gal that does your mom's hair thinks I have an odd-shaped head. Says we better not expose the world to it before we absolutely have to."

Matt's laughter started low and built up until he felt the tension from their earlier conversation drain out of him. "Let's go, Dad. Your breakfast is getting cold."

"Hey." He grabbed Matt's wrist as they headed toward the door. "I know I don't say it a lot, but I love you. You turned out well, despite your sisters."

Matt nodded his head. "Love you too," he said gruffly before leading the way to the kitchen.

Chapter Twenty-five

att and Lilia said a tearful good-bye to his parents before going to church. After Matt put the car in park, he buttoned the top of his shirt and knotted his tie. He tried not to think of his mom's assumptions about him and Meg.

His mom was definitely seeing something that wasn't there—most likely letting her own hopes color her vision. And as long as Matt didn't think about almost kissing Meg, he could discount his mom's words easily enough.

Matt grabbed Lilia's hand, and they walked into the chapel. He didn't question himself when he bypassed the pew in the back where he usually sat and instead found a seat in the third row from the front.

Lilia chattered about the new dress her grandmother had given her for Christmas, running her hands over the smooth ribbon that dangled from around her waist. Matt felt the ribbon when she told him to and then let it go as she switched topics to a movie she wanted to watch when they got home.

Meanwhile Matt looked casually around the room. He fidgeted with his scriptures, unzipping the case and flipping mindlessly through the pages. He read a scripture that didn't register, closed them, and zipped the case shut. Lilia talked on, unaware of her distracted audience.

Finally Meg walked in one of the back doors and headed toward the front of the room. She wore a red shirt with a denim skirt and had her hair pulled up in a curly ponytail. She caught his eye and smiled shyly at him as she continued up to the stand to post the hymn numbers.

Matt wanted to talk to her, but he didn't really have anything to say. He found himself just wanting to hear her voice. Now that Matt could watch Meg move around and set up a music stand, talk to the organist, and sit with an open hymn book in her lap, time went fast until the meeting started.

As the beginning notes of the opening hymn played through the chapel, Meg stood. Matt wanted to hear her sing. She raised her hands and opened her mouth, but Matt didn't hear any sound come out. She didn't meet his eyes until the song was done, and once she did, she gave him a small, tired shrug.

He wished he could pull her into a hug and . . . do what?

He was letting his mom get to him. He couldn't have feelings for Meg. It wouldn't be appropriate. What was he thinking—getting close to her, watching for her, wanting to see her so badly?

He bent his head over his lap and rubbed his hand behind his neck. He needed to stay away from Meg, if not for his own good, then for hers. The more time he spent with her, the more likely it became that he was going to do something stupid.

Matt avoided eye contact with Meg for the rest of the meeting, but his traitorous ears still listened for her sweet voice. It never came. Once sacrament meeting was over, Matt deposited Lilia in Primary and went to the Gospel Essentials class.

"Hey, Matt," Meg's voice rang out as she walked into the classroom.

Matt nodded his head and buried it in his lesson manual. He'd already read the lesson through twice, and it was one he was familiar with from his mission, but he proceeded to try to read it a third time.

Meg stood in front of him for a second before she sat and introduced herself to one of the new sister missionaries in the ward.

Matt made it through the lesson, only looking at Meg when necessary and ignoring her smiles in his direction. It would be too easy to smile back, and then things would only go downhill from there.

After the closing prayer, Matt turned to the missionaries and asked about a new family they were teaching. Meg stood behind him for several minutes, seeming determined to talk to him.

"Are you mad at me?" she asked as soon as the door closed behind the sisters.

"No." Matt busied himself with erasing the chalkboard.

"Then why won't you look at me?" She sounded hurt.

Matt put the eraser down and turned to Meg. His eyes were drawn to her mouth as she bit her lip.

"Where's Johnny today?" he blurted out.

There was an awkward pause before Meg said, "He didn't come today. He had to stay in Phoenix this weekend."

"Oh."

"Is something going on, Matt?"

Matt debated addressing his concerns. "Meg," he said, "I think it would be best for us to keep our distance for a while."

He saw the mortification cross Meg's face as understanding dawned. She reddened and backed up toward the door. "I'm sorry, I didn't mean anything."

"No, Meg, it's my fault." He rolled the chalk nervously between his hands. "Dr. Cohen gets back from vacation this week. I'm going to talk to her tomorrow about transferring your care to her."

"You don't want to be my doctor anymore?"

"It's not that. It's just better this way."

"How is it better? I have to switch doctors in the middle of my pregnancy because of something that didn't happen?"

"It's because of something that almost happened, Meg."

"Right. Sounds like you have it all figured out. I guess I'll see you around."

He started folding chairs to avoid looking at her as she closed the door behind her. He waited for the relief to hit him. He shouldn't have to see Meg again, except for at church. He wouldn't have to worry about what he was feeling for her. He could focus on Lilia and on Lydia's memory. He bit back his unwanted disappointment when he stepped out of the classroom and saw that Meg was gone. Still he waited for a relief that never came.

Chapter Twenty-six

*M*eg's heart pounded in her chest as she raced to the University Medical Center in Tucson. After school let out, she listened to the voice mail Johnny had left while she was teaching sixth period. His dad was in the hospital, and he wanted her to come.

Johnny had only called her a few times in the past month, each call becoming shorter and more distracted. She still didn't know if she wanted to be with Johnny because she liked him or if it was because she didn't want to be alone. She missed having someone to talk to, especially since her friendship with Matt had become awkward—if it could even be called a friendship anymore.

The drive to the hospital seemed to take forever. She called Johnny's cell phone over and over, but he wouldn't answer. She pulled into the parking lot and ran through the front doors. The front desk attendant directed her to Brother Peters's room, and she made her way there, her mind reeling with possibilities of what she might see.

She steeled her courage to open the door to his room. A clipboard in a tray screwed to the door rattled, and Johnny's head shot up. Meg closed the door behind her and took another step into the room, her gaze fixed on Brother Peters. He was so silent and still that she had to look at the monitors to make sure his heart was still beating.

"You're here," Johnny said, coming toward her with open

arms. His undone tie hung around his neck, and dark shadows had already formed under his eyes.

Meg put her arms around Johnny's waist and rested her head against his chest. His heart beat a steady rhythm against her ear. He buried his face in her hair and held her tight.

"Have the doctors told you anything?" she asked, tilting her head up toward him.

Johnny let go of her but grabbed her hand. Meg squeezed it and led him over to the two chairs by his father's hospital bed.

"Dad had another stroke." He paused. "They're not sure if he's going to make it this time."

Meg's eyes burned with tears that threatened to spill over. She held them back by squeezing her eyes shut. She didn't want to make things harder for Johnny by crying in front of him. Her heart was breaking for this man who had already lost his mother and was now facing the loss of his father.

"I need to get out of this room," Johnny said, pulling her up from her chair.

"You don't need to be here?"

"No, I've been with my dad since six this morning. Let's leave."

"Where do you want to go?"

"Anywhere that's not here. I just can't be around this anymore right now." He gestured toward the still form of his dad.

"Are you hungry?"

"No." He shook his head. "Let's just go somewhere and walk."

"How does the university campus sound?"

"Anywhere's fine. Let's go."

❧❧❧

Johnny took Meg's hand as they walked between the tall buildings past Campbell Avenue. "I have to go back to work tomorrow."

"You can't leave your dad like this."

"I have to. I was lucky I could get away today. I'm working on a project with an impossible deadline that I have to meet."

181

"But if you talked to your boss, I bet she would understand—"

Johnny laughed shortly. "I doubt it."

"Can you really work for a company that puts deadlines over your dad's health?"

"I have to. I can't lose this job. My brother David and his family are driving in tonight. They'll probably get here around midnight. He can take care of everything that needs to be done. I'm only a two-hour drive away if anything happens."

"He can get away from his classes at NAU?"

"I guess."

And you can't get away from your work for a few days? Meg bit back the question that sat on the tip of her tongue. Her lips tightened, and she saw Johnny glance down at her mouth. She turned and pretended to study a modern-style sculpture in front of her. Johnny moved behind her and wrapped his arms around her waist. When he kissed her neck, she briefly leaned into him before pulling out of his arms.

Johnny caught her hands and held her before she moved as far away as she wanted. "What's holding you back?"

"I told you—it's too soon. I'm sorry if I've been leading you on, but I still need time."

"Time for what, Meg?" Johnny snapped. "Are you waiting to see if your ex-husband comes back to you?"

Meg blinked back her tears, hurt by Johnny's tone. He took her arms in his hands and pulled her toward him. She resisted for a moment but let him pull her close.

"Do you think he's coming back?" he said softly against her temple.

She shook her head. "He made his choice clear."

Johnny sighed and kissed her forehead. "I don't mind giving you time as long as we're moving forward. I want you to be comfortable with me."

"I'm starting to be—" Meg began before Johnny's cell phone rang. Johnny let go of Meg to pull it out of his pocket. He looked at the screen and then held it in his hand as if debating.

"Go ahead and answer it."

"Peters," Johnny barked into the phone.

"I've missed you today," Meg heard the tinny voice of a woman on the other line pouting.

"This isn't a good time."

"You know it's always a good time with me, Johnny," she purred. Meg stiffened and Johnny pulled away from her so she couldn't hear anymore of the conversation.

"My dad's in the hospital, Sam. I'm not sure when I'll be back."

Meg prepared a stony expression to mask the hurt she was feeling. Johnny hung up the phone and slipped it into his pocket. "What were you saying earlier?"

"Who was that?" she asked in a flat voice.

"No one. Just my boss."

"Your boss. Okay," she nodded slowly. "Do you think I'm an idiot?"

"Of course not." Johnny frowned as Meg continued to glare. "Look," he continued, "I don't know how much you heard, but you're taking it out of context."

"Really? Please put it in context for me, then."

"Samantha and I had a thing going for a while."

"A while," Meg repeated.

"Yes, but it's over."

"She doesn't seem to think that it is."

"I can't help what she thinks, Meg." Johnny's tone had an edge.

"When did it end?"

"It doesn't matter," he said evasively. "It's over now."

"I need to go." Meg turned and started walking away from him.

"Wait," Johnny ran after her and grabbed her arm.

Meg shook it off. "I can't be with someone I don't trust."

"You can trust me."

"When did it end, Johnny?"

"It's been over for about a month."

Meg took a deep breath. "You were still dating her at Christmas?"

"Yes." He shrugged. "But we aren't dating anymore. Maybe

Sam still wants to be together, but I'm done. I chose you." He stepped closer and brought his hand behind her neck.

Meg laughed shortly. "Am I supposed to be happy that I was 'chosen'? You were dating both of us at the same time!"

"Why are you being so sensitive about this?"

"I've been cheated on before, Johnny. I'm not interested in experiencing it again."

She began to walk away, but Johnny called out after her, "You're one to talk."

Meg stopped walking and whirled to face Johnny. "Excuse me?"

"Does the name 'Matt Wilkes' ring a bell? Every time I turn around he's at your house, with you at church, or you have another appointment with him."

"We're friends," Meg said through gritted teeth.

"Friends," Johnny snorted derisively. "And how many of his patients is he friends with?"

"What are you implying?" Meg's venomous voice surprised even her. Johnny ran his hand through his hair and took a deep breath.

"I'm not implying anything," he said steadily.

"Oh really? Because you're always implying things about me. You think the worst of me, Johnny. And after I'm with you, I think the worst of myself." Her words were low and accusatory.

"I only tell it like I see it," Johnny snapped back.

Meg reeled back as if he had slapped her. The anger she felt turned to hurt, and she pivoted away from him. "So that's how it is?"

"I guess so."

"Fine. We're done."

As she walked away, she waited for him to run after her, grab her arm, offer her assurances that Sam meant nothing to him, that he didn't mean the things he'd said. Her lone footsteps tapped against the sidewalk, her ears straining for the rushed sound of someone running to her, but it never came.

Chapter Twenty-seven

Meg looked at herself in the mirror, hating every inch of the reflection that glared back at her. Her stomach was growing, but she didn't look pregnant yet. She just looked fat. Her clothes were too tight, but she didn't have enough money to get more. Her hair was too long, her skin was splotchy, and her chest and back hurt.

No wonder no one wanted to be with her.

She found herself on more than one lonely night holding the telephone, debating whether or not she should call Johnny and work out their fight. She didn't want to be the desperate girl who chased a man who didn't want her. But she really didn't want to be alone.

Dark-circled eyes reflected back at her. There must be something she was missing, or something she had that made it so that men couldn't stand to be with her. First Austin left, then Johnny. Even Matt didn't want anything to do with her. She wasn't good enough for someone to love. She was broken.

Cliff barked at something in the backyard, startling Meg from her session of self-criticism. It wasn't accomplishing anything other than making her feel more depressed than she'd already been feeling in the several weeks since she and Johnny fought.

Nothing. She hadn't heard anything from him since she walked away from him. Not that she expected to. Or wanted to. Unsolicited, her mom had told her that Johnny's dad had come home from the hospital, but she hadn't seen Johnny at his house.

Meg left the bathroom and dragged her feet to the kitchen. At least she could eat now without feeling sick. She could be grateful for small miracles anyway.

She heated up the leftover chicken she had from the night before and gathered the music folders that were resting on the counter. Curling onto the living room couch, she ate a small bite of her chicken and thumbed through the sheet music. A couple of young women in her ward had volunteered to sing in sacrament meeting but needed help finding a song.

A few songs caught her eye, and she sat at the piano and plunked them out. They weren't exactly what she was looking for. She set the sheets of paper aside and pulled out her hymnal. Flipping through it, she waited for something to grab her eye. About a third of the way through the hymns, her hand stalled on "Abide With Me."

She set the book on the piano stand and began to play it. On the second time through, she found the words slipping out of her mouth.

Pulling her hands from the keys, she looked around the room guiltily when she realized that she had sung. She cleared her throat, remembering that no one could hear her. Putting her fingers back on the keys, she expanded on the melody and, for the first time in a long time, she began to sing.

Her voice faded as the last notes rang from under her fingers, and Meg gasped as she felt a sharp jolt from her stomach. She splayed her hands across her abdomen, wishing for the baby to move again. Another kick pressed against her palm.

"Do you like music too, little one?" She imagined a tiny, developing baby spreading out within her stomach, its perfect fingers and toes begging to be caressed. Unable to repress her the urge, not even wanting to anymore, Meg began to sing a primary song she remembered her mother singing to her as a child. "I am a child of God . . . ."

Peace took root in her chest and spread its warmth throughout her body as she finished the final verse, still looking at her stomach, imagining the precious baby snuggled within her.

The young women were going to sing this song, and she was going to play her own arrangement for them.

And this Sunday, as she led the music, she would sing.

"Try the red one first," Missy ordered. Meg heard her sister's feet shuffle away from the dressing room and knew that she would still expect Meg to come out and model the clothes even if she was halfway across the store. With relief, Meg finally removed Tom's oversized T-shirt.

When she'd woken up that Saturday morning, she realized that her clothes situation had escalated into a serious problem. Somehow, overnight, her stomach had expanded to a point where she could not get the bottom of her shirt to meet the top of her unbuttoned, dangerously low-riding pants.

She thought that one slightly panicked call to Missy would solve her problems. She figured she could borrow Missy's maternity clothes for a while, just until she could save some money.

Unfortunately, she forgot a couple small details. Missy was four inches shorter than her, and a size smaller. She tactfully reminded Meg of this fact and then spent another five minutes trying to backtrack and say that the clothes would probably fit her just fine.

Instead, the only thing they could come up with was for Meg to borrow one of Tom's T-shirts and keep her pants unbuttoned. As long as she pulled her shirt down low over her belly, no one could tell that one good tug would have her showing off her leopard print underwear.

Now in the dressing room, she pulled the stretchy red T-shirt over her head and turned to look at her reflection in the mirror. Not bad. Especially when coupled with some maternity pants that had about five inches of elastic that rested under her enlarged belly.

She walked barefoot out of the dressing room and waved her hand to catch Missy's attention. Missy smiled and walked toward her with a huge pile of clothes draped over her arm.

"You look amazing. Red is really your color. Johnny is going to die when he sees you in this."

"I don't care what Johnny thinks of me."

"I knew you were holding out for Matt!"

"Missy!" Meg looked around the store to make sure no one had overheard her sister's remarks. "I am not holding out for him, and he for sure doesn't care about me."

"Right," she said, unconvinced. She handed Meg the armful of clothes and turned to head back into the gaping jaws of the store.

"Missy, I can't afford this much."

"It doesn't cost anything to try it on," she countered over her shoulder.

Meg closed the dressing room door and studied her reflection. With clothes that fit comfortably, she didn't feel like an incredible blob anymore. The shirt fit snugly over her shoulders and chest and allowed room in the stomach for growth. Most important, though, the pants fit.

She settled on three pairs of pants, six shirts, and a dress. She never would have thought that so few items of clothing could get her through three months, but she was on a budget. Times like these almost made her wish that she would have fought Austin for some money. Almost, but not quite. It was better to be completely separated from him. Fewer reminders, fewer ties, fewer reasons to think he might come home.

"Let's grab some dinner at the food court," Missy suggested. She hooked her arm in Meg's, and they walked toward the scent of several foods all mixed together into what should have been an unpleasant aroma, but made Meg's stomach growl.

"How does a salad sound?" Meg suggested.

They found a deli counter that served salads and lemonade and sat at a table in the corner.

"So what happened with you and Johnny?" Missy asked between bites.

Meg glared.

"What?" Missy asked.

"You're really going to start the conversation with that question?"

"Come on. You know that we're all dying to know what happened. It seemed like you two were together, and then all of a sudden he disappears from your life."

"It just didn't work out between us."

"Okay," she said, rolling her hand for more information.

Meg sighed. "We had a fight when his dad was in the hospital. We both said some things that we probably shouldn't have when things got a little heated, but it came down to the fact that we don't trust each other."

"He didn't trust you? Did he think you were seeing someone else?"

"It was so ridiculous. He was upset whenever I spent time with Matt and Lilia. I tried telling him over and over that we were just friends, but he didn't want to listen. I just got sick of it."

"Maybe he saw something you didn't."

"Not you, too! There's *nothing* there," Meg said slowly and pointedly.

"I see how he looks at you."

Meg's heart skipped, and she laughed to hide her reaction to Missy's words. "And how does he look at me?"

"Like you're the last sip of water after he's worked in the summer heat all day."

Meg snorted. "Yeah right, Missy. Maybe you need to get your eyes checked."

"You can deny it all you want, but I know what I've seen."

"He wouldn't be looking at me in any other way but disgust. Trust me. We already had to have an awkward conversation in church last month about how we're only friends and he couldn't be my doctor anymore. Plus, he's still not over his wife. I don't think he'll want to look at any woman for a long time."

"Wait." Missy held up a hand. "Why did you have to have a conversation about being friends? That's why he's not your doctor anymore?"

Meg mentally kicked herself. Why had she even brought that up? She shrugged and tried to glaze over the subject. "It just came up."

"I don't buy that." Missy sat back in her chair and brushed her perfect blonde hair off her shoulders. A group of college-age guys walked by and checked her out. She smiled when one of the boys nearly tripped over a chair trying to look at her.

Meg sighed, used to being overlooked. Then her sister's attention was back on her, and Meg debated. What would it hurt to tell someone?

"We may have almost kissed one day, but I don't know."

"What?" Missy shrieked and grabbed Meg's hand. "I need the details."

"There are really no details to give." Meg regretted bringing the subject up even more. "I already told you he fixed my dishwasher."

Missy nodded and leaned closer.

"When he finished we started talking and we had a—I don't know—a moment." She shook her head. "It's silly. We just got carried away, and nothing really happened, and nothing will ever happen again. I'd rather not talk about it."

Missy looked like she had more that she wanted to say but sighed instead. "Fine. I'll let you off the hook for now, but this subject is not closed forever."

"Great." Meg would worry about deflecting her sister later.

"I just have to say—"

Meg groaned.

"Listen," Missy insisted. "I don't think you should completely write off the possibility of something between you two. Remember, I've seen how he looks at you."

"Missy," Meg warned.

"That's it. I'm done." She took another sip of her lemonade and smiled teasingly. "So Larry came into the bank yesterday . . ."

PART FOUR

The Third Trimester

Chapter Twenty-eight

"Just make sure that there's enough water for everyone to drink," Tony Alvarez instructed Meg before he began to count the water bottles a second time. Meg knew that he was worried about being in charge that morning. Only fourteen years old, he had sped through scouting and was already doing his Eagle project.

Tom worked with him in scouts and had convinced Meg to help out. They were putting up a fence behind the church, separating the state land from the church land. Tony's counting ended, but he still stood poised by the refreshment table.

Meg took in the four five-gallon jugs of ice water and the fifteen packs of twenty-four water bottles. Even with the warm morning, they had plenty.

"I think we're going to be okay," she assured him.

Tom walked over and grabbed a donut from an open box. "The auger just got here, and the cement and poles are ready to go," he told Tony. "You need to start delegating tasks. The man with the auger will drill a hole at the places you marked this morning, someone will stick a pole in the freshly dug area, and then we'll fill a wheelbarrow with cement and shovel it around the pole."

Tony nodded and his gaze skittered back to the water bottles.

Tom pushed him toward the cement truck. "Meg will keep an eye on the water. Hey, guys," he yelled to two other young men standing around the donut box, "we need some manpower over here."

"Just a minute, Brother Baker," one of them called out through a mouthful of food. They refilled their cups with water from the jug and ran over to help.

As the morning drew on, Meg tapped her fingers on the table, pulled her hair into a ponytail, rechecked the nearly full water jugs, and then perched herself at the end of the table again. Meanwhile, everyone worked hard. Sweat and dirt streamed down faces. Muscles ached from continuous heavy lifting. Yet Meg sat, nearly as fresh as she'd been when they pulled into the church parking lot an hour before.

Spotting a full wheelbarrow waiting at a hole, she looked furtively around. Everyone was busy, and she didn't anticipate a run on the water. She slinked to Tom's truck and wrestled a shovel out of the bed.

Meg ran her hands over the smooth wood of the well-used shovel. It didn't look too hard to lift cement into the hole. It would give her something to do besides standing around. She needed to be useful.

"I can do this," she muttered as she dipped the end of her shovel into the grayish mixture in the red, rusty wheelbarrow. She then lifted the filled shovel and the contents plopped unceremoniously into the hole. Not bad.

Meg put her hand on her back and stretched it before trying for a second shovelful. She felt a small bead of sweat at her temple and ended her rest with satisfaction. Once again, she hefted the heavy shovel back into the wheelbarrow.

Matt pulled into the church parking lot and absently searched for Meg's car. Since he'd actually heard her singing the past several Sundays, he couldn't get her out of his mind. He'd wanted to talk to her about it, ask her what had changed, but each time he was tempted, he stopped himself. In the Gospel Essentials class, Meg wouldn't look at or talk to him unless he called on her, but he always looked forward to seeing her there. He unbuckled Lilia's booster seat, and then a sliver of disappointment stabbed him when he realized Meg's car wasn't there.

Matt dropped Lilia off with the other children and was looking for someone in charge when he spotted her. Meg stood at one of the fence-post holes, hefting a shovel into a wheelbarrow. She took one hand from the shovel and pushed back some stray curly hairs that had escaped her pony-tail. He saw her put her hand to her lower back and stretch before taking a deep breath and straightening her shoulders. When Matt realized her intention to lift the shovelful of cement from the wheelbarrow, he jogged over to her side.

"What do you think you're doing?"

Meg's wide blue eyes turned up toward him. "We're putting in a fence," she answered, using the side of the wheelbarrow as a fulcrum to lift the full shovel.

"I know what the project is." Matt took the shovel from her hands and let it fall back into the wheelbarrow. "You shouldn't be dragging a heavy wheelbarrow and lifting dense mounds of cement."

"What do you care? It's not like you're my doctor anymore."

Matt gritted his teeth. "I may not be your doctor, but I still care about you. I don't want you to hurt yourself. You need to be careful, Meg."

"I am being careful. I'm not filling the whole shovel up; I'm only lifting small amounts."

"Even small amounts are heavy."

"It's not that bad. You try it and see."

Matt took the proffered shovel and loaded it full of cement. He felt the muscles in his arms tense as he lifted it from the wheelbarrow and dumped the cement into the hole. One shovelful told him what he needed to know. It wouldn't be safe for Meg to do this.

He put the shovel back in the wheelbarrow, making sure to keep one hand on it. He caught Meg staring at him when he turned around, and her cheeks turned even more pink than they already were from being in the hot sun.

Meg cleared her throat and held her hand toward the shovel. "My turn."

Matt kept his grip on the wooden handle. "Meg, it's not safe."

"I'm only going to put a little cement on the shovel. I won't put as much on as you did." Her chin tilted as if preparing for battle.

Matt hesitated. He really couldn't force her not to work just because it worried him. "It's your decision, but I strongly advise against it."

"I want to help."

"There are other things you can do to help."

"Like what? Watch the water table?" She gestured to the refreshment area.

"You could help Tony's mom with the kids."

"I don't want to do that. They have too much energy for me." Meg looked over Matt's shoulder, and the fight from her expression dropped. She bit her lip, and Matt felt the urge to save the soft pink skin from the worry of her teeth. Stopping short of pulling her lip free with his, Matt tried to redirect his thoughts.

"Where's your boyfriend today?"

"What?" Meg's startled look met his.

"Johnny—is he here?"

Meg shifted and attacked her lip again. Matt almost groaned in self-restraint.

"He's not here." She paused. "I don't know how together we ever were, but we are definitely done now."

"Good," Matt said with an intensity that surprised him. Prompted by the injured look she gave him, he continued, "I never understood why you were with him. You're too good for him."

Meg gaze remained guarded. "Right." She said it slowly as if she didn't believe him.

"I'm serious, Meg." He paused, studying her distrusting face. Did she really not understand that she deserved better than Johnny?

"Come here," he said.

Meg allowed Matt to pull her closer to him. He dropped her arm and leaned toward her. "Maybe we can work together."

Meg looked over his shoulder at something behind him. "I thought we needed to keep our distance."

Matt dipped his head until his mouth rested by her ear. "I don't want to keep my distance, Meg. That's the problem."

Meg's head snapped up, her eyes wide.

Matt stepped back and grabbed the shovel. "I can't in good conscience watch you lift a heavy shovel again and again. We can take turns shoveling the cement into the hole, but you have to make sure that you only lift a small amount of cement. And you have to promise me that you'll stop when you get tired."

"There are other shovels in the truck. We can work at the same time."

"I'd rather share with you. That way I can make sure that you're taking breaks."

"It'll take longer this way."

"I'm not in a hurry." Matt shrugged. "Do you want to go first, or should I?"

Meg didn't answer for a time. Matt let the silence between them stretch, trying to interpret Meg's expression. Her eyes squinted as if assessing him and then finally softened into something that caused him to grip the handle of the shovel until his knuckles turned white.

"What?" he asked when she didn't look away.

"You're just being so nice. I don't know why I'm surprised. You're always nice to me."

"Is it such a change to have someone treat you nicely?"

Meg took the shovel from his hands and stuck it in the wheelbarrow, breaking their eye contact.

"No, not really. My family treats me well most of the time. When they acknowledge I'm there, you know. It's not all their fault. I push them away." She turned her back to Matt to empty the cement into the hole. "But you're not family."

"Why do you push your family away?"

"Because every time I'm with them I realize that I can't squeeze myself into their ideal mold. I just don't fit."

"They want you to be exactly like them?"

"Well, not exactly." She punctuated each word with a little shake of the shovel to get the last of the cement off.

She rested the end on the ground, out of breath, and Matt took the handle from her. She was winded but otherwise okay. Still, his concern prompted him to wait until her breathing evened before he began to fill the hole.

"What is it then?" he asked as he worked.

"I just see everything I'm missing when I'm with them. Look over there." She put her hand on his forearm and pointed discretely toward Tom and Missy. Missy was laughing at something Tom had said, and he looked down at her with pure adoration on his face.

"They're not newlyweds anymore, but you wouldn't know it just by looking at them. They've been married six years and have had their share of problems in that time.

"Missy can't have any more children," she continued to explain. "She had a difficult pregnancy and late miscarriage before Kaitlyn, and the doctor needed to remove one of her ovaries as a result. She finally conceived Kaitlyn but spent most of her pregnancy in the hospital. After she gave birth, the doctor talked to her about removing her other ovary. She and Tom wanted five kids, but now all they'll ever have is Kaitlyn. Yet, look at them. They're happy together in spite of their disappointments."

Matt leaned against the shovel and waited for Meg to finish. Her longing gaze didn't leave Missy and Tom. "Every time I'm with them it makes me think of what could've been."

"You can still have a relationship like theirs."

"Right." Sarcasm dripped from her tone as her look of yearning gave way to a sardonic smile. "My track record sure proves that. I've decided that there are no good men left in the world. They're all married or otherwise unavailable."

"Ouch." Matt rubbed his chest like she'd just hit him. "So that's what you think of me."

Meg laughed and snatched the shovel from Matt's hands. "You fall under that 'otherwise unattainable' category."

"Whew, that's a relief." Matt wiped his brow with mock relief. "So why do I fall under that category?"

Meg tucked some stray hairs behind her ears. Her eyes darted around behind him before landing on her feet. Still, she didn't finish her thought.

"What?" he encouraged with a small lift of his brow.

"Your wife," she finally said.

"My wife," he repeated, waiting for the pain that usually accompanied her memory to assault him. Unsettled when pain didn't pierce him to the core, he grasped at the memories of constant aching that had been his companion for so long. Then Meg, caught in the sun's glow, tipped her head with a wistful smile, and his aching fell through his clenched fingers like droplets of water.

"Yeah, I can just tell how much you loved her. If you ever decided to be with someone again, she would have to be an amazing person."

"She would," he agreed, still torn between holding onto his stinging loneliness and letting it all go for something more.

"So that's why you are 'otherwise unattainable' but still a good guy. I know I like being with you." She threw a guilty look in his direction as the words popped from her mouth.

Matt warmed at her sudden confession and relaxed his fists. "Thank you, Meg."

"Just don't let it go to your head."

"Too late."

Meg handed Matt the shovel and pushed him toward the hole. "Now are we going to stand and talk all day about my lack of a love life, or are we going to fill some holes?"

"Fill holes, ma'am," he said with a salute and a mirthful smile. He stuck the shovel in the wheelbarrow and peered over his shoulder at Meg. "For the record, I like being with you too."

Chapter Twenty-nine

"I think I need to take a break," Meg groaned as she clutched her aching side.

"Are you okay?" Matt set the shovel down and put his arm around her waist.

"I'm fine. I just need to sit down for a minute." In reality, she felt like something in her side was about to snap like a stretched-out rubber band, but she didn't want to appear overdramatic.

"There are some seats over here in the shade." Matt led her to an area that was set up like a makeshift nursery so the children could play without getting in the way.

Meg sat in a folding chair and felt the morning's work starting to catch up to her. Lilia waved to her from where she and Kaitlyn were playing a running game. Meg waved back halfheartedly, wishing for a strong blast of air conditioning in her face.

"I'll get you some water." Matt headed off in the direction of the refreshment tables. Meg couldn't help but watch him walk away. The sun cast the perfect glint on his dark hair, betraying just the slightest touch of gold. While they worked, she'd noticed how his muscles grew taut as he lifted the heavy shovelfuls of cement. It seemed impossible, but she believed he looked even better sweaty and casual than dressed up and put together for work. Almost, anyway.

"Thank you for coming, dear."

Meg reluctantly pulled her eyes away from Matt's retreating

form and looked up to see a sixty-something-year-old woman standing in front of her. She had an armful of chunky jewelry and short, spiky hair. This woman looked just spunky enough to get away with the combination.

"Tony's my grandson. Are you in his ward?"

"Yes. My brother-in-law is his Young Men's leader."

She nodded and gestured toward Meg's stomach. "So is this going to be your first baby?"

"It is."

"How far along are you?"

"About seven months."

"Oh! You seem so small." Meg could have kissed her spiky head for that comment. She felt anything but small with her stomach stretching the elastic on her maternity pants. "Do you know what you're having?"

"No, I want to be surprised."

"My daughters could never wait to find out. I don't think I could've either if they had that technology back when I had my kids. I've never been a patient person."

Tony's grandmother looked up at something to Meg's right and leaned down quickly. "That husband of yours sure is a handsome man," she said in a conspiratorial tone.

"What?" Meg asked, thrown off guard.

"Try to drink all this water, Meg. Are you feeling any better?" Matt passed her the water cup and placed his strong, sinewy hand gently behind her neck.

"I'm feeling a lot better," Meg said as she mentally willed Tony's grandmother away from them before she said anything embarrassing.

Matt noticed her standing there and held out his free hand. "Matt Wilkes."

"Sonja Alvarez. I've just been getting acquainted with your wife here. She's such a darling girl. You take good care of her." She patted Matt on the arm.

He looked more amused than surprised.

"We're not married, but I do try to take care of her. She's a tough one, though. She pushes herself too hard." His thumb rubbed Meg's shoulder, and she began to feel light-headed as all the blood rushed from everywhere in her body and straight to where his hand was.

"Oh?" Sonja raised her eyebrows. "And why aren't you married?" she asked Matt, pointedly looking at Meg's stomach and back at him.

"He's not the baby's father," Meg broke in, mortified. "I'm divorced. We're just friends."

"Friends," she nodded and winked at Meg. "It's just a matter of time, then." She faced Matt, "I was watching you two out there fill your holes. It was so sweet to see you working together. I can tell you love her. You two have *it*."

"It?" Matt asked. Meg buried her face in her cup and pretended she was drinking the last miniscule drop that slowly flowed from the bottom onto her tongue.

Sonja winked at Meg. "She knows. Don't you, honey?" Sonja looked at her until Meg moved her head in a way that Sonja might have been able to construe as a nod. Someone called Sonja's name over by the trenches, and she waved at Meg and Matt as she walked away.

"Matt," Meg said, humiliated beyond belief. "I am so sorry."

Matt waved good-bye as the small woman walked away from them. "Why?"

"I can't believe she thought we were married."

"We've been working together all morning. It was an easy assumption."

"I'm so embarrassed," Meg groaned. "And then she was talking about how much you love me. I wanted to crawl into my cup and drown."

"Is the thought of me loving you so devastating?"

Meg ignored his attempt to tease away her humiliation. "I'm more worried about what people will think of you."

"Meg," Matt crouched in front of her chair and took her hands. "Worse things have been assumed of me than my being in love with a wonderful woman."

Meg got lost for a moment in the sincerity of his gaze. Her heart started to beat wildly, and she fought the urge to lean closer to him. Forcing a laugh, she pulled her hands away from his. His closeness was making her flustered. She was having a hard time thinking straight.

"Wow." She cleared her throat. "No wonder I like hanging out with you so much."

"Same here."

Meg was starting to feel breathless under his direct stare when he jumped up.

"But there's just one thing I want to know."

"What?" Meg asked

"What is the 'it' Sonja was talking about?"

"How should I know?"

"You agreed with her that we had 'it.'"

"I'd have agreed to anything to get her to leave." Meg looked for more salvation from her cup, but amazingly enough, no water had mysteriously appeared to refill it and give her an excuse to drink instead of talk.

Matt snatched her cup from her hand. "I'm getting you some more water and taking you home."

"How do you know I didn't drive myself here?"

"I didn't see your car in the parking lot when we drove up," he said as he walked away.

Interesting. He'd looked for her car when he came. Maybe he was just doing a scan to see who was going to be there. Probably. Still, she could think what she wanted, although recently her ego was becoming smaller in proportion to her growing stomach.

"Are you ready to go?" Matt's low voice interrupted her search for confidence.

She took a deep breath and used his outstretched hand to pull herself up to standing. "More than ready. I just need to tell Missy I'm leaving."

"I already told her. She was getting a drink when I went over to the table."

"Thanks." Meg rested her hand behind her back and groaned. "Do you know how lucky you are that you never have to be pregnant?"

"Trust me, women remind me of that fact all the time."

"I love feeling the baby move. But some of this other stuff," she made a large circle around her stomach, "not so fun."

Matt laughed and put his hand on the small of her back to lead her to his car. Lilia waved good-bye to her friends and ran over to them. It surprised Meg that she didn't throw more of a fit. She mentioned it to Matt.

Matt smiled as he opened the car door for Meg. "It's a little parent trick I'm sure you'll learn pretty quickly."

"Oh? What is that?"

He leaned in close enough for her to smell his minty breath. She could see the amusement in his eyes by the way they crinkled slightly at the edges. Her face flushed as she wondered what it would be like to kiss him. She forced herself not to look at his lips and to even out her ragged breathing.

"Bribery," he said conspiratorially.

"Hmm?" She managed to get through her muddled brain. She totally failed in her efforts not to look at his mouth. Just a few inches closer, and she would know.

"Bribery," he repeated, a little louder. "You'll see. It works every time. You shouldn't use it too much or it loses its effectiveness. But every once in a while . . ."

His words jarred her gaze from his lips. She was seriously losing it. She needed to get home and lock the doors.

"So what did you bribe her with?" she forced out hoarsely when she realized he was looking at her as if waiting for some kind of response. She coughed to relieve the tightness in her throat.

"Lunch at McDonald's. Are you up to coming with us? We could stop at the drive-through on the way to your house."

There was a good chance she would lose what was left of her sanity if she spent another minute in Matt's presence.

"Wouldn't Lilia rather eat there so she could crawl around in the play place?"

"I think she would rather play with Cliff. But if you're not up for it, we'll come over some other time for her to play."

Meg leaned back even more as she thought about the invitation. Being alone in her house for even one more minute did not sound appealing. Yet, with the way her pregnancy hormones were flaring up, maybe it wasn't such a good idea. And she still hurt a little from his rejection after they almost kissed.

"So are we friends again?"

Remorse passed across Matt's face. "We always were. I just needed some time to work things out."

"Did you work them out, then?"

He nodded his head slowly. "I think so."

"Okay. Then I'd love to have you two over for lunch." Her breathing hitched again when Matt's fingers brushed across her cheek. They lingered at the corner of her mouth for a moment.

"You had a little dirt there," he said, brushing his thumb across her bottom lip. Meg thought her heart might leap right out of her chest.

"When are we going to go?" Lilia's head popped up from the backseat.

Matt quirked an eyebrow at Meg before dropping his hand.

"Right now, sweetie. Climb into your seat."

Chapter Thirty

Meg set her scriptures down on a bench and scanned the chapel for Matt and Lilia. She needed to get ready to lead the music soon but wanted to give Lilia a picture she'd printed that morning. She looked down at it again, loving the wide smile on Lilia's face as she kept her arm around Cliff.

"Hey, Meg."

Meg gripped the picture tighter and turned to Johnny. "Hey."

"We need to talk."

"About what?"

"About what happened at the hospital."

"That was months ago, and you want to talk about it now? I think we said everything that needed to be said."

Johnny looked around the room and dropped his voice to a whisper, "Look, Sam won't be a problem anymore. We are definitely over now. Let's go somewhere and talk."

Meg's irritation flared. "I can't, Johnny." She pulled her hand away from him. "They need me to lead the music."

"Someone else can lead just this once."

"But I don't really want to talk to you."

"Sorry to interrupt, Meg, but Lilia wanted me to ask you if she can come see Cliff sometime this week."

Meg sighed with relief as Matt stood next to her. "Sure. I should be home most evenings, and I don't have anything going on next weekend."

"You're sure it's okay?"

"You know you two are always welcome. Cliff will be ecstatic."

"How are you?" Matt extended his hand toward Johnny for a brief handshake.

Johnny snorted in disgust as his eyes darted back and forth between Meg and Matt. "Never mind," he said, ignoring Matt's question. "I can see you're still too preoccupied to talk to me."

"What's that supposed to mean?" Matt asked, an edge appearing in his voice.

"Yes, come to her rescue. The high and mighty doctor ruins our relationship and then swoops in to help the girl."

"What are you talking about?"

"Meg didn't tell you? Maybe you aren't as close as I thought."

Meg glared at Johnny. "Leave it alone."

He ignored her. "Meg broke up with me because of you."

"It's not the way it sounds," Meg said furiously. "You read too much into mine and Matt's friendship, and you insulted my character and Matt's integrity."

"Friendship?" he pointed to Matt's hand resting on Meg's back.

Meg shook her head at Johnny. "I don't think we have anything more we need to say."

"You're right. There is nothing more to say. Forget that I wanted to talk to you. I'm better off without you." Johnny angrily walked down the aisle and left the chapel.

Meg blinked away the sting of Johnny's words. They shouldn't have come as a surprise to her. Hadn't her ex-husband basically felt the same way? Maybe all men would.

"Are you okay?" Matt asked once Johnny left the building.

"I'm fine. He's just a jerk. Forget about him," she said, trying to convince herself as well as Matt. She absently handed Matt the picture of Lilia. Meg started to walk away but felt her hand suddenly pulled back toward Matt.

"Hey, it's Lilia's birthday in a couple of weeks, and I'm not sure what kind of present I should get her. Would you be willing to go to the store with me on Friday night?"

"Sure."

"I'll pick you up at six then."

"All right," Meg agreed. She let her hand swing down from Matt's and felt the cool air touch it. They'd been together many times with Lilia, but this was the first time he'd ever asked her to do something with just him. She smiled shyly at him and walked away, excitement replacing her former dejection.

❦

Matt threw his scrubs in the wash and pulled a dark blue polo shirt and a pair of cargo shorts out of the dryer. He ran a hand over his chin, glad he'd had time to shave that morning before work.

Sarah and Lilia sat at the table, each scribbling on a page out of a coloring book. He smelled garlic bread cooking and saw steam rising from a boiling pot of water on the stove. His stomach growled, and he knew he was going to have to add dinner to his and Meg's plans.

Matt leaned over Lilia and gave her a hug. She pressed her cheek into his chest and resumed coloring.

"I shouldn't be too late tonight. Thanks for staying," Matt said to Sarah.

"Hey, for what you're paying me, I'll stay as long as you want." She smiled and got up from the table. She lifted the lid on the spaghetti sauce and took a wooden spoon from a canister on the counter to stir it. "Go have fun on your date," she urged him, putting the lid back on the sauce.

Calling it a date was a stretch, but Matt liked how the words sounded, so he didn't correct Sarah. "See ya, Lils." He waited for a crayon-filled hand to wave at him before he let the door shut.

Matt backed the car out of the garage and started driving toward Meg's place. He knew it was low to use his daughter's birthday as an excuse to spend more time with Meg, but he couldn't bring himself to feel bad about it.

He parked his car at Meg's house and knocked on the door. Cliff's barking began almost instantly, and a few seconds later he heard Meg ordering Cliff to sit. She opened the door and stuck her head through the crack. "Let me put Cliff in the backyard." She closed the door and reopened it less than a minute later.

Her curly brown hair folded over her shoulders in soft ringlets that contrasted her pale yellow shirt. Matt couldn't take his eyes off her as she turned her back to him to lock the front door. He smelled some type of flowery perfume and resisted the urge to move closer to her.

"Have you decided what you want to get Lilia?" Meg asked as he opened the car door for her. She slid into her seat, and Matt got in on his side before answering.

"Not yet. She needs clothes, but I don't know what she'd like. I'm sure she'll want some type of girly toys. A doll maybe?"

"Where do you want to go?"

"The mall." Matt had already decided. The thirty-minute drive with Meg in the car was reason enough to want to drive into Tucson to do his shopping. She agreed that this was a good idea and settled in for the ride.

The drive passed in companionable conversation that was only interrupted a few times by Matt's persistently loud stomach. Meg laughed when it growled once again as they pulled into a parking spot. "I think we'd better find somewhere to eat first, before your stomach starts eating itself."

"Good idea." He opened Meg's car door and took her hand as they walked toward the mall. He interlocked his fingers with hers and couldn't hide a smile as he felt her delicate fingers clasp tightly between his.

They decided to go to a Baja grill inside the mall. Matt hated letting go of Meg's hand so that they could sit on opposite sides of the booth, but they quickly attacked the chips and salsa that the waitress delivered to their table.

"Tell me about your wife," Meg said after the waiter brought their meals.

Matt automatically moved his thumb to his ring finger to rub it against his wedding band before remembering that he'd pulled it off earlier that week. "She was the only person I ever met that would make goals and then always complete them. She was organized; everything had to be in its place at all times. Our house was always spotless. She put a lot of pressure on herself to be perfect. Yet, she knew how short life could be, so she always made sure that Lilia and I knew how she felt about us."

Matt took a drink of water before continuing. "Her dad died of a drug overdose before she was born, and her mom died of breast cancer when she was nineteen. I'd known Lydia most of her life, and I'd just gotten home from my mission when her mom died. We were married two months later."

"Wow," Meg said, setting down her fork. "That's quick."

"We knew it was right. We were in love. She was all alone, and she needed me."

"Your mom told me you've always liked to take care of people," she said, her voice strained. Then she seemed to shake off her weird change in mood. "Is it too personal to ask why you didn't have more children?" Meg took a drink of her soda, her blue eyes piercing Matt to the core.

He cleared his throat. "We waited until I was almost done with medical school to have Lilia. Lydia never really had a chance to do what she wanted while she was growing up. Her mother found out about the cancer when Lydia was fourteen, and from that time on, Lydia cared for her mom. After we got married, she needed some time to learn who she was without having to take care of someone."

"But she had you," Meg pointed out.

"Yes. But I did everything I could to make sure that she got to have new experiences and freedom from cares to just discover what she wanted to do with her life. I never pressured her to have children, and at times I thought that it might never happen. When she told me that she was pregnant with Lilia, it was one of the happiest days of my life."

Matt paused, debating if she should tell Meg the rest. He'd never told anyone before, but when she reached across the table and wound her fingers through his, he decided that maybe he should.

"Lydia was pregnant when she died."

"Oh, Matt . . ."

"She was in her first trimester. No one knew. There was so much to deal with that I couldn't add one more tragedy to the list."

Meg's grip tightened on his hand, and he watched as she brushed a fallen tear from her cheek. Matt swallowed his emotion and let the silence rest between them.

"You didn't tell anyone?" Meg finally asked.

"Not until now. You're the only other person who knows everything I lost that day."

Meg set her fork down and slid out of her bench. She sat down next to him and wrapped her arms around his waist. Matt hugged her tight against his chest, wishing they weren't in a crowded restaurant but somewhere quiet and private where he could hold her tight and never let go.

Meg pulled back when the waiter stopped by their table to fill their water glasses. She turned her flushed face toward the table, and Matt reluctantly let her go.

"I guess we should finish eating," she said, going back to her side of the table.

"Thank you for listening, Meg. I didn't mean to go on about my wife."

"You can talk to me anytime, Matt. It sounds like she was an amazing woman."

"She was."

Matt wanted to move the conversation to lighter topics, so he asked her about her classes, and a smile lit her face again. He laughed as she told him about some of the funny things her students did. The rest of their meal flew by, and Matt was surprised when the waiter brought him their check.

As they left the restaurant, Meg surprised him by sliding her arm around his waist and hugging him with her head against his shoulder.

"Thank you, Matt."

"For what?"

"For telling me about your wife. For being my friend."

Matt looked at her for a moment before he slowly bent down and put his mouth by her ear. His senses went wild when he absorbed her perfume and her smooth skin against his chin. "Haven't you realized yet how much I like being with you?"

He gave into the urge to kiss her cheek. Her eyes widened, but he just grabbed her hand and began pulling her toward the stores. "C'mon. Let's go get Lilia's presents."

Chapter Thirty-one

*M*eg noticed the unfamiliar car in her driveway as Matt turned the corner onto her street. It was a bright blue, Mustang convertible. Too flashy and pricey for anyone she knew.

"Are you expecting someone?" Matt asked as he pulled into the driveway alongside the car.

"No. I don't know whose it is, and I don't see anyone by the door."

She waited while Matt got out of the car and walked around to open her door. Again his words from earlier that night crashed down on her while she watched him walk around the car. He'd explained that he married his wife because she was alone and needed him. She finally understood why he wanted to be her friend. He couldn't resist a person in need. She was someone he could fix.

He opened her door and held his hand out to her. When she slipped her cold hand into his warm one, and he tugged her against him, she didn't care *why* he wanted to be with her. She was just glad he was there.

"So do you think I got too much?" Matt asked as Meg rifled through her purse to find her keys.

"Yes." Meg looked up from her search to smile at him. "But she's going to love everything. And it's hard to count the clothes as gifts. Those were needed."

Matt laughed. "Thanks for helping me justify spending all that money tonight."

"It's what I do best," Meg said before she finally found her keys wedged in the pages of her never-used day planner.

Matt slipped his fingers in the edge of her purse. "What in the world do you have in there?"

"Nothing." Meg pulled her purse a little closer to her body.

"Really . . ." Matt stepped closer, and Meg backed away until she bumped into the wall. She put the purse behind her back, not stopping to wonder why she was baiting him.

Matt leaned in and reached around her back teasingly. He grabbed the bag with one hand, so she pulled it to the other side of her body, and he reached his other arm behind her as well. She stifled a nervous giggle as both of his arms came around her and gripped the purse behind her back.

"Now, this is a predicament," she said, biting her lip.

"No," Matt said as his glance dropped to her mouth. "This is right where I want to be."

Meg's breath caught in her chest, and she felt a pleasant shiver run down her spine as she saw desire flicker in Matt's eyes. He slowly leaned closer, and her eyelids fluttered shut.

"Isn't this cozy?"

Matt jerked his head up and turned toward the voice that Meg had thought she would never hear again.

"Austin," Meg whispered. She took in his blond wavy hair and straight smile that didn't quite reach his granite eyes.

He stood in the open doorway of Meg's house, leaning against the post. His gaze traveled down Meg's body, halting at her rounded stomach.

"What are you doing in my house?" Meg asked coldly.

"I thought this was our house, honey."

Meg folded her arms over her stomach when she noticed his gaze falling to it again. "I didn't realize I was going to have to change the locks after the divorce. I thought you'd be too preoccupied with your new wife to worry about pestering me."

"I'm not pestering you. Who's this guy?"

"None of your business."

"I'm trying to be polite. I want to know your friends." His voice had an edge to it that Meg hadn't heard before.

"Austin, why are you here?" Meg asked, furious that they were having this conversation with Austin in the house and her standing outside. Her feet and legs were killing her from walking around the mall, and she needed to use the restroom.

"She needs to get inside," Matt barked when Meg leaned into him. Austin moved aside so that Matt and Meg could slip past him. "Should I call the police?" Matt murmured against Meg's ear.

"He won't hurt me."

"There are more ways to hurt a person than physically."

Austin sat in his favorite recliner when he went into the living room. The chair rocked back as he rested his ankle on his knee in a relaxed pose. Meg tried to pull away from Matt and head toward the hall, but he wouldn't relinquish his hold.

"I need to go to the bathroom," she whispered.

Matt released her, but she felt his gaze as she walked down the hall. She worried about leaving the two men together but hoped they would be civil. Austin should be too laid-back to get into a fight, and Matt was too responsible. But both had looked like they were on the verge of losing their cool just moments before.

When Meg came back, she steeled herself for a fight. "Tell me what you're doing here, Austin."

"Let's talk about this privately."

"No."

"Please, Meg."

Meg let herself fall briefly into his ocean blue eyes and found herself capitulating. "Fine. We can talk in the kitchen." She lagged behind until Austin left the room. "Will you stay?" she asked Matt.

"I'm not going anywhere."

Meg impulsively leaned over the couch armrest and gave him a hug. She pulled away before he had time to put his arms around her.

"What's going on with you two?" Austin drilled as soon as Meg stepped into the kitchen.

"How many times do I have to tell you that it's none of your business?"

"It *is* my business. I love you, Meg."

"I'm sure you do."

"Really, I do. I was a fool. I admit it. We had something good together, and I blew it. I just want to talk, work things out."

"What, no note this time?" she began bitterly. "That was real classy, Austin. Way to show how much you love me by dumping me without even a word."

The baby kicked her soundly, and Meg put a hand on her stomach with a gasp. Austin put his hand on her shoulder.

"Are you okay?"

"Don't touch me."

"I want to be with you."

"I want you to leave." Meg pushed him away from her and moved to the other side of the kitchen. "You cannot use your key on my house."

"This used to be our house."

"Used to be." She emphasized his words. "So are you just here to flatter me with words of undying love?"

Austin took a deep breath and drummed his fingers on the counter. "I left Carmen."

"Oh, did she get pregnant too?"

"Meg." Austin sighed in frustration. "I didn't know you were pregnant when I left. Carmen and I didn't click. I think she was seeing someone else."

"You're not looking for pity from me, are you?"

"No, that's not why I'm here. I can't stop thinking about you. About what we had. I never had that with her. I guess I—"

"Stop." Meg held up a hand.

Austin ignored her and grabbed the hand she held up. "I guess I never stopped loving you. And seeing you pregnant with this baby, our baby . . . Meg, it's incredible."

Meg yanked her hand away from Austin. "So you want the baby now. When my lawyer called you to tell you I was pregnant, you wanted me to get an abortion."

"I didn't know what to think. I thought you were using birth control. I figured this was some stunt to trap us in a relationship. None of that matters now. I want you back."

"What makes you think I want you back?"

"You love me. I know you do. That doesn't just go away."

"I did love you. And maybe sometimes I still do," she acknowledged. "But I don't trust you. I don't like you. I don't like what you did to me, to my self-esteem, my personality, my life."

"Give me a chance to prove to you—"

"To prove what? That you'll stay until the next Carmen comes along? Austin, I could never trust you again. Every time you leave the house, I'll doubt if you're really going where you say you are. When you're late coming home from work, I'll have to wonder if you're coming home at all. If I call, I'll wonder if you've changed your number. If I get pregnant again, I'll wonder if you want me to get an abortion?"

"It won't be like that. I know I made some mistakes, but I'm still the same Austin you fell in love with."

"But I'm not the same Meg," she said quietly.

Austin paced before coming to a stop inches from where Meg stood. He put a hand on either side of her, trapping her against the counter.

"I will be a part of your life, Meg" he threatened before crushing his lips against hers.

Meg gripped the counter when Austin broke away from her. He left without a backward glance, slamming the door behind him.

"You okay?"

Meg's head flew up when she heard Matt's voice from the kitchen doorway. She rubbed her forehead and pushed away from the counter. "Sure, fine."

"What happened?"

"He said he still loves me." She shuffled past him in a daze, and he grabbed her arm.

"Wait . . ." he said.

She looked down at his hand on her arm. He let go of her and brushed some of her hair out of her face. A pleasant shiver traveled down her spine when his knuckles grazed her cheek. When she didn't move away, he leaned closer. Matt's warm lips covered hers in a soft kiss that deepened when Meg wrapped her arms around his neck.

"Meg," he murmured against her mouth. "Please tell me you

don't still love him."

Meg drew back and put her fingers over her trembling lips. "No, no." She shook her head. "I don't know."

"You can't seriously be thinking of going back to him after everything he put you through." Matt pulled her close to him again.

"I need time to think."

"What is there to think about? He left you. That's reason enough to not give him another chance."

"That's easy for you to say." Meg pulled her arm away and began walking to the door. She heard Matt behind her, and she swiveled back toward him. "And what if Lydia came back? Wouldn't you want to have her if you could?"

"It's different, and you know it."

Meg regretted making the comparison. Before she could apologize, Matt pulled her into his arms again.

"I wish you could see yourself how I see you. You've grown so much, come so far since he left. You don't need him. I don't understand why you'd even need to think about it."

He kissed her again, and tears built up behind her eyes. She pulled back and buried her head in his chest, groaning as confusion swirled around her. "You don't want me. I'm broken."

"I *do* want you. I want you any way you come."

Meg shook her head. "No, I know you. You're a nurturer. You think I need you, so you want to fix me."

"That's not true."

Meg pulled away from him and opened the front door. "Please, go."

"Meg—"

"You can't fix everything, Matt."

A chill spread through Meg when Matt pulled away and left without another word. She stayed in the doorway but averted her gaze when he looked back at her one more time. It was safer to make him go before he rejected her too. Her bruised heart wouldn't be able to recover from it. The sound of him shutting his car door echoed long after he drove away.

Chapter Thirty-two

*M*eg's phone was her new enemy.

Austin called every day, leaving messages about how much he loved her and wanted her back. She eventually stopped listening to them. He had come back to the house once, but she'd threatened him with a restraining order and hadn't seen him since.

Meg groaned when the phone rang again. She saw Matt's name on the caller ID and put the phone face-down on the table.

He'd been trying to call her for several days, but she ignored every call. She listened to his voice messages, though. She was weak.

Her phone beeped, indicating that Matt had left a message. She dialed in the voice mail service and berated herself as she lifted the phone to her ear.

"Hey, Meg. I know you don't want to talk to me. I'm going to take the hint and stop calling you so much. I need you to know that I think you're perfect the way you are. I really do not want to fix you, or whatever you're thinking." He paused for a moment. "I want to see you. Please call me."

She knew he deserved to hear from her but she wouldn't know what to say. Her lips still tingled when she thought of their kiss. Her feelings for him were starting to grow stronger and would only end in her getting her heart broken anyway.

Meg found the sister missionaries right after sacrament meeting so that she could walk with them into the Gospel Essentials class.

Meg plied Sister Harrison with questions about the MTC as they walked into the classroom, making sure to keep her eyes averted from the front of the class. She felt Matt watching her, and her face grew warm when she again recalled their kiss.

She opened her manual, torn between relief and disappointment when Matt didn't come and talk to her. Then she fiddled with one corner, fanning the pages against her fingers.

"Today we are going to talk about the Atonement," Matt began as the class quieted. "Why is the Atonement necessary for our salvation?"

He turned to the board to write some scriptures for the class to look up, and Meg took the opportunity to study him. It hadn't been that long since she'd last seen him, but she drank in the sight of his broad shoulders and thick brown hair. Meg followed the course of his long fingers as he pulled at the neck of his suit coat. Startled, she realized that he had removed his wedding band.

Matt unexpectedly turned from the board and caught Meg staring at him. She averted her eyes and picked at an imaginary piece of lint on her skirt. Her breathing sped up just at the accidental glance they shared.

Meg spent the rest of the lesson studying the picture in her manual of Christ kneeling in Gethsemane while she listened to Matt. Her heart warmed as he explained the principles of the Atonement, and for the first time, Meg began to realize that it was important for her individually.

"Meg, could you please read Alma 7:11 for us?"

"'And he shall go forth, suffering pains and afflictions and temptations of every kind; and this that the word might be fulfilled which saith he will take upon him the pains and the sicknesses of his people.'" She read through the scripture again, recalling the pains she'd experienced throughout the past year. She looked up at Matt as she was struck with hopeful understanding.

"The Atonement is all-encompassing. Christ not only suffered for our sins, but for our hurts, pains, sicknesses, and sorrows. He loves each and every one of us individually and wants us to come to him with enough faith to let the Atonement work in our lives."

Their eyes met as Matt finished speaking. From the corner of her eye, she saw one of the sister missionaries raise her hand. He paused for a moment before tearing his gaze away from Meg to call on the sister.

Meg let out the deep breath she'd been holding and listened to the discussion flow around her. Matt's words and the scripture she read went through her mind for the rest of class. Disappointment stung when Matt didn't attempt to talk to her following the closing prayer. She slipped from the classroom, looking back at him one last time, but their gazes didn't meet again.

When she got home, she carefully pulled the picture of Christ kneeling in Gethsemane from her manual. Finding an old frame in the closet, she stuck the picture in it and placed it in the kitchen where she would see it often. Looking at it again, she thought about the Atonement, wishing she had enough faith to let go of her hurt so that Christ could heal her.

Matt was trying to give Meg some space.

He paced the kitchen with the phone in his hands. Lilia was already asleep for the night, and Matt debated calling Meg. He hadn't expected to feel pain gnawing at his heart at Meg's absence from his life, but he did. He hadn't talked to her in several weeks. Seeing her in church every Sunday almost alleviated his longing, but the silence between them made it harder to watch her run from the classroom immediately following the lesson, as if she was afraid he'd talk to her.

He needed to figure out how he was going to convince Meg that he didn't want to fix her. She said that she wanted time to think, and he needed to respect that. Putting down the phone, he picked up his joint knife to slap putty on the walls in the living room. He ran the tool with the thick putty over the gouges until they were smoothed from sight. Working his way steadily across the wall, he filled in the holes, bit by bit. The tension eased from his shoulders, and he sat back on his heels to take a break.

He fingered the tool in his hand, thinking about Meg's accusation. The words shot in his mind: *You can't fix everything.* He ran his hand across one of the gouges in front of him. He did like to fix things—to help people. That was why he became a doctor.

But it was not why he was in love with Meg.

He fell back into the rhythm of filling holes with putty, leaving the one deep gouge alone. When he finished, he stepped back and felt satisfaction in the one imperfection left. It gave the wall character, it gave it story. It reminded him of his devastation when he first walked into this house and discovered its condition. It held the story of how fixing up this house had been a journey of healing for Matt. He laughed when he remembered Meg noticing the gashes on his walls the first time she came over. Most of all, it bore a poignant reminder that although he liked to fix things and help people, he was not the ultimate Healer.

He set his joint knife down on the counter and put the lid on the putty. His life didn't feel right without Meg. He needed to find a way to show her how much he cared for her and loved her for who she was.

PART FIVE

The Delivery

Chapter Thirty-three

*M*eg awoke with an uncomfortable tightness in her abdomen. She put a hand on her taut stomach until it relaxed a few seconds later.

A dry mouth and an urge to go to the bathroom propelled Meg from bed. Her bare footsteps on the carpet and kitchen tile rustled through the silent house.

Meg filled her glass with water from the fridge and took it with her to the bathroom. She checked out her reflection in the mirror. In profile, it looked like she had stuffed a basketball under her shirt. Her stomach had made up for lost time and grown huge during the past month. She felt the consequences of a full pregnant belly everywhere. Her back ached, her ankles had swelled, and her energy dried up long before the end of the day.

Her stomach tightened again as she studied her image. She put her hand on the counter and bent over in pain, her fingers curling over the cool marble edge. The aching gradually eased, and she straightened her back with a stretch.

Dr. Cohen told her that the preparatory Braxton Hicks contractions could be painful, and they definitely did not make her look forward to real contractions. She had already told the doctor that she wanted pain meds the minute she stepped foot in the hospital.

Meg tossed and turned the rest of the night, only catching sleep in little portions here and there. Her whole body ached by the time light streamed through her window. Pulling the quilt over her head, she decided that there was no way she was going to church after the night she'd just had. She knew she needed to call someone to lead the music for her, but she'd left her cell phone plugged into the charger in the kitchen. It would just have to wait.

Meg's phone rang a few hours later, but the thought of hauling her body out of bed to get it did not appeal to her. Whoever called would just have to leave a message. She curled up into a ball when a really hard contraction split across her abdomen. The thought that had been flittering in the back of her mind most of the morning forced its way through.

This couldn't be real labor. Her due date was a month away. Her water hadn't broken yet. She didn't own one baby item. There was no bag packed. She didn't even have a plan.

She moaned as the hardest contraction yet hit her lower abdomen like a punch to the stomach. She held her breath for as long as she could and let it out in a gasp before taking another deep breath. Her toes curled under the thick blanket, and she buried her face in the soft folds of the pillow.

"Okay." She breathed heavily and swung her feet from the bed. "I need to call someone."

She shuffled to the kitchen where her phone was plugged into the charger. The shifting of the lock on the front door begged her attention, but she doubled over with a moan before she could see who came in.

"Meg, we are going to talk this time. No more avoiding me." Austin's arrogant voice could hardly be heard over Cliff's barking.

"What can I do to make you go away?" Meg's aching added a healthy harshness to her words. She shook his hand off her back and moved away from him.

"I'm not going away this time, Meg. I'm here to stay. I don't know how to make you believe me except by proving to you that I won't leave this time." Austin's eyes held shadows, and it looked like it had been too long since his hair had seen a comb or his face a razor.

Meg shuffled out of the kitchen, slumping into the couch when she reached the living room. Austin wisely sat in the recliner across from her and rubbed the back of his neck. "I feel like I haven't slept in weeks. You won't answer any of my phone calls. I had to come see you in person again. Tell me what I can do to get you back, and I'll do it."

"Just leave me alone," she pleaded as another contraction hit. She hunched over in a dry heave as the pain wrenched her stomach.

Austin jumped up from the recliner with a disgusted expression. "I'll come back later . . ."

Meg looked up at his pale face as he edged toward the door.

"Austin, I think I'm in labor." She wanted to kick herself for whimpering. She couldn't show any weakness in front of him. She needed to prove to him that she was strong, that she could handle this. "Get my phone for me. I dropped it on the floor in the kitchen."

Austin handed it to her a few seconds later and then retreated to his position in front of the door. Meg waited for another painful contraction to pass before she called her mom's house. The answering machine picked up after five rings. Calling her mom's cell phone yielded the same results. She rested her head against the armrest of the couch as tears filled her eyes. Where was her mom? She dialed the house again and let it ring twice before she remembered.

It was Sunday. Her mom was at church.

Austin was going to have to take her to the hospital. The man who wasn't there the whole time she was pregnant, who left her right when she needed him the most, was going to swoop in and save the day. She wanted him out of her life, not more deeply imbedded in it.

She buried her face in her hands and allowed her tears to fall. This was not how having a baby was supposed to be. It should be happy and exciting with loved ones all around. Thankfully, Austin didn't try to comfort her while she reconciled herself to the reality of her life. She silently said a prayer for strength and wiped her eyes on the sleeve of her shirt.

"I need you to take me to the hospital."

Austin pulled out his keys from his pocket. He jogged to the car and got in while Meg waddled out of the house. She opened his car door, a sarcastic thanks for his help on the tip of her tongue, when a familiar car pulled in behind Austin's.

"Mom?" Meg stumbled away from Austin's car and into her mom's arms.

"What's wrong?" her mom's voice held a hint of alarm as she pulled back from Meg's embrace to study her face.

"Meg thinks she's in labor." Austin's words trailed off as her mom's venom-filled glare hit him.

"Let's get to the hospital," she said, ushering Meg to her car.

"I don't have a bag packed."

"Missy can pack a bag for you before she comes to the hospital."

"I'll follow you over there." Austin jumped back into his car.

Meg and her mom ignored him.

Meg felt another contraction hit and held her mom's hand until it passed.

"How did you know, Mom?"

Meg's mom looked over at her, releasing a heavy sigh.

"All morning I felt like I should call to check up on you, but every time I went to pick up the phone, something happened. Your dad spilled orange juice on his shirt. Then a lady I visit teach called and asked me to substitute for her Primary class. And then I couldn't get my curling iron to turn on. Finally I figured I would just talk to you at church.

"I didn't see you when we got there, and by the time Bishop Miller began announcements I started to worry. I had decided that I would stop by your house after church to see if you were sick when I felt impressed that I needed to go to your house."

"You left church to check on me?" Meg's disbelief echoed through her tone.

"Of course. Nothing could make me ignore such a strong feeling that you needed me. I kept thinking the worst."

Meg ingested all that her mother told her. She leaned over and hugged her as tight as she could without compromising her mother's driving.

"Speaking of the worst, what's Austin doing at your house? Did he do something to put you into labor?" Her controlled tone barely belied the anger that showed on her face.

"No." Meg paused. "He wants to get back together."

"And what do you think about that?"

"Oh, Mom," Meg cried. "I wanted it so badly for so long. I dreamed that he would come back to me, and we could get together again—raise this baby like a real family, you know? Instead of being born into divorce, this baby could have a mom and dad. But I can't do it. I am in a different place now than when we were married. If he hadn't left me for another woman, I'd have done everything I could to keep us together, but he did. He left, and I changed my life. I don't want to go back to how things were."

"Hmm." Her mom swerved into the next lane.

"You don't think I should give Austin another chance, do you?"

"Heavens no. You're right. You've changed a lot since he left, and I can tell that you finally like yourself. If I'm not mistaken, though, there's another man out there who wants to have a chance."

Meg turned toward the window. "I don't know, Mom. I'm not sure anyone would want to deal with everything I would bring into a marriage."

"I can't speak for him, Meg. But I'll tell you this—I wasn't the only one who was worried when you weren't at church. In fact, I was surprised not to see Matt Wilkes's car pull in behind mine when I got to your house."

Meg glanced at her muted reflection in the tinted car window, mulling over her mother's words. Another contraction hit, and she heard the car moan as her mom accelerated.

"Don't go into labor in this car. I don't know how to deliver a baby."

Meg kept her hands folded over her aching stomach and concentrated on her breathing. She pushed down panic at the thought of the baby she wasn't ready for but who was coming already. How could she take care of this baby by herself? Why hadn't she prepared yet? Could she survive this torture much longer?

As pain sliced her body, Meg glanced at her determined mom—who was actually speeding. Peace trickled into her heart as she realized that even if she didn't have the answers to all her questions, at least she had someone who loved her along for the ride.

When Matt saw Sandra Pierce bolt from the chapel, he knew he needed to follow her. All morning he'd had Meg on his mind, and the moment he'd seen that she wasn't sitting on the stand, preparing to lead the music, his worry enveloped him. He couldn't be sure that Sandra was going to Meg's house, but he knew that was where he needed to go.

He stood up with Lilia in his arms and walked over to her Primary teacher. She agreed to take Lilia home with her and watch her until Matt could pick her up.

Sister Forrester caught up with Matt as he left the chapel. "Where are you going?"

Matt clenched his fist, willing himself to have patience. "To a friend's house."

"I can call my Kendra to watch your daughter while you're gone."

"No, thank you. Lilia's Primary teacher already agreed to watch her."

Sister Forrester folded her arms with a glare. "Well, what kind of friend would take you out of sacrament meeting?"

"The kind I'm in love with."

He slipped past a sputtering Sister Forrester and got in his car.

He backed out and kept his foot firmly on the gas until he reached Meg's house. No one answered his persistent knocking, so he tried turning the handle. It twisted easily in his hands.

"Meg?"

Cliff bounded over to Matt, jumping up on his legs. Matt absently rubbed the dog's ears and walked down the hall, calling Meg's name. After a thorough check, he felt satisfied that she wasn't there. Visions of Meg lying hurt somewhere in her house cleared from his mind.

He filled Cliff's food and water bowls and took him into the backyard. He tried calling Meg's cell again and heard the ringing on the couch. Wherever she was, she'd left her phone at home.

He brought Cliff back inside before he left Meg's house, locked the door behind him, and sat in his car. She probably just went for a walk or something. It was ridiculous that he was so worried about her. Just because she wasn't home didn't automatically mean that something was wrong.

Matt considered calling several of the hospitals in Tucson to check for her. He dialed information on his cell phone. A blue convertible pulled into the driveway next to his car as Matt connected with the first hospital on his list. He hung up his phone and got out of the car to face Austin.

"What are you doing here?" Matt asked, filtering his worry into anger toward Austin.

Austin sneered. "Grabbing a few things for Meg."

"She's not home."

"I know. She's on the way to St. Joseph's to have my baby." Austin walked to the front door and tried opening it. He swore when he realized it was locked. "I left my key in the house."

"Is she driving?"

Austin shook the door handle. When it yielded no results, he turned his attention to Matt. "No, her mom came and picked her up."

Relief filled Matt. Sandra would make sure that everything went okay.

"Where are you going?" Austin asked as Matt got back into his car.

"To check on Meg."

"I can take care of her."

"I know how you take care of her," Matt said.

"What's that supposed to mean?" Austin moved toward Matt's car, and Matt got out of it again. He hadn't been in a fight since junior high, and now was definitely not the time to be in one again. But as Austin clenched his fists, Matt's irritation won over good judgment.

"You can take care of her?" Matt asked angrily. "So, where

were you when Meg found out that she was pregnant? Or when she was so sick the first few months that she couldn't keep anything down? How about when her boss told her she couldn't miss any more days of school?"

He stepped closer to Austin and anticipated how satisfying it would be to bury his fist in Austin's face. "I didn't see you with her when she had her first doctor's appointment or at any of her ultrasounds. You weren't there the first time she heard the heart beat and felt the baby move. She did all that by herself. So tell me, how did you take care of her?"

"This is none of your business," Austin growled.

"I actually *do* care about Meg, so that makes it my business."

"I'm here to take care of her now."

Matt glared with disgust at Austin and relaxed his fists. He needed to see Meg, not have the cops called on him for fighting with her ex. "Maybe she doesn't need you to take care of her anymore. She's learned to take care of herself."

Austin backed away as if he had been punched. Matt got into his car and turned it toward the hospital. A part of him still wished he would've thrown at least one good fist at Austin's pretty-boy face, especially after Austin's car rode his tail the entire way to the hospital.

Matt arrived at the hospital in record time and parked in physician parking when he couldn't find any visitor spaces open. He'd glanced behind him to see if Austin's blue convertible was still following him. It was.

Somehow, Austin found a parking spot, and both men entered the hospital. Austin followed Matt as he walked toward the labor and delivery unit. Matt waved at the security guard, who recognized him from how often he was there for deliveries. Austin tried to follow Matt into the restricted section of the hospital, but security detained him. Matt heard him arguing but quickly went out of hearing range. He was done with Meg's ex.

Chapter Thirty-four

"I want the epidural," Meg cried to the nurse who helped her from the wheelchair into the bed.

The nurse adjusted the pillow behind Meg's back. "It's too late for that, sweetie. This little baby is on the way."

"I need something for the pain," Meg begged her.

"The only way to stop the pain now is to have the baby." The nurse searched Meg's arms for an acceptable vein for an IV. She found one that must have pleased her because she pushed on it a few times and grabbed a needle.

"I'm not ready."

The nurse didn't look up until after she stuck the needle into the full vein. She taped it down and hooked it up to a bag of fluids. "The doctor just got here. She'll come and check on you in a moment."

Meg laid her head back on the starchy pillow and tried to pray away her contractions. It didn't work. She moaned and rolled into a ball on the bed. Her mom held her hand.

Dr. Cohen walked into the room with two nurses behind her. She pulled on gloves, checked the IV fluids, and asked the nurse about Meg's blood pressure.

"How are you feeling?" she asked Meg.

"Horrible."

"Dr. Cohen," a nurse said from the doorway. "There's a man out here that says he's the baby's father."

Dr. Cohen looked at Meg who shook her head violently.

"Tell him to wait outside," the doctor ordered.

"I did, but he's insistent."

"No," Meg whispered through ragged, painful breaths.

"Tell him to sit in the waiting room, or you'll call security." Dr. Cohen's tone allowed no room for argument.

The nurse closed the door, and Meg felt another contraction. She grabbed the edge of her mattress, her fingers clutching the top sheet.

"It will all be over soon. I can feel the top of the baby's head. This baby is ready to come."

"It's too early."

"Meg," Dr. Cohen said firmly. "You're bleeding more than we like to see. If it gets worse, I'm taking you in for a C-section. When you feel your next contraction, I need you to push."

Meg felt a contraction building a few seconds later, and the nurse reminded her to push. Everything hurt so badly that she wanted to give up, but another part of her longed to get the baby out.

"I don't think I can do this," she brokenly cried after she pushed as hard as she could. She laid her head back on the bed and panted. Her hand shook as she brought it up to her face to wipe away the sweat and tears from her eyes. Another wave of nausea caused her to gag.

"Get her a wet cloth," Dr. Cohen ordered one of the nurses. The nurse came back with a cool cloth that she patted against Meg's forehead. Meg shuddered through a few deep breaths as the nurse tried to coach her. She cried out when another contraction began.

"You can do this, Meg. Push again. The head is almost out. It looks like the baby has your brown hair."

Meg steeled her mind against the pain and forced her body to work on having the baby. She pushed through several more contractions until she perspired, cried, and gasped for air. The hospital gown stuck to her sweaty body. Her lungs screamed for oxygen, and her body begged for a rest.

"One more push, Meg. Just one more." The voices in the

room swam together, and she wasn't sure if it was the nurse or the doctor or even her mom telling her to push.

She pushed as hard as she could. She thought about the pain of the baby and the man who fathered it who was the cause of this pain but didn't share in it. She thought about the pain of loneliness over the past several months and the pain of realizing that in her time with Austin she'd become someone she didn't know. She cried out as she pushed with everything she had, knowing that it had to be the last push because she couldn't take anymore.

Oh, God, help me.

She didn't know if she said the words out loud or not. She saw stars behind her eyes and felt like a part of her head was going to explode before her body gave out on her, and she let her muscles rest. She couldn't do it anymore. Her whole frame shook, and hot tears streamed down her flushed cheeks. Her rapid breathing coupled with high-pitched gasping was the only noise in the quiet room.

Finally a tiny wail pierced through the silence of the room. It was weak and sporadic and quieted down after only a few seconds.

Dr. Cohen handed the baby to a nurse, and she gently set the wiggling body on Meg's stomach as the doctor cut the umbilical cord. Meg took one of the baby's shaky fists in her own trembling hands.

"It's a girl," she whispered thickly. She looked at her mom. "Did you see her?"

"She's precious," her mom whispered back as she also wiped tears from her face.

Meg let go of her baby's hand when the nurse picked her up. She carried the baby to a small crib in the corner of the room.

The baby cried as one nurse cleaned her body while another took her blood pressure. Meg dropped her head against the bed and closed her eyes as the room began swimming.

"Get her some oxygen," Meg heard Dr. Cohen bark. Something clamped over her mouth and nose and a sound of wind filled her ears.

"She's still bleeding."

Meg groaned as something pressed down hard on her stomach. A cool sensation drifted through her vein and down her arm. The weight against her abdomen increased, and she felt her mom's comforting hand against her forehead.

Matt donned his scrubs, prepared to help Dr. Cohen if needed. He paced in front of the room, knowing that Dr. Cohen was a competent doctor, that the nurses were trained to help, and that he would only add more stress to the situation by barging into the room feeling the way that he felt at that moment.

It had been ten minutes since the nurses came out of the room, pushing Meg's baby in a heated crib. He'd stopped them for an update, hearing nothing after the word *hemorrhaging*.

A nurse tentatively touched his shoulder, and he whirled toward her, as taut as a rat trap ready to spring. "There's a man in the waiting room asking for you. Says that he's this patient's husband. He's pretty insistent."

Matt clenched his jaw. "Fine. Come get me if anything—I mean *anything*—changes. I'll be right back." His anxiety mounted the further he moved from Meg's room. He found Austin lounging in a waiting room chair with his ankle resting on his knee. Austin was flipping through the pages of a magazine.

"What do you want?" Matt growled.

Austin flipped another page before looking up. Matt almost yanked him from the chair when his arrogant stare met Matt's. "I want to see my wife."

"You brought me out to say that! Your *ex-wife* is hemorrhaging right now."

Austin's face paled. "What?"

"I need to get back in there."

"Wait!" He jogged after Matt and grabbed his arm. "Is she dying?"

"They're doing what they can to make sure that doesn't happen."

"She can't die. I can't take care of a baby all by myself. I never wanted a baby."

Matt shook his hand off and released his frustration with a solid punch to Austin's face. "Besides Meg, that baby would be the best thing that ever happened to you, you selfish—"

The security guard pulled Matt away from Austin, who grabbed his bleeding nose. He turned and ran out of the door before the security guard could stop him. "Dr. Wilkes," the security guard began before Matt interrupted.

"I can't believe I did that."

"To tell you the truth, I can't believe you did it either."

"I guess you're going to kick me out now."

The burly guard blew air through his teeth. "That is policy."

Matt rubbed his raw fist. Because of his impulsivity, he would miss what happened with Meg.

"But," the guard continued, "seeing as how this is your first infraction, and no one else saw it," he motioned to the empty waiting room, "and I've been wanting a reason to get rid of that idiot all morning, I'll let you go back in. If you promise that it won't happen again."

Matt ran his thumb and finger against his eyes. "I can wholeheartedly promise that I will never punch someone in this hospital again if you don't kick me out."

The guard pushed open the door that led to the delivery room, and Matt slipped past him with an emotional thanks.

Chapter Thirty-five

"How are you holding up?" Missy leaned over Meg's shoulder and let Melody hold her finger.

Meg stilled the rocking of the chair and watched Melody's small hands clasp so tightly that her little fingers turned white at the tips. Meg shrugged in response to Missy's question. She blinked back the tears that had been too near to the surface since she had Melody three weeks ago.

Since they'd come home from the hospital, Meg had finally begun to understand the reality of being a mom. A lonely, single mom.

She tried to sleep when Melody slept, ate whatever food she had left in her house after not going to the grocery store in almost a month, and briefly showered in any other time that she found.

As a result, she was unclean, underfed, and exhausted.

Missy let go of Melody's hand and rubbed Meg's shoulders. "You don't look like you're doing so great," she said kindly.

Meg shrugged her sister's hands off. "I'm fine."

"Can I hold my niece?"

"It's almost time for her to eat."

"Then I'll just hold her until it's time to eat," she pressed.

Meg held Melody for another moment before reluctantly handing her to Missy.

"How are you, Princess?" Missy cooed. She took the baby out of the room and walked down the hall.

"Hey, where are you going?" Meg pulled herself out of the rocking chair she'd been parked in all morning.

"To the couch," Missy called back. "I need more sunlight."

"There's plenty of sunlight in the baby's room," Meg grumbled.

"Take a shower," Missy ordered Meg when she finally dragged herself into the family room.

"I can't. I need to be with Melody."

"Melody is having some quality aunt time. I don't know when I'll ever get to hold a little baby like this again." She looked lovingly down at the wrapped bundle in her arms.

"Are you sure? It's almost time for her to eat again."

"Go!"

"Okay, okay." Meg laughed for the first time in weeks. "Just don't blame me if she starts crying in a few minutes."

"I won't."

"But if she starts crying in a few minutes, could you knock on the bathroom door—"

"Meg," Missy sounded exasperated. "We'll be fine, I promise. I think she's almost asleep. You can take a nice long shower. Relax."

"But if she cries—"

"I'll come get you."

"All right," Meg said reluctantly. She inched toward the bathroom to make sure Melody didn't start crying before she made it down the hall. When no wailing followed her exit, she figured it was safe to go into the bathroom.

She sighed a few minutes later as she rolled her neck to let the hot shower spray soothe her sore shoulder muscles. She loved having Melody, but she had to admit she was lonely. Her thoughts rewound to that moment when Matt had kissed her and then how she had ruined everything by pushing him away. She couldn't risk letting him get too close and then having him leave her. After one kiss with Matt, she felt more emotion for him than she'd felt for Austin in their whole marriage.

Meg cracked open the door of the steamy bathroom to listen for cries, but all she heard was the soft humming of the ceiling fan in the living room. She dressed quickly so that she could check on Melody.

Peering into the family room, she didn't see Missy so she turned around to head toward Melody's bedroom. The doorbell rang before she went too many steps, and she ran to get the door before they could ring it again and wake up the baby.

She opened the door, surprised to see Austin. His crooked smile seemed a little more crooked than usual. When she stepped closer, she noticed that something was wrong with his nose.

"Austin! What happened to you?"

Austin put a hand on his nose, glaring at Meg. "Your boyfriend sucker punched me in the face. The idiot broke my nose."

"What are you talking about?"

"At the hospital. I was just trying to get back to see you, and he lost it."

Meg shook her head, disbelieving. "Matt?"

"Yes, Meg. How many boyfriends do you have?"

She ignored his sarcastic tone and leaned against the door. Matt had been at the hospital. He had gotten in a fight with Austin and broken his nose. Her heartbeat accelerated.

"Is Matt okay?"

"Lucky for him, the security guard stepped in before I could fight back or I would've made his face look even worse than mine does."

Unexpected sympathy rose in her when she looked at Austin's broken nose. "Would you like to see Melody?"

"Who's Melody?"

Meg's sympathy shriveled. "Our daughter."

"Why would I want to see her? I came here to see you. I thought you were going to die in that hospital, Meg. I don't know what I would've done if you had."

"You don't want to see your own daughter?"

"Why do you keep bringing that up? I'm here to see you, to be with you."

Meg backed up. "Melody and I are a package deal, Austin."

"I never wanted a baby, but if you want her, fine. I won't question it. We can still be together."

"If you decide you want to see Melody, your lawyer can call mine. Otherwise, I never want to see you again."

"Wait, Meg—"

"The worst part of this," Meg interrupted, "is that you don't even realize what you're missing."

"I can't give up on you."

"If you ever come into my house uninvited again, I will get a restraining order. We're over forever, Austin, and that is never going to change." Meg slammed the door and slid the dead bolt in place for good measure.

"Austin?" Missy said from behind, startling her.

Meg nodded. "Where's Melody?"

"Asleep in her crib."

Meg went down to the baby's room to check on her. Melody's soft pink lips pursed in her sleep, and Meg resisted the urge to run her fingers across them. She hummed a quiet lullaby and kissed her softly on her downy head.

She found Missy a few minutes later, straightening up the kitchen.

"Why didn't you tell me that you don't have any food?" Missy raised her eyebrows in accusation.

"I have food."

"Really?" She yanked open the empty fridge.

"I just haven't made it to the store yet."

"I've been to the grocery store three times this week already. I could've picked something up for you."

"I don't need you to go to the store for me. I can do it myself when I get the chance."

"Why do you feel like you have to do everything yourself?"

"Because I always have. If I don't have to rely on anyone, then it's less likely I'll be disappointed or get hurt."

"I won't hurt you."

Meg sighed. "It's hard to change when I've been doing something for so long."

Missy nodded and turned her back to Meg to continue wiping the counters clean.

"Um, Missy?"

"What?"

"Did you by chance see Matt at the hospital when I had Melody?"

Missy set her rag down and turned around. "I did."

"Matt was there, and you didn't tell me?"

"He didn't want you to know. He left church right after Mom did. He was outside your hospital room the entire time you were in labor and after you hemorrhaged. When I got there, his face was so white I thought they were going to have to check him in too. Once they stopped the bleeding and moved you to postpartum, Matt talked to Dr. Cohen and left. He asked me not to tell you that he was there. Why would he do that?"

Meg fell into a chair while her sister was talking and rested her head in her hands. "I told him that I needed to think about our relationship, so I wanted some space. I can't believe he was there."

"I can. Anyone can see that he's in love with you."

Meg swiped her hands against her wet eyes. "Did you know that he broke Austin's nose?"

"No, but I like him better for it."

Meg started crying in earnest, and she felt her sister's arm go around her shoulder. "Hey, what's wrong?"

"Matt's not in love with me. He just wants to fix me. He can't help finding someone who is broken and then helping them to feel better. That's just who he is."

"Meg, you listen to me. You are not something broken that he is trying to fix."

Meg lifted her head to look at her sister. "Yes, I am. My life is a mess. I'm all alone. I'm a young, divorced, single mom."

"Okay, so you may be a little dented."

"Thanks."

"We're all a little dented. It's the dents that give us character; they're what make us who we are. Having a few dents doesn't make you broken." Missy hugged her again. "And what's all this alone business, anyway? You have me and Mom. And Dad, Tom, Kaitlyn, Melody, Stan—"

"It's not the same."

"—and Matt."

"I don't have Matt."

"You do, if you're willing to let go of your fear that he'll leave you. Trust him, Meg. He loves you. He broke your ex-husband's nose for you. He stood outside your hospital door, scared to death that you might die, and then left without seeing you because he was respecting that you needed time."

"What if he leaves me?"

"He won't."

"Missy—"

"Then you have me and Mom. And Dad, Tom, Kait—"

"Okay, okay. I get it."

"He won't leave you, Meg. Trust him."

Missy hugged her again and looked at her watch. "I need to pick Kaitlyn up from Mom and Dad's. Are you going to be okay?"

"I will." She walked with Missy to the door. "Wait!" she called before Missy got in her car. "Can you get me some food the next time you're at the store? Apparently I'm all out." She swallowed. "And I could use your help."

Missy nodded. "I'd love to, little sis."

Just after Meg shut the door, Melody began to cry. Meg hurried down the hall, and as she nursed her daughter, she thought again of Matt waiting outside her hospital room, worried about her. He had always treated her kindly. And what had she done? Turned him away when he put his heart out for her to take.

She fiddled with her cell phone and set it down on the arm of her chair without calling. He probably didn't even want to hear from her anymore. She was too much work. Yet regret gnawed at her insides. She didn't know if she could handle one more rejection.

Meg sighed as Melody fell asleep against her chest. She looked to where Matt had sat the last time he was at her house and longed for him to be a part of this. Tears fell down Meg's cheeks as loneliness overwhelmed her.

Meg eased Melody onto a blanket and went into the kitchen. She stopped when she saw her picture of Christ kneeling in

Gethsemane. Remembering the scripture Matt had her read during that class, she fell to her knees, pouring her heart out in prayer. *Please, Father, give me the faith I need to let Christ heal me.*

Peace wrapped Meg in a comforting hug as she tried to let go of some of her hurt. She remained kneeling for another moment, letting peace dispel her pain and loneliness.

Meg wiped her cheeks on her sleeve and stood. She tiptoed into the baby's room and retrieved her phone. She scrolled down to Matt's name but chickened out before she could press *send*. She needed a few more prayers for courage before she could make that phone call. She pushed the down arrow and called her mom instead.

"Meg!" her mom answered. "I was just going to call you. You'll never guess who I ran into today."

"Do I really want to know?" Last time her mom had said that, it was Johnny Peters, and Meg didn't want to go there again.

"Irene Forrester."

"From church?"

"Yes. I think I could just slap that woman silly. Just a second. Let me say good-bye to your sister."

"You can call me back."

"No, hold on."

Meg heard her mom say good-bye and then the rustle of a hug. She was surprised when her mom came back on the phone within a minute. She couldn't remember a time when she and Missy had said good-bye so quick.

"Okay, where was I? Oh, yes. That meddling Irene."

Meg stifled a laugh. "What happened?"

"She tells me that she took her daughter, you know Kendra, over to Matt Wilkes's house a couple of days ago and that they really hit it off."

Meg felt a sick jolt in her stomach. "What?"

"I told her that you and he were together, or whatever you call it these days. She stormed away in a huff, and it made me wonder how great that meeting with Matt really went. Poor Kendra. Her mother has always pushed her around."

"Mom, Matt and I aren't exactly together right now." Her gut wrenched. "Maybe they really did hit it off."

"Megan Pierce, you listen to me. That man paced outside your hospital room for hours. He didn't want me to say anything, but I am your mother, and I will say what I want. I've never seen someone so worried. The poor guy is lucky he has any brown hairs left after all the stress you've put him through."

Meg didn't know how to respond. "It's Megan Sanders, not Pierce," she finally said.

"Is that the only thing you heard? Meg, if you don't go over to Matt Wilkes's house and tell him that you love him, then I am going to pull an Irene and drag you over there. None of us wants me to turn into Irene, heaven forbid."

"I'll think about it."

"You'd better do more than think about it."

"I love you, Mom."

Her mom sighed. "I love you too."

Chapter Thirty-six

"Grumpy Daddy," Lilia pouted when Matt snapped at her for dumping a bowl of dry cereal all over the floor he had just swept. "I'm going to Grandma's."

Since his parents had moved to Arizona just a few weeks ago, that had been Lilia's biggest threat when he was in a bad mood.

"You can't go to Grandma's until you've cleaned up this mess." Matt heard Lilia muttering as he went into his bedroom to cool down. He had been less patient with Lilia than usual.

It had been a month since he'd seen or talked to Meg, and he missed her more than he thought possible. He hadn't realized how much he wanted—needed—to be with Meg until she wanted space.

Matt groaned. It wasn't like him to sit around and do nothing.

Then, with Sister Forrester and her daughter's visit, he felt like the vultures were circling. He had been surprised when Kendra turned out to be a nice girl. He had expected her to be a mini version of her mom—overbearing and aggressive. Instead, she had turned out to be pleasant, although a bit shy. He could even admit she was pretty. But she didn't have long, curly hair, blue eyes, or a cute freckled nose. She didn't bite her lip when she was concentrating or trying not to smile. She didn't have that maddening tilt to her chin when she was being stubborn. She didn't make him feel breathless with just one look.

"It's all clean. I'm sorry, Daddy."

Matt sat up and motioned Lilia to come closer. He pulled her into a hug. "I'm sorry for being so grumpy." He kissed her on the forehead. "Let's do something fun today. Anything you want."

Lilia clapped her hands. "I want to go see Meg's new baby!"

Matt's heart dropped. "Uh, anything but that."

"You said we could do what I wanted, and that is what I want to do!"

It was what Matt wanted to do, too. As he fought with himself, his daughter looked up at him with pleading eyes. "Please, Daddy."

"Let's go."

Determination welled inside Matt, and his heart felt lighter than it had in a long time as they drove toward Meg's house. He parked in Meg's driveway and opened Lilia's window. "I'm going to go to the door first, okay? I'll come get you in a few minutes if it's okay for you to see the baby."

"Of course it will be okay. Meg loves us!"

"I hope you're right."

Meg finished writing the letter and read through it one more time. Missy had accused her of being a coward for writing a letter, but it was going to take all of Meg's courage just to drop it in the mailbox. Her family would be there in a few minutes to take her out to dinner for her birthday. She'd finished it just in time.

She folded it and dropped it into an addressed and stamped envelope when someone knocked at the door. Grabbing the letter, she went to answer it.

"Matt," she whispered as she opened the door, the letter falling from her fingers. Her heartbeat quickened when she saw the man who occupied her thoughts completely. "What are you doing here?"

"I know you asked for time, but we need to talk."

He reached down to pick up the envelope before she could stop him. He glanced down at it and stopped moving when he read the envelope.

"You wrote me a letter?"

Meg tried to get it back from him, flustered. The whole point of the letter was that he would read it when she wasn't present.

"Daddy! Is it okay?" Lilia called from the open window of the car.

Meg plucked the letter from his hands and slipped it into her pocket when he turned around. "Just a minute, Lilia."

"Is what okay?"

"Lilia wants to see Melody."

"Oh." Meg bit her lip and nodded. Matt wasn't there to see her. He had come to please his daughter. "Sure. Come on in, Lilia!"

Lilia scrambled out of the car and ran into the house, giving Meg a hug that brought a lump to her throat.

"I've missed you, Meg. Where have you been?"

Meg bent to wrap her arms around Lilia's neck. "I've missed you too." Her eyes met Matt's. She pulled her gaze away and swallowed her emotion. "Melody's in here." She led Lilia and Matt into the family room.

Lilia knelt beside where Melody slept on the floor. "Can I hold her?"

Meg hesitated for a moment, but Lilia's hopeful gaze won her over. "Sit on the couch, and I'll hand her to you."

Meg set Melody in Lilia's outstretched hands. Lilia kissed Melody on the head. "Her eyes are open!" She stayed close to Melody's face. "Hi, baby," she cooed. "I'm Lilia, and I'm five years old."

Lilia began to squirm when Melody's eyes drifted shut again. "Does she do anything but sleep?"

"Babies sleep a lot," Matt explained. "Do you want me to take her from you?"

"Yes. Can I play with Cliff?"

"If it's okay with Meg."

"Sure. He's out back."

Lilia ran out the back door, leaving Meg and Matt alone.

Matt cradled Melody in the crook of his arm as he sat on the couch. She stuck a couple of her fingers in her mouth and snuggled into his chest.

"Matt . . ." Meg began, not exactly sure what she wanted to say but liking the feel of his name on her mouth. And loving how he looked holding Melody in his arms.

"You have a beautiful baby, Meg," he said softly. He ran the backs of his fingers across Melody's cheek. "She's perfect."

Meg's heart fluttered as she watched Matt tenderly holding Melody. He leaned down and softly kissed the downy top of her head. A shiver of longing ran through her as she wished his kiss had been on her own forehead instead. Or on her lips.

Matt's loving gaze lifted, arresting Meg. Tense silence vibrated between them until Melody let out a cry.

"She needs to be changed," Meg choked out.

Her hands grazed Matt's arm as she lifted Melody, and she knew he could sense the suddenly rising temperature in the room as well. She walked on shaky legs to Melody's room. As she set her on the changing table, she leaned down and kissed her cheek, inhaling the sweet scent of baby. Meg took a deep, relaxing breath to steady her racing heart rate and began to sing a soft lullaby to Melody as she changed her diaper.

"I love hearing you sing."

Meg swiveled around and found Matt standing in the doorway.

"Matt!" She held a hand to her neck. "I think you like startling me."

Her senses tingled in awareness as Matt walked closer to her. She couldn't move—didn't want to move—as Matt raised his warm hand and softly touched her cheek before sliding it behind her head. Meg's heart beat wildly as he wrapped his other arm around her waist and pulled her close to him. His mouth lowered, and he softly kissed her lips. He pulled a fraction of an inch away, and Meg wrapped her arms around his neck. She raised her head, and he retook her mouth in a kiss she eagerly responded to.

When Matt ended the kiss, he still held Meg close. Meg forced her eyes open, having a hard time believing that Matt actually came back.

"I know you were there," she whispered.

"What?" He took a step back, but Meg held onto his forearms.

"I know you were at the hospital. Why didn't you come see me?"

"I was giving you space to think."

Meg swallowed and gathered the courage to say what was in her letter. "I don't want space, Matt. I want you."

Matt wrapped her in a tight hug, his mouth close to her ear. "You don't know how much I've wanted to hear you say that. Meg, these past few weeks without you . . ."

"I missed you."

"I love you," he answered huskily. "I think I've been falling in love with you little bits at a time since I first saw you."

"I love you too." She bit her lip to keep her smile under control. Matt used his thumb to gently tug her bottom lip from her teeth before kissing it.

"I've wanted to do that for a long time," he murmured against her mouth.

Meg smiled and entwined her fingers in his hair.

"So, when's the wedding?" A loud voice sounded, and Meg pulled away from Matt with a shriek.

"Tom!" she yelled when she realized who it was.

"What?" he asked. "All I've got to say is, finally! We've all been wondering when you two would figure it out."

"Tom!" she yelled again in mortification as her face reddened. "Who let you in anyway?"

"Your mom. The door was unlocked, and we saw Lilia playing in the backyard with Cliff." He laughed and backed up. "Your mom sent me in to tell you that we're ready to go when you are. I'll let her know you need a few more minutes." He winked and sauntered down the hall.

Meg put a hand up to her forehead. "I'm so sorry about that. Tom is such a loudmouth. If he knows, pretty soon everyone will know."

"I'm okay with that." Matt pulled her close to him again. Meg reveled in the feeling of being near him and decided that she was definitely okay with everyone knowing.

Melody started fussing, and Meg groaned, reluctantly pulling herself away. "How would you like to go out to dinner with my family for my birthday?"

"I would love to."

Matt picked Melody up from the changing table and handed her to Meg. He put his arm around Meg and dropped a quick kiss on her lips as they walked out of the room, leaving her longing for more.

"At least Tom's interruption gave us something to think about," Matt whispered teasingly before they walked into the living room where she could hear her family talking.

"What's that?" she asked, her voice still breathless.

"When's the wedding?" Matt took her hand and raised his eyebrow.

Meg couldn't help the smile that spread across her face. And the smile stayed there as Missy noticed her walking into the room and announced to everyone that she was there. Meg kept Matt's hand tightly in hers as they greeted her family.

Lilia hugged Meg's legs before running off with Kaitlyn and Cliff. Her mom made sure everyone knew where they were going for dinner so they could meet there. Tom nudged Missy, and when Meg heard her squeal, she knew that Tom had just informed her of the kiss. Meg squeezed Matt's hand and caught his eye.

Soon, she thought. *Very soon.*

Book Club Questions

1. Music plays an important role in Meg's life. How does it impact how she's feeling? How she sees others? Her testimony? What role does music play in your own life?
2. What are some ways that Matt handles his grief? Is Lilia grieving as well? How do you respond to tragedy?
3. When she goes back to church for the first time in two years, are Meg's fears of being judged by others justified? Have you experienced the feeling of being judged?
4. After Missy accuses Meg of changing for Austin, how does Meg begin to find herself again? Is her pregnancy a help or a hindrance?
5. What causes the strain in Meg's relationship with her mother? What role do expectations play in their relationship? What is your relationship like with your mother?
6. Why do you think Johnny was so persistent in trying to get Meg to date him? Why would Meg give into his attentions if she doesn't have strong feeling for him?
7. Do you think Austin really loved Meg? Why would he come back to her when he was feeling low? Do you think he will continue to appear in Meg's life?
8. Do you think Matt loved his first wife, or did he just want to heal her? Is his desire to heal what draws him to Meg? How does he deal with not being able to heal his father?
9. What led Meg to struggle with feelings of low self-worth? Do you think she comes to terms with who she is by the end of the novel? How do you handle similar feelings?
10. Meg finally realizes she doesn't have to do everything alone. How does letting other people into her life help her? What role does Matt's lesson on the Atonement play in this realization? Do you have a hard time letting others help you?

About the Author

Kaylee Baldwin grew up in Mesa, Arizona, and graduated summa cum laude from Arizona State University with a degree in English literature.

She currently lives in southern Arizona with her husband, Jeremy, and her three children. When she is not writing, Kaylee enjoys reading, starting new craft projects, and spending time with her family.